ACCLAIM FOR **E. LYNN HARRIS** AND

Any Way the Wind Blows

"E. Lynn Harris delivers juicy tales . . . laced with romance and spiked with sexual encounters. He also has a knack for creating characters that readers love to hate."
—*The San Diego Union-Tribune*

"A gripping revenge yarn." —*New York Daily News*

"E. Lynn Harris . . . has been called the Luther Vandross of literature." —*Entertainment Weekly*

"Harris's books are hot, in more ways than one."
—*The Philadelphia Inquirer*

"Harris is a great storyteller who knows how to tug on the heartstrings with wit and sensitivity." —*USA Today*

"[E. Lynn Harris] tucks in plot twists bound to keep his readers turning pages late at night." —*The Washington Post*

"Filled with sensuality, deception, friendship, and love." —*Ebony*

"Harris is a wonderful writer. His romantic scenes, whether between men and women or men and men, are always touching." —*San Francisco Chronicle*

"Harris's ensemble of characters—gay or straight—are entertaining, outspoken, and colorful." —*Black Issues Book Review*

"What's got audiences hooked? Harris's unique spin on the ever-fascinating topics of identity, class, intimacy, sexuality, and friendship." —*Vibe*

E. LYNN HARRIS

Any Way the Wind Blows

E. Lynn Harris is a former IBM computer sales executive and a graduate of the University of Arkansas at Fayetteville. He is the author of seven previous novels: *Any Way the Wind Blows, Not a Day Goes By, Abide with Me, Invisible Life, Just As I Am, And This Too Shall Pass,* and *If This World Were Mine.* His most recent novel is *A Love of My Own.* In 1996, *Just As I Am* was named Novel of the Year by the *Blackboard* African American Booksellers, Inc. *Abide with Me* and *If This World Were Mine* won the James Baldwin Award for Literary Excellence. In 2000, E. Lynn Harris was named one of the fifty-five Most Intriguing African Americans by *Ebony* and inducted into the Arkansas Black Hall of Fame. Harris divides his time between New York City and Atlanta.

Also by E. Lynn Harris

Any Way
the Wind
Blows

Any Way the Wind Blows

a novel by

E. LYNN HARRIS

Anchor Books

A DIVISION OF RANDOM HOUSE, INC.

NEW YORK

FIRST ANCHOR BOOKS EDITION, JULY 2002

Copyright © 2001 by E. Lynn Harris

All rights reserved under International and Pan-American
Copyright Conventions. Published in the United States by Anchor
Books, a division of Random House, Inc., New York, and
simultaneously in Canada by Random House of Canada Limited,
Toronto. Originally published in hardcover in the United States by
Doubleday, a division of Random House, Inc., New York, in 2001.

Anchor Books and colophon are registered trademarks of
Random House, Inc.

Song lyrics to "Any Way the Wind Blows" by Bobby Daye.
Copyright © 2001 BobbY DayE MusiC, Inc.

The Library of Congress has established a record for this title.

Anchor ISBN: 0-385-72118-8

www.anchorbooks.com

Printed in the United States of America
10   9   8   7   6   5   4   3   2   1

It's All Love

This novel is dedicated in alphabetical order to a trio of three wonderful human beings who have impacted my life by sharing their lives with me. Troy Donato (a.k.a. my Jared) for being my most trusted friend for more than fifteen years, Charles Flowers for sharing his brilliance, friendship and kind, gentle spirit and Janet Hill for friendship, leadership and class second to none.

In Memory
Andrew Harvey (Grand-daddy)
Julian Richardson
Heath Williams
Donald Vincent Welcher

Acknowledgments

It's a blessing to have a career that I love even on the tough days. I am thankful to my savior, the Lord Jesus Christ, for granting me this blessing and helping me to realize I'm not special, just blessed.

I am thankful to have a wonderful family who supported me when nobody knew my name. There are too many family members to mention here (you know who you are), but I must thank my mother, Etta W. Harris, who taught me to be grateful and humble; my most special aunt, Jessie L. Phillips, who taught me the power of love; and Rodrick L. Smith for support that can't be described with mere words. My life is better because of these three very special people.

I have wonderful friends. Thanks for being so understanding when I go into writer's hibernation: Troy Donato, Vanessa Gilmore, Lencola Sullivan, Blanche Richardson, Robin Walters, Cindy Barnes, Garbo Hearne, Debra Martin Chase, Dyanna Williams, Yolanda Starks, Ken Hatten, Regina Daniels, Carlton Brown, Rose Crater Hamilton, Lloyd Boston, Christopher Martin, Sybil Wilkes, Derrick Thompson, Deborah Crable, Brian Chandler, Brent Zachery, Anderson Phillips, Kevin Edwards and Reggie Van Lee.

I also must thank my new friends in Chicago who have welcomed me and offered me treasured friendships. Thanks, Vince Williams, Dexter Arrington, Linda Johnson-Rice, Bonnie DeShong, Desiree Sanders, Stella Foster, Sandy Matthews, Sonya Jackson and Juanita Jordan.

I have been with my publisher, Doubleday/Anchor, for more than nine years and they've become my family. I'm proud to work with people who care deeply about the authors they publish. I extend my thanks to: Stephen Rubin, Michael Palgon, Jackie Everly, Bill Thomas, Suzanne Herz, Jenny Frost, Linda Steinman, Laura Wilson, Roberta Spivak, Pauline James, Gerry Triano, Jen Marshall, Judy Jacoby, Kim Cacho, Marni Lustberg, Amy C. King, Allison J. Warner, John Pitts, Anne Messitte, Luann Walther, Ari Jones, Rebecca "The Magician" Holland, and Emma Bolton, whose smile the first time I entered the building made me feel like I was home. I must offer a special thanks to Alison Rich, publicist extraordinaire, for her hard work, professionalism and friendship. Thanks also to the newest member of the family, John Fontana for his patience and a beautiful cover.

I must also give special thanks to my Doubleday Canada family, especially Adrienne Ball and John Neale, for their hard work and kindness during my Canadian tour.

Thanks also to Chris Fortunato and his team.

I have a tremendous support staff of talented people who make my life manageable, and who are wonderful friends as well: my assistants, Anthony Bell and Laura Gilmore; my agents, John Hawkins, Moses Cardona and Irv Schwartz; and my attorney and accountant, Amy Goldsend and Bob Braunschweig. Special thanks to Tony Hillery and his guys at TRZ.

There are several other people (good friends as well) and organizations that have offered me support and love for which I am most thankful. Shannon Jones, Sherri Steinfield, Smith & Polk Public Relations, Taurus Sorrells, Janis Murray, Bobby Daye, Tom Kochan, Yvette Cason, Matthew Jordan Smith, Susan Taylor, Deborah Gregory, Patrick

Henry Bass, Monique Greenwood, Stanley Bennett Clay, *Essence* magazine, *Ebony* magazine, *SBC* magazine, *The Doug Banks Morning Show, The Tom Joyner Morning Show, The Isaac Hayes Show, The CBS Morning Show, The Steve Harvey Show,* Frank Ski and his morning team, Ryan Cameron and his team, Skip Murphy and his crew, Donnie Simpson and his staff, Cliff and Jeanine. I also wanted to thank the numerous booksellers and book clubs, as well as Sigma Gamma Rho, Zeta Phi Beta, Alpha Kappa Alpha, Alpha Phi Alpha, Kappa Alpha Psi and Delta Sigma Theta, the Links and the NAACP. I also must mention the staff at the Trump International Hotel, especially Suzy, Pamela, La Tanya, Dennis and Carlos.

Since I've had only two careers, I must turn to others for my characters. These people offered me their time and friendship, and for this I am thankful. Thanks to football greats Robert Bass and Sean James for the sports agent information. The novel benefited from details provided by Dr. Arthur Smith, Rosalind Oliphant and Michel, a young man from Motown whose card I lost but who was so helpful with information on the recording business.

I am proud to be a part of a writers' community that would make James, Langston and Zora proud. I must make special mention of my mentees, talented writers R. M. Johnson and Bryan Gibson, for teaching me more than I could ever teach them, and Kimberla Lawson Roby and Tananarive Due for always being a smile and a phone call away. And Terry McMillan, Iyanla Vanzant, John Edgar Wideman and Walter Mosley for leading the way with talent and class.

I am thankful for two amazing people, Janet Hill, Doubleday/Harlem Moon Vice President, Executive Editor, and Charles Flowers, Associate Director, the Academy of American Poets, to whom I dedicated this book, for their dedication to my novels and a friendship I depend on more than they know.

Finally, I thank each of you, the readers, for all your prayers, love and continued support. It meant so much ten years ago and means even more today. Thanks for letting me know that I am blessed, I am loved.

That's it for now . . . e. lynn harris . . . New York City.

Any Way
the Wind
Blows

Side A

Yancey's Big Reign

When I walk into a room, other women either leave or gather into small groups. That's the kind of woman I am. So imagine my surprise when that stopped happening when I moved to the West Coast. I was used to the seas parting for me. But I guess LaLa Land hadn't been warned about me.

About a month ago, my record company gave a listening party at one of Hollywood's newest eateries, Reign, for my soon-to-be-released CD, *I'm Not in Love*. The party was swimming with members of Hollywood's black elite and their flunkies and was a west coast version of a Ghetto Fabulous plush bash. It was a great event, but if I had to rank them, it was the second-best party where I was the guest of honor. The *best* party I ever attended was the day before I was *supposed* to get married. We had a spectacular party at Laura Belle, in New York City, and as delicious as that party was, my wedding day was an equal disaster. My groom-to-be dropped a full-tilt nuclear assault bomb on me: He decided the morning of our wedding that he would rather spend the rest of his life flip-flopping between the beds of both men *and* women instead of sleeping with just me.

But when I really think about it, Basil and I had more problems than a college entrance exam. He had a difficult childhood. I had a miserable one. He lied about his past. I embellished mine. He wanted children, while the only thing I desired with the letter *C* was a Career. And not just any career, mind you, a C-A-R-E-E-R that would rival that of any diva, living or dead.

My name is Yancey Harrington Braxton, now known to the recording world as "Yancey B," pop singer fabulosa. (Move over, Whitney. Step aside, Mariah. J-Lo, get outta my way.) I relocated to Los Angeles a day after being left at the altar, and it has turned out to be the *best* move I've ever made—that is, if you don't count not speaking to my former fiancé and my mother.

I arrived in LaLa Land with no agent or manager, no permanent residence and very little money. Thank God the real estate market in New York was so hot; I was able to get a much-needed equity loan against my East Side town house. The L.A. weather was so inviting when I arrived that it was hard to close myself off from the world, as I had intended. I went to Malibu, did lots of window shopping and started reading the trades looking for work. The only contact I had with New York was a call every other day from my good friend Windsor, who was staying in my house until the right offer to sell came along.

One night I found myself having dinner alone at the hotel's Polo Lounge restaurant. After finishing a chicken caesar salad, I went into the bar, had a drink and soon found myself singing and confiding in the piano player. Turns out Bobby Daye was not only a talented piano player, but a wonderful songwriter as well. After he finished his set, he took me to several other clubs while I told him my life story. When he dropped me off, he looked at me and said, "I'm going to write some songs for that voice." I thought it was the liquor talking, so I was shocked when he showed up a week later at my suite with five songs written just for me. Three weeks later, we were in a West Hollywood studio recording a demo. One month later, not only did I have a record deal with Motown Records, but an agent and manager as well. Who said dreams can't come true in Hollywood anymore?

Right now I'm living right in the middle of Beverly Hills, in a lovely two-bedroom guesthouse behind the mansion of my manager, Malik Jackson. Malik (a.k.a. Roosevelt) stopped counting birthdays some fifteen years ago but looks to be in his early fifties. I get to live rent-free; I just have to perform a few duties for Malik every once in a while. Trust me when I say I'm not talking about cooking and cleaning.

I've been so busy recording my CD that I've had very little time to concentrate on my movie career, but that will come soon enough. I do know that Hollywood is a lot like New York. A few divas (Angela, Nia, Lela, Ms. Jada and Vanessa L.) get all the work while the rest just pray the unemployment checks come on time.

I'm an actress and a damn good one. And if my word isn't enough, just ask anyone who was at my wedding. Even though Basil had drop-kicked me unmercilessly that morning, I'm a diva and the show must go on. So after all the guests arrived, I stood at the head of the table, poised like I was one of the last two beauties standing in the Miss America pageant, confident that my name would be called after they announced the first runner-up. I told the assembled guests and press that I had had a change of heart and had decided *not* to marry John Basil Henderson. Damn . . . if Julia Roberts could leave Kiefer Sutherland on their wedding day, then why couldn't I leave Basil? At least I showed up. I shared with a few of my guests the exciting news that I had been offered the lead role in a movie being filmed in Toronto based on the life of Lena Horne. I reported that I had beat out Vanessa L. Williams, Halle Berry and Sanaa Lathan. I asked them to keep my news on the QT since the producers hadn't told the other ladies I got the part. In front of the press, I acknowledged, softly, that Basil was heartbroken and had left the hotel in tears. I even bit my lips as my own tears appeared on cue. I encouraged them to keep Basil in their thoughts and wish me much success. And then I greeted my guests, each one of them, accepting their hugs and kisses for over an hour.

So after a year I think I'm ready to return to the scene of my greatest acting triumph ever. In conjunction with my debut CD, the record company has decided to film my first video in New York City as well and has set up media interviews with BET, VH-1 and MTV. We're releasing a house version of the first single a couple weeks before the single is dropped. The A&R manager thought it might make sense to do a couple of performances at some gay clubs in New York and Washington, D.C. He told me if the "kids," as he called them, loved the song, then it would be *Billboard* number one here I come.

I am a little nervous about returning to New York. But I knew I couldn't stay away forever. I can't wait to visit with Windsor, eat some of her cooking and stroll through Shubert Alley. I plan to stop at the stage door of the theater where I first heard the sounds of thunderous standing ovations.

There are a few places I want to shop and some scores I need to settle. Damn . . . now I'm sounding like my mother, the been-done, broke-down diva Ava Parker Middlebrooks. There was a time when I would have said that with great pride. But every time I breathe the air and look at the sun, I shed layers of Ava. I know that one day very soon, I will finally be the marvelous, amazing and incomparable Yancey I was placed on earth to be. And trust me, *everyone* will know my name—coast to coast. The real reign of Yancey B is just beginning. To update a line from one of my favorite movies, *All About Eve,* Strap on your seat belts. And don't say you weren't warned. . . .

Bart's Sweet Revenge

If anyone ever tells you revenge ain't sweet, don't believe him. Just ask me, Bartholomew Jerome Dunbar, a.k.a. Bart. How else can you explain that I'm looking in the mirror and feeling sweeter than a Krispy Kreme double-glazed donut?

It's been about a month since I returned from Atlanta, where I spent the weekend in the minimansion that my ex-lover, Brandon, shares with his wife and two children. It had been over seven years since I had seen Brandon Roberts, the first real love of my life. We met during our freshman year at Morris Brown College in Atlanta, while both grabbing the last biology book at the campus bookstore. We shared three glorious years together, and I was expecting to spend the rest of my life with him.

So forgive me for being a little surprised when Brandon announced one day in our apartment that he was marrying some lady from Spelman who he had been secretly dating for two years. No matter how much I pleaded, cried, pleaded and cried, Brandon told me his decision was final. In an instant I had become invisible. I was devastated. When my GPA hit 1.3, I got kicked out of school, so I moved to New York. Brandon and I had always planned to move there once we'd completed our education.

Just when I was finally getting him out of my system, some seven years later, he calls and tells me he still loves me and needs to see me. He'd recently seen me in a magazine layout (I'm a model/waiter/actor), and Brandon had gone to great lengths to track me down, calling over ten model agencies in New York City. When he finally reached my agency he called every other day. Eventually, I relented and called Brandon back at his office. The first thing out of his mouth was "Bart, you look so tight, I've been having wet dreams about you for weeks."

Brandon's wife and kids were in Paris so I hopped a plane to Atlanta, where for three days we ate, slept and fucked (not "made love") like we used to, in the bed he shared with his wife. On the day I left, I asked for his home phone number and he told me he didn't think that was such a good idea and that he would get a voice-mail box so I could leave him private messages. What kinda guy did he think I was? Obviously not a very smart one.

I was so angry I didn't know what to do. I had to show Brandon he couldn't treat me like crap. I was fed up with brothas touting that bogus, down-low bullshit. I wanted to scream from the bottom of my vocal cords, "Pick a team and play!"

While Brandon was in the shower, I dialed my home number from his phone. I was planning to harass him with phone calls and hang-ups, late at night, once the wife and kids returned. I had learned from our conversations over the weekend that his wife was a stay-at-home mom, and that he spent long hours at his office. Before I went home, I couldn't resist leaving Brandon and the Missus a little gift.

When I got back to my Harlem apartment, Brandon's number was on my caller I.D. I couldn't believe he wasn't smart enough to have a restricted phone number. I guess having a B.S., an M.B.A. and a law degree didn't give Brandon a whole lot of common sense.

I dialed the number, and sure enough wifey answered the phone.

"How are you doing?" I asked.

"Fine. Whom am I speaking with?"

"You don't know me, but I know you," I said.

"How may I help you?" she asked.

"Oh, you can't help me, but maybe I can help *you*." I wanted to mess with her a little more, but she lost patience and demanded to know who I was.

"Are you in the bedroom?" I asked.

"Listen, if this is some kinda sick sex call, then I'm warning you, my husband is an important man in Atlanta and we will get you."

"I know who your husband is," I said. "Are you in the bedroom?" I repeated.

"Yes," she said. If I were her, I would have hung up, but I guess she liked my voice.

"I was in your bedroom recently, and since you weren't there, I decided to leave you a little gift."

She didn't respond, so I continued.

"Why don't you look underneath your mattress?" I suggested. There was silence for a few moments and then I heard an audible gasp.

"Did you find the present I left you?"

"Who are you?"

"Just answer my question. Did you find my black Lycra Jockey boxers I left for you and Brandon? He really seemed to like them. I know Brandon only wears Calvin Klein briefs. You buy them by the box. Right?"

"Who are you and what were you doing in my bedroom?"

"Are you holding them?" Oh Bart, you are a bad, bad boy.

"Stop it," she yelled. "Who are you and why are you doing this?"

"Ask your husband, and ask him to tell you how he was screaming my name so loud I'm surprised you didn't hear me all the way in Paris."

"What are you saying?" she asked. She had begun to cry, but I didn't give a flying fuck. I doubt she would've cared that for years I'd cried myself to sleep over losing Brandon to her.

"Ask your husband to tell you about Bartholomew Jerome Dunbar," I said. And then I hung up, sweetly satisfied.

When I told my best friend, Wylie, what I had done, he called me everything but a child of God. "You've most likely destroyed a family. Ain't you got no shame?"

When I defended myself by telling Wylie how Brandon and his wife had destroyed my life, first with their affair and then with their marriage, Wylie responded, "That was years ago. Grow up and get over it!"

Get over it? Get over this: At twenty-one, I believed in love lasting forever. At twenty-eight, I know nothing lasts forever . . . except maybe revenge.

Basil's Back

Have you ever heard news so shocking that you feel like someone has pulled the rug out from under you, then picked up the table and pimp-slapped you upside your head? Two months ago that shit happened to me, and I'm still trying to recover.

I was rolling out of bed with my special lady friend, Rosa Matthews, after some pulse-popping sex. She had that special afterglow I've been known to lay on the ladies, and a few men for that matter.

"I've got something to tell you," Rosa said. Despite the sleep in her eyes, Rosa was beautiful. Her long black hair was pulled back and she was wearing one of my T-shirts. I looked up at her as I launched into my preshower round of 200 sit-ups. (I do them in the nude, of course, to make sure my body stays tight.) I am proud of the fact that despite being thirtysomething, I don't have an ounce of fat on my 6'2", 215-pound body.

"What? You got another weeklong trip?" I asked. Rosa is an international flight attendant for United.

"Basil, I'm pregnant," she said calmly.

"You're what?" I stopped mid-crunch.

"I'm pregnant," Rosa repeated.

At one point in my life those words would have made me angry and fearful, but recently I've harbored the strong desire to have kids, and Rosa would make a great mother. I grabbed Rosa and pulled her toward me and kissed her passionately, but she pushed me off and pulled away.

"How many months are you?" I asked.

"Three."

"And you're just telling me?"

"I wanted to make sure everything was all right. I went to the doctor yesterday and actually heard the baby's heartbeat."

"You did! I want to hear it," I said as I moved my ear down toward Rosa's stomach, but she brushed my head away.

"What's the matter?" I quizzed.

Rosa was silent, and tears started to roll down her face.

"Baby, what's the matter? Everything will be fine. You know how much I want children. Is there something wrong with the baby?" Rosa didn't say anything, and while I was trying to figure out why she was crying, she said, "Basil, it's not your baby." Her voice was so soft, a whisper, and I wanted to make sure I had heard her correctly.

"What did you say?"

"It's not your baby."

This time I heard her loud and clear.

"What do you mean it's not my baby?" I said, suddenly feeling rising anger. Since the first time we met, almost a year ago, Rosa and I had been talking about how much we both loved and wanted children. It was one of the reasons I was attracted to her.

How could she give me this kind of news now? A few months earlier my sister Campbell's husband was promoted and the family relocated to Pittsburgh. I'd told Rosa on numerous occasions how much I missed my nephew Cade, and she had even offered to give me flight passes so I could visit him on a regular basis.

"Basil, I'm sorry. But I thought we'd agreed we weren't ready to be exclusive, especially with both of our schedules," Rosa said, never raising her eyes. Good, at least she was feeling guilty. Yeah, we'd agreed not to tie each other down. I loved the fact that Rosa was independent. I didn't need a woman who wanted to be my shadow. I'd gotten used to getting calls from her telling me she was on her way to Paris to shop on her days off. Sure, I was still dibbling and dabbling with some of my female freaks I kept on the side, but I wasn't having unprotected sex with them.

Rosa and I had actually talked about having a child together, although neither one of us wanted to be married. We'd discussed hiring a nanny and getting our child into the best schools in New York, and we even kicked around names. Rosa was such a cool lady, I was convinced coparenting would have worked.

Lately, though, my business was growing by leaps and bounds, and I found myself spending more and more time on the road and longer evenings in the office when I was in New York. My company, XJI (Ex-Jocks Incorporated), had opened two more satellite offices and hired additional staff. We were battling the big sports agencies player for player.

It'd been months since we (my partners, Brison, Nico and I) had lost a player we wanted to one of the large agencies.

"Yeah, but I didn't know you were out there having unprotected sex with some dude you met on a layover." There was a part of me that wanted to grab her and shake her and make her tell me what all our baby-planning conversations had been about. How could she be certain the child wasn't mine? I had used condoms when we had sex, most times. But there were several shower sessions where we had only soap and water for protection. Had Rosa been diddling with me the whole time? Was she playin' me?

"Basil, look, I still want to see you. We can work this out," Rosa pleaded.

"You want to see me? Well, sweetheart, you better take a good long look right now, because this is the last time you're going to see me and this jimmie," I said as I headed to the bathroom. I knew Rosa was smart enough not to still be sitting on my bed when I returned.

When I walked back into my bedroom after a long shower, I realized I was right about Rosa. Not only was she gone, but so were her clothes and personal items she kept at my place.

Good. I'm cool with that. I'm ripe for another ride on the rough-and-ready freeway of love. Oh, my bad. I mean, that good old freeway of lust. I'm going back to my old motto: I'm sexing *everybody,* and the good ones twice.

Motown's New Diva

I overheard two women whisper, "That's Yancey B," as I walked into the conference room at Motown Records' Los Angeles office and took my seat at the head of the table. Some little skinny assistant with bad skin, named Lucy or something, looked at me and said, "That's Mr. Hudson's chair."

"Oh, it is? I'm sure he won't mind," I said as I sat down without hesitating and opened my purse for a mint. A few minutes later, Marc Hudson, a big bear of a man, walked in cheerfully and took the seat right next to me. I wanted to whisper to him that suspenders didn't look good on big men, but I resisted.

"So you ready to rock and roll, Yancey B?" he asked with a huge smile.

"As ready as I'm going to be." I smiled.

"Then let's make some money," he said as he opened his leather portfolio.

"Lucy, can you get me a notepad and some carrot juice?" I asked. She looked at me, rolled her eyes and then looked to Mr. Hudson for confirmation.

"You heard our new star, Lucy. Get this lady a pad and some juice. Let's go over the plans."

This was the final meeting before the official launch of my album. My first single was due to be released in a couple of days, and I was ready to meet and greet my fans. There were five other people besides Lucy and Marc sitting around the table. They all had pads of paper and held their pens nervously like anxious executives on the brink of losing their jobs if they didn't come up with a fresh idea soon.

"Anthony, what was the feedback from the listening party?"

"Very, very positive. Everyone loved the album, and they're all on board for the promotions," Anthony said.

"So are we all agreed on the first single?" Marc asked.

"Yeah, everyone loved 'Any Way the Wind Blows.' Everyone thinks it's going to be a big hit," Anthony added.

"Is anyone concerned about the lyrics?" I asked.

"Great question, Yancey," Marc said with another smile. He then turned to a plump sista who was obviously a member of the Fake Flowing Hair Club and quizzed, "Vivian, what are the radio programmers saying?"

"Well, Marc, they think it will be controversial, but it's such a beautiful song, and Miss Yancey B delivers on the vocals. Bottom line, they think it will help . . . if . . . ," Vivian said.

"If what?" I asked.

"If you're willing to talk about the contents of the song," Vivian said as she looked down at her yellow pad.

Before I could answer, Marc's strong voice boomed, "Of

course she'll talk about it. With the song and the video we plan to shoot, everyone will be talking about it."

"I'll do whatever it takes to sell records," I said, making eye contact with everyone at the table to let them know I meant business. Lucy came back into the conference room with the carrot juice and a fresh legal pad and placed them in front of me.

Anthony reviewed the cities where I would do promotional performances and record store signings.

"Of course, we'll do the key major markets, New York, Chicago, Atlanta, Detroit, and since Yancey is from Tennessee, I thought we'd add Memphis," Anthony said.

"How does that sound to you, Yancey B?" Marc asked.

"That's great, but what about Los Angeles? And do we have to do Memphis?"

"Oh, I'm sorry. Of course we'll do Los Angeles. And if not Memphis, how about Nashville? I think we need to do New York first, so we can kill two birds with one stone by shooting the video and having the showcase performance in the same week."

"Let's just skip Tennessee altogether," I said. Then turning to Marc, I asked, "What's the concept for the video?"

"If you think the song is going to be controversial . . . wait for the video." Vivian laughed.

"We are ready for you in New York," said Michel Rodriguez, a small cute Hispanic man who was going to be my main contact in New York. He had come out the day before, and the two of us enjoyed a "get-to-know-you" lunch at the Peninsula Hotel in Beverly Hills.

"Any Way the Wind Blows" was a beautiful ballad that told the story of a young woman, me, whose groom leaves her at the altar for another man. It was one of the first songs Bobby had written for me after I told him what my ex-fiancé, Basil, had done to me.

The plan was to shoot me all dolled up, in fabulous gowns, with a large canopy bed in the background. When I hit the final note, I was going to turn with a forlorn look on my face toward the bed and discover two well-muscled and good-looking men going at it, while tears rolled down my face.

I didn't know if I was ready to talk about my personal life and would have preferred that the company make my cover of "I'm Not in Love" the first single, but it was their record company. I just hoped the world, and especially Basil, was ready for the way the wind was about to blow.

· · ·

My ringing phone awoke me from a sweet dream. I was dreaming that I was at the Grammys receiving an award for Best New Artist from Lenny Kravitz. Just when I was about to make my acceptance speech, the phone rang.

I rolled over and picked up the phone. "Hello," I mumbled. I figured it was Malik trying to get a little sumthin' sumthin' early in the morning, but then I remembered that he had a key and his wife was in town.

"Do you miss me, Mommy?" the voice of a little girl asked.

"Who is this?" I asked as I sat up straight in my bed.

"Do you miss me, Mommy? I miss you."

"Who is this?" I demanded.

There was silence for a few moments, and then an adult female voice came over the phone and said, "I'm sorry. My daughter is playing with the phone."

I was quite relieved. "You need to keep your daughter under control!" I said as I hung up the phone.

Drop 'Em, Bart

The third week of January was proving to be much better than the first. I had been able to pick up two night wait shifts and had two "go sees" in one day. I knew that didn't mean I was going to get the job, but at least I was getting in front of clients.

I showed up ten minutes early at CBS Music on Avenue of the Americas, where I was welcomed by a lobby of good-looking black men. The same ones I saw on most calls. From the look of the lobby, the client hadn't specified light or dark, since the room was filled with men with skin tones that ranged from vanilla-yellow to chocolate fudge. I nodded and gave my fake glad-to-see-you smile to a couple of guys I always saw on castings. I checked in with a receptionist who seemed to be enjoying all the male company, took a seat and pulled out *USA Today.* I had just finished the Life section and was looking over the front page when the receptionist announced, "Bart Dunbar! You're on." I grabbed my bag and rushed to the desk.

"Someone will be out here in a few seconds," she said. A few moments later, a short black girl dressed like a boy said,

"I'm Audrey. Come with me." I followed Audrey down a long hallway and then into a conference room.

"This is Bart," Audrey said to a tall, thin white boy with slouching shoulders and a big-boned, brown-skinned sister with an auburn pageboy wig on that didn't fit her round face.

"Come on in, Bart. I'm Steven, the casting agent."

"Nice meeting you," I said as I shook his frail hand.

"This is Suzy, the casting assistant," Steven said.

"Nice meeting you, Suzy."

"Have a seat. Did you bring your book?" Suzy asked.

"Sure," I said as I pulled out the large black binder filled with pictures of yours truly. I passed the book to Suzy, and she and Steven began to look at my photos.

"Oh, that's a nice one. Great-looking body," Steven said to Suzy. They both were acting as though I wasn't there. When they finished they looked at me like I was a piece of prime sirloin hanging in a meat freezer.

"We're looking for someone to be in a music video. Can you dance?" Steven asked.

"I do all right," I said. Great, I thought, a video, which meant if I wasn't cast as a principal, I would end up making about two hundred dollars for unlimited hours of work.

"You've got to have a great body," Suzy said.

"No problem," I replied quickly and confidently.

"Do you mind standing up, taking off your sweater and dropping your pants to your knees?" Steven asked.

"Sure," I said, grateful I had decided to wear underwear. I stood up, pulled off my navy blue turtleneck and dropped it on the table and then unbuckled my belt and dropped my jeans, not to my knees but to my ankles. I figured they should see the entire package. I gave Steven a look like if Suzy weren't here, I would make sure you gave me this job in sixty seconds.

"Turn around," Steven directed.

I turned around slowly like I was on top of a music box, and then back again.

"You have a great body," Steven gushed.

"Thank you. Do you need to see more?" I asked with a wicked smile.

"Oh, no. You can pull your clothes back up," Suzy said.

"Do you mind answering a few questions?" Steven asked.

"No."

"Tell us about yourself," Suzy said.

"I'm from Cleveland," I said, thinking, Oh no, this is one of those let's-play-male-beauty-pageant calls. I could anticipate the next question.

"Give us one word that describes you," Steven said.

"Expensive." I smiled.

"How long have you been modeling and acting?" Suzy asked.

"I don't consider myself an actor. I've been modeling for about five years," I said.

"What type of music do you like?"

"All types, but mostly jazz and R and B," I said.

"Do you have any questions for us?" Steven asked.

"When are you going to make a decision?"

"In the next forty-eight hours," Suzy said.

"I would *love* this opportunity," I said. It always helped to beg for a job.

"We'll get back to you," Suzy said firmly. It was definitely a don't-call-us, we'll-never-call-you tone.

"Thanks," I said as I grabbed my portfolio and headed for the door.

Basil's New Year's Gift

Sometimes the best Christmas presents come after the holiday season has ended, like the end of January. And for someone in the competitive business of sports management, the best present comes in the form of a 6'4", 225-pound All-American tight end.

"So you're sure you want to do this?" I asked.

"Folks, are you crazy? Just show me where to sign, and it's goodbye CSU and bling, bling, hello NFL," Daschle said.

"You've read the contract?"

"Yeah, I read it. It's chill."

"And your mother approves?"

"Yeah, she's ready for a new house and a new car," Daschle said, with a huge smile on his face. A smile I'd seen several of my clients flash when they talked about their mamas.

I was thinking how many times I'd heard "gonna buy a house and car for my mama, and one for my girl." I wanted to make sure that I arranged a meeting with a financial planner immediately for Daschle Thompson, my first client of the year. I hadn't expected to sign Daschle so soon, since he was only a sophomore. I'd actually been trying to sign his roommate, who was a certain first-round choice until he had a career-ending injury during the third game of the season. I had mixed feelings about signing someone who had spent only two years in college, and I always made sure potential clients knew the moment they signed on the dotted line, or accepted a meal or trip from an agent, it was bye-bye college days. I also warned them that the NFL not only stood for National Football League but also Not For Long. A halfback from Itta Bena, Mississippi, Daschle had pulled in over eighty-two receptions for more than 1,200 yards and had been told by scouts he could be a certain first-round pick if he decided to leave college early. That was all D, as his friends called him, needed to hear.

Daschle leaned over my desk and signed his name very slowly. I wondered for a moment if he was having second thoughts. It looked as though he was filling in the holes on a test card rather than signing his name. When he finished, I looked at his signature and chuckled.

"Daschle, from the looks of this signature, if you don't make it as a football player then you could be a doctor. Your handwriting is bad," I joked.

"A doctor?" Daschle asked with a puzzled look on his face.

"Dawg, haven't you heard about . . . forget about it. I was just kidding," I said. I guess the doctors in Mississippi had good penmanship.

"I feel ya," Daschle said as he shook his head.

"So what do you feel like eating? We need to go out and celebrate," I said as I moved the signed contract into my *in* basket.

"Don't matter. Some chicken or maybe a steak or

sumthin'. I ain't choosy. I just want to go to a tittie bar and get me a private lap dance and then get some Z's," he said.

"I'll have my assistant find us a place that has both. I mean, chicken and steak. There are a couple of places we can go for a lap dance."

"Cool," Daschle said as he stood up and stretched his healthy body. He then walked over to my large picture window overlooking Columbus Circle and the entrance to Central Park and looked out onto the city.

"So how tight are you and your girl, Allison? That's her name, right?"

"My dip, yeah, that's her name and we tight. I ain't ready to walk down the aisle and shit, but she's cool."

"I hear ya," I said as I pressed the intercom button for my assistant, Kendra.

"Yes, sir," Kendra said.

"Kendra, see if you can get me a reservation at Jimmy's Uptown Café in about an hour."

"Yes, sir."

I looked at Daschle and said, "I think you'll like this place. It's up in Harlem and it's the top shit right now."

"Dude . . . Harlem. I've always wanted to go to Harlem." He had a child's smile on his face like I had just told him I was giving him an all-day pass to Disneyland.

"I'll even have my driver give us a little uptown tour. Harlem all of sudden is the hottest spot in New York City. Can you excuse me for a second?"

"Cool."

"Make yourself at home. If you need to use the phone or listen to music, go ahead. I shouldn't be but a few minutes. I need to talk with my partner, Brison," I said as I moved from behind my desk.

"Take ya time, dawg. I think I'll just enjoy this view," Daschle said.

I left my office and walked the few yards to Brison's office. His door was open and I could see him looking down at his desk. I knocked once firmly, and Brison looked up and motioned for me to come in. When I moved closer to his desk, I saw that he was studying a glossy color brochure.

"Basil, whatsup?"

"Trying to bring in some new business. What's that?"

"The competition is bringing in some new tools. Look at this," Brison said as he handed me the pamphlet.

"This is smooth," I said as I looked at the photos of athletes, both male and female, touting the services of PMK Management, one of the largest sports agencies in the country. PMK had made overtures to buy XJI, and we'd turned them down cold.

"You think we should do a brochure like this?"

"You bet. This is the shit. Something we can leave with potential clients. Make sure they won't forget us."

"I'll contact an advertising agency before I leave this evening."

"Sounds like a plan."

"How's it going with Daschle?"

"He's now a signed, sealed and delivered first-round pick," I said as I exchanged dap, the brotherman's hand-tap, with Brison.

"That's great news. So I guess you win the bet?"

"What bet?"

"Don't you remember? We said whoever signed the first client of the new year would get the largest office when we move," Brison said. Nico, our other partner, had convinced Brison that maybe we should move to a large suite of offices in the Times Square area. Rent in the area was off the hook, and sometimes I worried that we were moving a little too fast. We had already moved once in the last year to accommodate additional support staff.

"Aw, yeah. Cool," I said as I shook my head, recalling our friendly wager.

"Is Daschle still here?"

"Yeah. He's in my office. I think we need to get him with George real quick before old boy spends all his money before he's drafted." George Douglas handled the finances of most of our clients, even though a lot of them resisted his advice.

"Let me guess. He wants a car for himself. One for Mama. A car for his childhood friend, Pookie, and a car for his girl." Brison laughed.

"You got it."

"How long is he going to be here?"

"I can keep him for a couple of days. He's already dropped out of school."

"Where's he staying?"

"I think at the Hudson."

"Okay, I'll place a call to George's office and try to arrange a meeting tomorrow afternoon."

"Thanks, Brison," I said as I headed back to my office. When I reached for the door handle, I heard Brison's big voice call my name.

"Basil."

"Yep," I said as I turned around.

"Way to go. Looks like you're going to have another bang-up year. Before you know it, we're going to be buying up the competition."

"And you know that," I said with a confident smile.

• • •

When I got home from hanging out with Daschle, I was checking my e-mails when I ran across one from someone with the screen name SWALZ. The e-mail address wasn't one I recognized, so I started to delete it, but instead I opened it and began to read: *Hey Mister Sex Pro Football Star: When was the last time you kissed the boyz and made them cry? Whose heart are you holding hostage now?*

So I wrote back, *How are you doing, Yancey? I was wondering when I would hear from you. Glad to see you've joined the world of technology . . . Basil.*

I checked a few more Web sites like the football rating service on CBS SportsLine.com. They had Daschle rated as an 9, which was great because it meant he would definitely be a number-one pick. I spent about ten minutes checking out the ratings of a couple other players I was interested in representing and was getting ready to sign off, when I decided to check my mail again. There was another e-mail from SWALZ. I clicked it open and read: *Yancey? Who dat? A man or a woman? And just so you know, this is not Yancey. . . . But I'm watching you, heartbreaker.*

I chuckled and said, "Yeah right" to myself and clicked off my computer.

Love . . . Peace and Yancey B

When I was a young girl growing up in Jackson, Tennessee, *Soul Train* was my way of learning what was going on in the rest of the world. I heard songs that weren't played on our local radio stations. I learned the latest fashions and the newest dance steps. I dreamed of being a *Soul Train* dancer, moving my way down the line, causing both admiration and envy. When I dreamed of being a singer, I imagined Don Cornelius with his huge Afro interviewing me and saying, "Let's give it up for Miss Yancey Braxton."

That was a long time ago, so I was shocked when my manager told me I was doing the show. Not because I didn't think I was good enough, but because I didn't realize it was still on the air.

On my last day in Los Angeles before I left for New York, I taped two songs at the *Soul Train* studio. The first was the title track, "I'm Not in Love," and then I brought the house down with a dance version of "Any Way the Wind Blows." It was obvious from the reaction that most of the crowd knew what I was talking about. But I wanted to wave my magic wand over the rest of the crowd and tell the ladies with questionable-looking male dance partners, "Y'all not listening to this song, ladies."

It was also a special day because I met one of my favorite television performers, Shemar Moore, the host of *Soul Train,* and a star of the only soap I watched, *The Young and the Restless.* When he gave me a kiss on the cheek and whispered, "You look damn good, girl," I wanted to tell him we'd both look better on each other's arm.

The bad part of my day came when I returned home and Malik started pleading with me not to leave. When I told him I didn't have a choice, the record company was calling the shots, so I needed to be in New York for a couple of months, Malik tempted me with my own Beverly Hills apartment and an audition for the remake of *Sparkle.*

"*Sparkle*'s being remade? That's one of my favorite movies! You think I could play Sparkle?"

"Not Sparkle. That role's already been cast. I think it's one of those A or B girls. You know, Aaliyah, Brandy or Beyoncé. But you'd be perfect for the role of Sister, because you're beautiful, sexy and a woman who can sing her ass off," Malik said. Who did he think he was talking to? First, he was saying I was too old to play Sparkle, but just the right age for the older sister. Maybe it was just a twisted ploy to get me to stay in Los Angeles, but I had a song to promote, and not even an all-black remake of *Gone with the Wind* was going to keep me in Los Angeles.

"So can I come see you in New York?" Malik asked.

"It's a free country. Look, I've got a flight to catch. Call me on my cell if you need to reach me," I said as I gently pushed him out of the door.

While I was packing for my trip back to New York, I thought about my mother and how much she would have enjoyed the day I had. Not for me, but for her. The other day, an older black receptionist at Motown said, "Your parents must be so proud of you." I looked at her and smiled and said, "I hope they are." The truth is I never knew my father, and my mother, well, Ava's story is more than just a story, it's a miniseries. We *all* have baggage in our lives thanks to our parents. Some of us carry it in a change purse and others use a U-Haul. Me? I need a double-wide mobile home.

Bart Meets Miss Chicken

My friend Wylie David Woolfolk III is the kind of guy who can sometimes put on airs, but when he's drinking, he's always the life of the party. Wylie loves his "*cock*tails," as he calls his libations. He's a church queen and is always trying to talk me into going to service with him on Sunday morning and Wednesday evening prayer meeting. I am not into churches and all those hypocrites who pack them. Wylie comes from one of the most prominent African-American families in San Antonio, Texas, which was hard for me to believe since I had never heard of any well-to-do black families from Texas, period. His father and mother had created some magic potion hair product called Jeheri Juice Swirl, right before the hairstyle became popular and made millions. Looking at some of Wylie's pictures from his youth lead me to believe they used the poor child as a human hair tester. Wylie told me he gets a chill anytime he sees someone wearing his or her hair in a jeheri curl. "Then stay out of prison," I had jokingly warned him.

Sometimes it seems like Wylie is bragging when he talks about the private schools he attended. Not to mention the

Jamaican nanny who raised him, and the annual trips abroad he and his sister took with their parents. He graduated from Southern Methodist University and Columbia's J school. He's a partner in an up-and-coming public relations firm handling books and entertainment and he speaks three languages, actually four if you count moogie, the language of B-boyz in New York City and its surrounding boroughs. I knew he sometimes talked about his family's wealth just to make himself feel good. He suffers from time to time from LSE (low self-esteem). LSE is a common thing in the black gay community, so many of us struggle to find something to brag about. I remember a time when intelligence was considered hot in a man. Then you'd meet someone who couldn't spell cat (even when given the *c* and the *t*) and you'd suddenly find yourself dumbing down just for the dick. Today it's beauty, sex (which means a big dick or a mesmerizing ass) or wealth. Rarely does someone have all three, and a lot of the gay kids I know have none of the above.

Wylie does have a heart as big as Texas. Besides the free meals, he's always sending me books (which I never read) and CDs. I knew when we met he was interested in me for more than friendship, but I made it perfectly clear he wasn't my type. Maybe it was the gym shorts he wore that reminded me of a little girl's pleated skirt. He's somewhere between mildly attractive and cute. That's cool with me because I don't have to worry about who's going to be the beauty on duty.

• • •

Despite my better judgment, I decided to go to an DOS (old sissies) dinner party with Wylie. The party was just what I expected, a bunch of old unattractive sissies with boy-toy dates, putting on airs and drinking too much. There was only one woman, and she was wearing a big blond wig and a tight dress that held life-threatening breasts.

The party was in a brownstone on Strivers Row that would have been spacious except for all the antiques this man had crammed in there. The host, Lester Williams, owned several dry cleaners in Harlem and the Bronx. He was a tall, thin, balding man, with bad teeth and humming breath. I noticed just how stank his breath was when he came up to me and moved his eyes over my body like a bar-code scanner.

"So what do we have here?" Lester said to me while balancing a cigarette in one hand and a wineglass in the other.

"Are you talking to me?"

"Baby, as good as you look, who wouldn't want to talk to you?"

I was looking good in my white leather pants and body-hugging, pumpkin-colored sweater. Lester was standing closer to me than I felt was socially acceptable, but I let it go since he was the host.

"That sounded like a compliment, so I guess I should say thank you," I said.

"Oh baby, I only tell the truth. I'll get right back with you, but I see some of the other guests have arrived. Now, if you need anything, just wink, and I'll feel it, no matter what part of the house I'm in."

"Thank you, but I'm not that hard to please."

"And neither am I, especially after a few cocktails," Lester said, dissolving into laughter and swooping across the room with a feline quickness.

I always felt a certain sadness when I went to parties like this, because in many ways they predicted my future. Being old, gay and alone. Most of the older gay men who had survived the AIDS crisis had lost lovers and friends. The only way it seemed they could enjoy male companionship was by flaunting their material possessions. I saw many of them cruising Mount Morris Park with furs and jewels, hoping for quick sex with some young boy exploring his sexuality or a blue-collar married man looking for anonymous sex. Sometimes I despised straight folks for having so many options for real love.

I asked the bartender for a glass of red wine, and gave a polite smile to two men. One young, one old, one pretty great-looking, and the other so-so. They were also talking about some of the popular television shows.

"Have you seen *Queer as Folk?*" the younger man asked.

"I watched it once," his friend said. "I think they should call it *Queer as White Folks,* since I haven't seen any black people on the show. Last time I checked, there were black men in Pittsburgh."

"I guess it really is a homo version of *Friends,* since there aren't any black people living in New York on that show either."

"At least on *Will and Grace* you see black folks every once in a while. When I heard Gregory Hines was going to be on the show I got so excited, 'cause I thought Will had jungle fever. But I ain't mad at Grace for having the fever."

I walked around slowly, sipping my wine and watching Wylie and Lester move from group to group as Jill Scott's amazing and soulful voice covered the room. When I'd finished my wine, I was heading back to the bar when Lester rang the dinner bell. A crystal one, of course.

When the server lifted the steel covers off the entrée, I realized Wylie had had one *cock*tail too many. His voice didn't sound like the professional voice I heard when he was trying to impress people with his education and wealth.

"Oh my, my, look who's here. Miss Chicken! She is everywhere. I mean, you can be at the White House having dinner with the president and who's there . . . Miss Chicken. Honey, you can fry her, bake her, grill her, boil her, wing her, poach her. I mean, the bitch is *fierce*. You can be at yo auntie's house and who's there? Miss Chicken . . . there she is. Fried golden brown. You want to lose weight? Who you gonna call? Miss Chicken, boiled without her crispy coat, will do the trick. You want to impress your trade into thinking they getting something fancy, then throw some extra spices on Miss Chicken and maybe a can of concentrated orange or pineapple juice and she becomes a delicacy. Now, Miss Fish, you can't take her everywhere. Miss Chicken is the one. When was the last time you ate some boiled fish? I don't think so. And nobody beats that bitch Miss Chicken when she's fried. I mean, when was the last time you seen Church's fried fish? So, honey, let's give praise where praise is due," Wylie said as he raised his glass. "To Miss Chicken, the fiercest fowl around."

Many of the guests couldn't clink their glasses because everyone was holding on to their sides with laughter.

"To Miss Chicken," I said when I finally stopped laughing myself.

Calls Come . . . but Not the One

The inductees for the Pro Football Hall of Fame were announced today, and the name John Basil Henderson was not among them. I'm not sad or even slightly disappointed. At least that's what I tell myself. I've had to remind myself that it's rare when someone is selected the first time they're nominated. I decided not to go to the Super Bowl in Tampa Bay, because I was sure all my associates would be telling me how sorry they were I didn't make the hall. The truth is they'd be playa-hating if I had been selected the first time out.

If I'm feeling anything, it's what I felt when I was a sophomore at Raines High School in Jacksonville, Florida. Although I had broken the city's records for receiving yards during my first year, I didn't make any of the all-state or all-district teams because many of the coaches and reporters who voted for the teams thought I was too young. They didn't want me to get a big head.

Right now I feel out of sorts. The same way I felt the first season after I left the NFL. It was the first time since I was eight years old when fall arrived and I wasn't strapping on a helmet.

Not getting the call from the hall has its benefits. I did get phone calls from the two most important men in my life. Right after the inductees were announced on the Internet I got a call from my Pops, who tried to cheer me up just like he had during my sophomore year. I think he was really disappointed, but he assured me I'd make it into the Hall one day. And later that evening I got a call from my nephew, Cade. He didn't call to talk about the Hall of Fame, but to tell me he scored two touchdowns in the fourth quarter of his Pop Warner championship game. As he got off the phone he told me how much he loved me and it almost brought me to tears, just like when I watched the movie *Remember the Titans.* But I have a rule: Tears are the ultimate sign of weakness, and I am not weak.

When I was getting ready for bed, I got another call from another, kinda, sorta important man in my life. I picked up the phone immediately when I saw the Seattle area code.

"Is this who I think it is?" I said.

"If it's Raymond Tyler."

"'Sup, dude? How ya living?" I asked as I lay back on my bed, shirtless, with just my slacks and socks on.

"Just checking in with you," Raymond said.

"So you heard I didn't get in, huh?"

"Yep. You all right? I know how important it was for you," Raymond said.

"How'd you find out? It hasn't hit the papers yet," I said.

"My little bro told me he saw the list on the Internet. Kirby's down in Tampa for the Super Bowl."

"How is your little bro doing?"

"He's doing good. Had a great season, and getting ready for the arrival of his first child," Raymond said proudly.

"So you're going to be an uncle, huh? Are you trying to be like me?" I joked.

"You know that's what I do when I wake up every morning. Think of ways I can be like my guy, Basil Henderson," Raymond said.

"True dat," I said.

"True," Raymond said.

"Who did he marry?"

"A young lady he met on his first day in San Diego. She's the real estate agent who sold him his house," Raymond said.

"What happened to the Asian chick he was dating?"

"They broke up a couple of years ago. I can't tell you how happy my Pops is that he married a beautiful black woman. I keep telling my Pops he's a racist, but he tells me black people can't be racist." Raymond laughed.

"I know a lot of black racists. But most of them hate their own," I said as I smiled to myself when I heard Raymond refer to his father as "Pops." Raymond and I were alike in more ways than I wanted to admit to myself.

"I hear you. I hope I hang around long enough to see all these isms gone for good," Raymond said.

The conversation was getting a little deep for me, so I tried to change the tone and asked, "So how ya doing? It's been almost a year since we got to hang out in ATL at the Super Bowl." I had taken Raymond to the Super Bowl last year, and despite an ice-covered Atlanta, we had a good time. Just as friends, two men who enjoyed each other's company. Raymond had insisted on paying for his own and separate hotel room, even though I had a nine-hundred-square-foot suite at the Ritz-Carlton in Buckhead. I guess he didn't want to tempt himself, since I loved being butt-ass naked and did it every chance I got.

"All is cool on the home front," Raymond said. I guess he was trying to tell me that he and old boy were still going strong.

"That's cool."

"How about you? I know you got somebody up there to help console you," Raymond said.

"Naw, I just broke up with this honey I was seeing. You remember the flight attendant, Rosa? The one who backed out of the Super Bowl trip at the last minute? She's the reason you got to go," I laughed.

"Oh yeah, Rosa. Make sure you thank her again, but I know you got some pretty boy on the side," Raymond teased.

"You're the only pretty boy I would keep on the side, and you've made it perfectly clear I can't have you."

"So how is your father?" Raymond asked. I guess he wasn't going to respond to my flirting.

"He's cool, though I think he already had his suit picked out for the ceremony, so I feel bad not making it into the Hall."

"That's okay, next year he'll get the chance to wear it," Raymond said reassuringly. His support made not making the Hall a little easier to take. At least for tonight, I thought as I thanked Raymond and said good night.

· · ·

I was unable to sleep, so I got up and went online. I was secretly hoping there was some late-breaking news and that by some fluke I'd actually made the Hall of Fame. I logged on and checked a few sports sites. Nothing.

I checked my messages and saw there was a new one from SWALZ. I opened it and began to read: *Don't you know they don't let closeted bisexuals into the Pro Football Hall of Fame? Not on the first time. Not anytime soon.*

I started to write back a nasty response but still felt it was best just to ignore this asshole, so I clicked off the Net and climbed into bed and tried to give sleep another shot.

• • •

This is a real nice building," Sallye said as I opened the door.

"It's all right," I said as I handed my keys to the doorman and asked him to take my car to the garage.

While we rode the elevator Sallye Morgan, a young lady I had just met a few hours before, looked around like a little girl riding an elevator for the first time.

"I must say, Basil, you got it going on. Nice car and great building. What did you say you did for a living?"

"I didn't say, but I have my own business."

The elevator reached my floor, and I held my hand out so Sallye could walk out first and I could get another view of this tall and beautiful brown-skinned sister I had met at Lola's having drinks with some of her girlfriends. Sallye had saved me in a way. I was there checking out the new talent in town and drowning my Hall-reject sorrow in a few drinks, but all

I saw were a lot of women dressed like they were in an old Mary J. Blige video, wearing fake leather, knee-high boots, fake hair and colored contacts. I wanted to yell out, "Sistas, get a clue. Even Mary doesn't dress like that!"

A couple of days after I'd sent Rosa packing, I met a sister at Chaz & Wilsons on West Seventy-ninth between Columbus and Amsterdam, a club where a lot of the ball players go when they are in town for games. I spotted someone who looked good, but when we were getting ready to leave I gave her the weave test. I casually put my arm around her so I could check out her hair. It was long, but it was too scratchy to be the real deal. I decided to give the sister a chance, so I asked her if it was a weave, and she denied it. I then warned her by saying, "Sweetheart, if I get you home and there is anything fake about you, I'm sending you home quicker than you can say 'gold-diggers r us.'" She looked at me and started swearing at me like she had Tourette's syndrome. I left that bitch standing outside the club looking stupid and cussing at the wind.

Sallye and her friends were different. They were dressed in blazers and silk blouses. As I was going over to buy the ladies a drink, a woman walked up behind me and called out my name.

I turned around and asked, "Do I know you?"

"I'm Mandy. Remember? I work with Rosa."

"Oh yeah, excuse me I got to run," I said. The last thing I wanted to do was talk with one of Rosa's good friends.

"You should call Rosa," Mandy said.

I started to ask why, but thought quickly, What does it

matter? I had more immediate tasks to take care of, like finding some new pussy tonight. Rosa and Mandy were not going to get in my way.

When Sallye walked into my apartment she immediately dropped her coat, and I could see the profile of her breasts through her silky plum-colored blouse. Her hips and ass looked delicious in the tight knee-length black skirt she was wearing. I picked up her coat, took mine off quickly, then grabbed her wrist and spun her around toward me.

"I've been wanting to do this since I first saw you," I said as I kissed her lips and released the gold clip that was holding her long dark hair in an elegant ponytail. Her skin was the color of walnuts and caramel mixed together.

Sallye kissed me back like it had been a while, and I was feeling like I was getting ready to break the bank. I began to unbutton her blouse, and I felt her hard nipples through her sheer bra.

"Wait a minute," Sallye said as she moved my hand and pulled back.

"Am I moving too fast?"

"I need to ask you something?"

"What?"

"Are you married?"

"No."

"Engaged?"

"No, now come on over here and let me get started," I said.

"One more question," Sallye said.

"I'm listening."

"Are you gay or bisexual?"

I tried to keep my cool. "Damn, baby, if you thought that was the case, then why did you come home with me?"

"My girlfriends and I always ask these questions. You don't look or act gay or bi, but answer the question," Sallye said as she stopped unzipping her skirt from the back.

"No, I'm not either one of those things," I said confidently. As far as I was concerned, that was the truth. I wasn't gay or bisexual. She didn't ask if I was on the down low and I didn't tell her. Besides, she wasn't looking at my lips but at the bulge in my pants. I could have said "hell yeah" and Sallye would have heard "hell no."

I dropped my pants so she could see what she was staring at and my jimmie sprang out like the tongue of a snake.

"You are so phine," Sallye said as she slipped off her skirt to reveal violet see-through panties. I slowly removed her blouse and I could see that her breasts were small, but round and plump, not like the silicone-enhanced breasts I ran across from time to time.

I picked Sallye up and moved her to the sofa and laid her down. I began kissing her legs, starting with her knee. Her skin was soft and moist and I could smell the subtle fragrance of perfume.

"What are you going to do to me?" Sallye asked with eagerness in her voice. As I stopped exploring her, I looked at Sallye and said, "Baby girl, I'm going to eat you like you're a banana split with three scoops of chocolate." I then slowly removed her panties and sank my tongue between her legs.

An hour later and a couple of trips to paradise for both Sallye and myself, I got up from the sofa and went into the bathroom and removed the condom. I took a warm and damp washcloth and wiped myself off, then pulled a bath-sized towel out and walked back into the living area where a nude and smiling Sallye welcomed me.

"That was wonderful," Sallye said.

"I know."

"When can I see you again?"

"What?"

"When can I see you? I mean like a date?"

"Sallye, how old are you?"

"Twenty-three."

"Sweetheart, you're young so listen carefully. If a man brings you to his house, doesn't offer you a drink and doesn't play soft jazz or R and B while he's sexing you, that's not a good sign. You don't fuck a man real good a couple hours after you meet him and expect to see him more than once."

"What are you saying?"

"I'm looking for the mother of my children and you've just been disqualified for spreading your legs too quickly. The bathroom is that way," I said as I tossed her a towel and pointed toward a slightly open door off the hallway.

Yancey's First Family Dinner

My flight to New York had been delayed. But what else was new? I was sipping a club soda when I remembered the early-morning phone call I'd received a couple days before, which had frightened and annoyed me. Even though I was convinced it was a prank call, I wanted to make sure.

I pulled my cell phone out of my bag and dialed one of my ex-boyfriends. Derrick and I had dated seriously in college, but the birth of a child had sent us in different directions. About a year and a half ago, I discovered Derrick was actually raising the child I had given up for adoption. It was a big shock to me, and I was convinced that if the news got out it would end my career, but thankfully Derrick and I had come to an agreement. I needed to be certain he wasn't having a change of heart.

Derrick picked up his office phone after a couple of rings. "Derrick speaking."

"Derrick. This is Yancey. Is everything all right?" I asked.

"Everything's fine. Are you all right?"

"I'm fine. Everything is going great and getting ready to

get better. I just wanted to make sure you've been getting my packages," I said as I looked at the monitor and saw that my flight was getting ready to board.

"Yes, I've been getting them, and we're doing fine. I just opened up a savings account, and that's where the money is going. Is that why you're calling?"

"Yes," I said. I decided not to mention the weird wake-up call I'd received because I knew he would think I was giving him drama.

"Are you still in California?"

"Yep, but I'm on my way to New York right now."

"Have a safe flight."

"Thanks. Gotta run," I said, but then I asked quickly, "How's your mother?" wondering if Charlesetta had anything to do with the call.

"Why do you ask? You two aren't friendly," Derrick said.

"Just wondering. Okay, bye," I said, and just when I was getting ready to push the End button, Derrick said, "And Madison is doing fine, too."

• • •

When I got home to New York, I'd planned to just relax my first night back, and get reacquainted with Windsor. Instead, I walked into an Adams family reunion.

"Yancey! Welcome home. Why didn't you tell me you were coming?"

"I've been busy and I wanted to surprise you," I said. Well, I *was* the one who was surprised. I loved Windsor, but what were all these people doing in my house? There was an older man who looked vaguely familiar sitting in the living room watching *Wheel of Fortune,* and some crazy-looking older woman, with a bop in the step of her transparent orange-and-purple swirled heels, was bouncing around like she owned the place.

"Oh, Yancey! This is my family. You remember my parents, Mr. and Mrs. Adams, and this is my aunt, Toukie Wells, and my beloved fiancé, Wardell. Everyone, this is Yancey Harrington Braxton, now known as Yancey B!"

Windsor's family all said hello in one voice, which sounded like a choir warming up. Windsor's parents had attended my engagement party. Wardell, the man Windsor was always talking about, was a little older than I thought he'd be, but as long as he was good to Windsor it didn't matter to me. For a moment I thought I might have to find myself an older man, but then I remembered Malik and decided quickly I didn't want to do that show again.

Over the next hour, while Windsor was putting the finishing touches on her meal, I learned about the Adams family, Aunt Toukie and Wardell. Windsor's parents were from Detroit, having migrated from Columbus, Georgia. Her father was old enough to retire but still drove a city bus. Windsor's mother worked at a nursing home, and Aunt Toukie, who I learned had a fondness for tight clothes and Cadillacs, was a retired elementary school teacher and was the reason Windsor had decided to teach.

Dr. Wardell Pope was a widower and father of two grown daughters. He taught sociology at the University of South Carolina. He'd met Windsor when he was a visiting professor at New York University and Windsor had audited his class. Now he was back teaching in Columbia and had proposed to Windsor right before he left. I was enjoying the chatter of the older people talking about things back in "the day," but eventually the questions turned to me.

"So, Yancey B, how much rent do you pay to live here?" Windsor's aunt asked me.

"Toukie! You know you ain't supposed to ask questions like that!" Windsor's mother said.

I ignored Miss Toukie's question and said, "What's that scent you're wearing?"

"It's my new perfume. My first since Youth Dew!" Miss Toukie said proudly as she patted the side of her hair.

"And we're all thankful you switched scents," Windsor's mother teased.

"What's it called, Miss Toukie?" I asked.

"Call me Aunt Toukie, baby. My scent is called Zandria by Anthony Mark Hankins."

"Oh, I know who he is. He made a dress for me once." It was actually my engagement dress, but they didn't need to know all that.

"So Yancey, Windsor said you used to be in plays. Have you seen the musical play *One Monkey Don't Stop No Show*?" Aunt Toukie asked.

"No, I don't think so. Was it on Broadway?" I was trying to be polite; I knew she was talking about those bus–and–truck shows making money off black folks who didn't know better.

"How would I know that, since I ain't never been to Broadway? It was playing at the Fisher in Detroit. That girl who used to play Thelma on *Good Times* and all the Winans except CeCe and Bebe," Aunt Toukie said as she sat down at the table and kicked off her shoes.

"How many times did you see that show, Toukie?" Windsor's mother asked.

"Oh, 'bout four or five. It was *so* good. What about *Why Don't Mama Sing?* You seen that?" Aunt Toukie asked.

"Was that at the Fisher also?" Windsor asked.

"No, I saw that in Flint. My church group took a bus trip down there. It was good, too, but not as good as *One Monkey,*" Aunt Toukie said.

"So I guess you've become a patron of the arts," Windsor teased.

"You could say that," Aunt Toukie said, as she walked out of the kitchen, and I started to follow her.

Windsor and her mother were alone in the kitchen; at least they thought they were. I stood in the hallway between the dining room and kitchen and listened in. I didn't have a relationship to speak of with my mother, or any other members of my family, so I was curious about theirs. Through the crack in the door I could see Windsor put her arms around her mother as she asked, "So what do you think about your future son-in-law?"

"It don't matter what I think. You the one gonna marry him. What do you think of him?" Mrs. Adams asked.

"I love him, Mama. I love him a lot," Windsor said.

"Then that's all that matters, baby girl."

"What about Daddy?"

"What about him?"

"Has he said anything to you about Wardell?"

"Now, Windsor, you know your daddy and I don't do no talkin' until we go to bed. You know that's when we do our personal *business* kinda talking," Mrs. Adams said.

"Will you let me know what he says?"

"Not unless he tells me to," Windsor's mother said as she pulled the pitcher of lemonade out of the refrigerator. "Now, come on and let's go on out there. I'm hungry and I know your daddy is starving."

That was my cue to hightail it to my seat.

"I still think you should have let me and Toukie cook," Mrs. Adams said under her breath as she approached the table.

Windsor followed her mother out of the kitchen, and everyone else was already seated at the table. Mr. Adams was at one end of the table looking miserable, and Wardell was at the other end, forehead shiny and covered with sweat. Aunt Toukie was sitting in the middle, spreading butter on a piece of corn bread.

"Windsor, I hope you don't mind, but I'm having a little smidgen of your corn bread. Your auntie is famished," Aunt Toukie said.

"Toukie, why can't you wait for everyone else? And in front of company, too!" Mrs. Adams asked.

"'Cause she wouldn't be Toukie," Mr. Adams said, his voice sounding like he was coming out of some kind of trance.

"Louis, don't start with me. Don't let me remind you who drove you to the airport and who is supposed to take you back. I wouldn't feel nuthin' putting your ass on the airport bus when we get back to Detroit," Aunt Toukie said while pointing the butter knife sideways toward Windsor's dad.

"Toukie! Stop with that filthy language," Mrs. Adams screamed. "You know we don't talk like that."

"What did I say? All I said was 'ass.' We all got one.

Wardell, do you use the word *ass*?" When he didn't answer quickly, Aunt Toukie looked in my direction and said, "Miss Yancey, I know that word has crossed your lips a time or two, hasn't it?" I didn't answer but gave Aunt Toukie a polite *that's right, girl* smile.

Wardell still seemed a little startled but looked at Aunt Toukie, smiled and said, "I have used it on occasion."

"What about *shit*?"

"Toukie, please," Mrs. Adams said.

Before Wardell could answer, Mr. Adams looked at Windsor and said, "Let's hold hands and say grace. Father, we thank you for this food our body is about to receive, amen."

Mrs. Adams and Aunt Toukie looked at Mr. Adams in shock. Windsor had told me many times that her father was known for giving a five-minute sermonette at every meal.

"Eula, if you can get him to say grace like that in New York, then maybe y'all need to move here," Aunt Toukie said, and laughed.

For about five minutes, the dining room was filled with the sounds of utensils hitting plates and the subtle smacking of lips. Then Wardell looked up and said, "Windsor, the food is just delicious. You did a wonderful job."

"Thank you, Wardell," Windsor said as she put another spoonful of the macaroni and cheese on his plate.

"Can you cook, Wardell?" Mrs. Adams asked.

"Not that well, Ms. Eula," Wardell responded.

"You can call me Eula," Windsor's mother said. Her father was silent and eating very slowly, like he wasn't feeling well.

"Are you all right, Daddy?" Windsor asked her father.

"I'm fine, baby," he said softly.

"Windsor, honey, everything is just dee-lovely," Aunt Toukie began. "I would have put some onion and chives in my macaroni and cheese for more flavor, but you'll learn. I need to send you some of my recipes. You know, I been thinking about doing me a cookbook. What do you think, Wardell?"

"Can you cook as well as Windsor?"

"Honey, pleeze. What is Windsor puttin' on you besides food?"

Before Mrs. Adams could chastise Aunt Toukie, Mr. Adams's voice took on a deep and soulful tone. "Toukie, stop your foolishness or else you might not make it back to Detroit or anyplace else."

"Y'all know I'm just being playful. Why is everybody so uptight?"

After we finished dinner, I breathed a sigh of relief. I was tired and wanted to go to bed in a quiet house. To speed things along, I got up and helped Windsor clear the dishes. As Windsor reached for her aunt's plate, Miss Toukie looked up and said, "Now, I know we just got through eating, but Windsor, I thought you had been doing that Weight Watchers, baby. The last time I saw you I thought you had lost so much weight, *Jet* magazine was gonna be calling you to be their next beauty of the week."

Windsor was wearing a black turtleneck sweater and pants and didn't look to me like she'd gained any extra weight. But Windsor had always been a big girl, so who could tell if she'd picked up a few pounds?

"Aunt Toukie, I might have gained a pound or two over the holidays," Windsor said softly. She looked a slight bit embarrassed, as she was always proud of her shape.

"We all do that, Toukie," Mrs. Adams said.

"I know good black don't crack, but I guess it stretches pretty well," Miss Toukie said, and laughed. I thought she had finished, but then she looked at Windsor and asked in front of everyone, "Windsor, you ain't pregnant, are you?"

I was stunned. I couldn't believe Miss Toukie had come out of her face like that. I looked at Windsor. Then I glanced at her father and mother, and then at Wardell. They were all waiting for an answer. I don't think Windsor had ever lied to anyone, let alone her parents and Wardell. Was she pregnant?

Now, I liked drama, but this was more than even I could stand. I felt sorry for Windsor. She looked like a child who just got caught stealing gum from her mother's purse. Her eyes moved around the room like she was searching for an answer. Trying to decide between fact and fiction.

"Yes, I'm going to have a baby," Windsor said in a voice barely louder than a whisper.

Windsor's father put down his coffee cup and looked at Wardell. Mrs. Adams covered her mouth. Wardell glared at Windsor with a tightness in his face. But Miss Toukie had the final words for a little while: "Looks like our family is going to have our first Viagra baby."

For several moments the room remained quiet and no one, not even Aunt Toukie, said a thing. I didn't know what to say, but I knew I wouldn't get any sleep in this house tonight. As much as I wanted to stay and help Windsor, this was her family drama. So I picked up the phone and called the Trump International Hotel and Towers and asked for Megan, one of my dressers from my Broadway days, who worked part time at the front desk. I needed a nice little room for the night, and I needed one quick.

Bart's Big Day/
A Change in the Weather

I'd had a bad day. I had been on three model calls and I knew I wasn't going to get any of the jobs. All three clients had thumbed through my book and dryly replied, "Thanks for coming." It must have been high-yellow Tuesday. On my last call of the day, I heard a couple of models talking about a go-see for a sports campaign at an office located on Fifty-ninth Street near Columbus Circle.

As I rode down in the elevator, I pulled my cell phone from my bag and tried to reach my agency. I wanted to find out why I hadn't been notified about this potential job. My booker was constantly telling me that if I wanted to do more catalog work, I needed to lose some of my muscle mass. I resisted and sought out jobs where an athletic body was an asset, and now it looked like I wasn't even getting those opportunities. It was a little after 6:30, so I got the answering machine at the agency. But since I was my best advocate, I decided to take matters into my own hands and started moving toward the West Side.

The evening sky was heavy with snowflakes, some as big

as rose petals, falling around me to the ground. The streets were filled with people, and yet a winter stillness had settled over the city. I reached the building on Fifty-ninth and walked into the high-ceilinged lobby. I went to the directory and my eyes moved to the *X*'s. I had overheard the guy say something about XFL. After a few seconds, I didn't see XFL listed, but I did see a company called XJI. I walked over to the security guard and told him I was going to the twenty-ninth floor.

"I think they've all gone home," the security guard said. "Who are you going to see?"

I didn't know the name of the contact, but with my quick-thinking confidence, I said, "Ginger."

"I don't know everybody's name up there, but sign in and go on up," he said.

I signed my name and rushed to the elevator before the guard had a chance to check his directory and discover that there wasn't a Ginger on the twenty-ninth floor. As I rode the elevator up, I pulled out my portfolio and moved up a stunning picture of me wearing white nylon boxer briefs that covered everything but concealed nothing. I called it my money shot. I also made sure some of my more tasteful nude shots were in their proper place.

I walked off the elevator toward the double maple doors that announced XJI Sports Management in bold brass letters and rang the bell. A few minutes passed, and I began to knock on the door with balled fists. The day's frustrations had finally taken over, and my body began to slump toward the floor. This shit was tough. I was sitting with my back pressed against the door, when I felt a force pushing toward me. I quickly jumped up, and a few seconds later, I was standing eyeball to eyeball with a very handsome man. For a few seconds I couldn't stop looking into his mesmerizing gray eyes.

"Can I help you?" he asked.

"I came for the modeling call. I think I'm a little late," I said.

"The modeling call?" he said with a quizzical look on his face.

"Yes, sir," I said politely.

"Oh, that was over around four," he said.

"Did you hire someone?" I asked.

"I don't know. The ladies in the office were in charge."

"Can I leave my book or maybe one of my comp cards, just in case there's still a chance?"

"Sure, come into my office, and I'll give you the name of the person to contact."

I walked into a set of well-decorated offices. The wood paneling and leather furniture made the space feel masculine. Gold trophies and sports photos lined the walls. When the phone rang, the man said, "I need to get that," as he dashed into an open office. A few minutes passed and I took a seat in an armless black leather chair, picked up a copy of *Sports Illustrated* and mechanically thumbed through the pages. I had closed the magazine and put it back on the rack when His Flawlessness walked back out of his office.

"I'm sorry. That took a little longer than I expected. Here's our marketing director's card. Give her a call and see what she can work out," he said.

"Who shall I say gave me her number?" I asked.

"Tell her Mr. Henderson, Basil Henderson. I'm one of the partners."

"Thank you, Mr. Henderson."

"No problem. Sorry about the mix-up," he said.

I was heading for the door when I turned to get one last look at Basil Henderson. I wanted to see if I could memorize his handsome face so I could remember it on one of my lonely winter nights. When I turned, he was standing so close to me I could feel his warm breath caress my face.

"Would you mind looking at my book to see if I even have a chance at this job? I understand you're looking for someone with an athletic body," I said.

"Yeah, we're looking for an ex-football player," he said.

"Then I'm your man. Why not take a look?" I asked as I passed him my book.

"You played ball?" He looked skeptical, but I figured I had nothing to lose.

"Yes," I lied.

"Where?"

"Morris Brown."

"What position?"

I knew only two football positions, so I quickly said, "Tight end."

"That's the position I played. Come on into my office, and I'll take a look," he said.

I followed Basil into a large room with an oval-shaped glass table, a softly glowing computer screen and a breathtaking view of a snow-covered Central Park. He sat in a black leather chair and began looking through my book. He began nodding to himself and then he said, never raising his eyes, "Nice abs."

"Thank you," I said. I wanted to tell him he could drop a quarter on my stomach and it would bounce twice before it found a home.

"Yeah, you got some nice shots here," he said. If I wasn't mistaken, he had looked through my entire book and then started again. I didn't know many straight men who enjoyed my photos, especially the nude ones, as much as Mr. Henderson appeared to. As he pored over my book, I had a chance to study him. His skin was so golden brown, he looked like he had been scrubbed in sunshine. He was wearing a cobalt-blue business shirt, a lemon-yellow tie, with dark suit pants. When he looked up at me, my knees buckled, and his sexy smile revealed two perfect rows of white teeth. Fuck this job. What I really wanted was a gig with the handsome Mr. Henderson, but I had to be quick.

"I'm sorry, I didn't get your name."

"Bartholomew," I said.

"Is that your last name?" he asked in a very seductive tone.

I prayed he was looking for something more than a last name, but I said, "Dunbar."

"As in Paul Laurence Dunbar," he joked.

"The same," I said as his sensuously full lips mesmerized me.

"Ahh . . . I don't want to keep you. Give Sherrie a call tomorrow," he said.

"Sherrie? Who's Sherrie?"

"The marketing director. Her name's on the card," he said.

"Oh," I said.

"Thanks again," he said. I thought I detected some nervousness in his voice, like he might be fearful of my seductive powers. I decided there was only one way to find out.

"Mr. Henderson, in case I can't get in touch with Sherrie, maybe I should let you tell her what she missed."

I sat on the edge of the black chair, pulled off my Timberlands, and threw them like they were trick-me-fuck-me boots. I stood up and unbuttoned my skintight black jeans and pulled them to my ankles, then reached up and pulled off both my candy-red sweater and thermal nightshirt with one swoop. I was thrilled I wasn't wearing any underwear. When I looked at Mr. Henderson with a confident smile, I could tell he was happy as well.

"So what do you think?" I asked as I turned slowly to give him a view of the back. When I turned around, he was leaning back in his chair licking his lips. I stepped out of my jeans, then walked over toward his desk with the speed of a character from *The Matrix.*

"You didn't answer me, Mr. Henderson."

"Call me Basil. Your body is sweet," he said.

I took his very large hands and whispered, "Touch me." His hands were both smooth and hard as I placed them on my stomach and then my ass.

"Stand up," I said.

Basil stood up, surrendering himself as I unloosened his tie. I slowly began to undress him, like he was a long-lost lover. I undid his belt buckle and then allowed his suit pants to drop to his ankles. I slowly unbuttoned each button on his shirt like they were precious diamonds. I removed the shirt from his broad shoulders, then moved to my knees as I slowly pulled down his body-hugging gray-and-black boxer briefs. His dick was swinging like a saloon door, and my manhood was hanging stiff and long. Basil's body was amazing, every muscle, so perfectly proportioned. I was about to climb on top of him like he was a ladder, when he finally spoke again.

"Do you have protection?"

"No, but I'm clean. I get a checkup every six months."

"Sorry, dude, but as much as I want to, I can't swing without a coat."

"Can I just taste it?" I pleaded like I was a little kid wanting to lick the icing from the cake bowl.

"How bad do you want it?" Basil asked.

"Bad . . . real bad," I said.

Basil bent over and pulled up his underwear and pants, then reached for his shirt.

"I think you should put your clothes on. I mean, if you want it . . . *real* . . . *real* bad," Basil said.

"What do you mean?"

"If you can get your clothes on as quick as you took them off, then maybe, just maybe you might get to taste something real good."

I almost tripped over my own boots as I raced for my clothes while shouting, "You ain't got to tell me but once."

Stop in the Name of Lust

I imagine it was probably a woman who said men in unexpected situations think with their third dangling leg. And as much as I hate to admit it, she was probably right. I mean, how else could I explain the man, with a banging body, now in my bathroom using one of my spare toothbrushes, pink no less, that I reserve for my female first-timers? Explain to me how I came closer than a condom on my jimmie to smashing this dude in my office without even thinking about how it would look if one of my partners or assistants or the cleaning crew came in unexpected. To make it even worse, I'm pretty sure this Bart is at the very least a white liar, since he told me he had played college football but later he didn't know the difference between the wishbone and the option formation. I mean, you learn that shit as a kid in Pop Warner football.

I was in my kitchen sipping some coffee when Bart walked in with just his jeans on. I looked down, not wanting to look at his face or that fabulous fat ass of his. I had broken not only one of my mofo's rules to live by, but a second one when I allowed him to spend the night. Yeah, he was sexy as fuck (as dudes go) and knew how to please, but after I had gotten off twice, I was ready to say, "Would you like a glass of water before you leave?" When I looked out the window and saw a fast driving snow, I guess I felt sorry for old dude, knowing it would be days before a black man got a taxi on a night like that. But I can't figure out what made me begin a conversation that make it sound like I was concerned about his life. I even quit doing that shit with females a long time ago. What got into me? I can't drink anymore on work nights. I'm gonna have to leave those concoctions of cognac and Alizé called Thug Passions alone.

"So did I get the job?" Bart asked as he walked over toward my kitchen counter.

"Yeah, you got the job," I responded, even though I didn't know what he was talking about. I supposed he meant head jimmie sucker for the next three months or so.

"I enjoyed talking with you last night. I mean, great-looking and smart, too. I hit the jackpot," Bart said.

"You think so?" I mumbled under my breath.

"When I woke up this morning and I was looking at you, I thought for a moment I knew you from somewhere," Bart said.

"I used to do television. Maybe you saw me there."

"Maybe. Besides, it's not a good memory, so I'm glad it wasn't you."

"If I was a bad memory, you would have remembered," I said.

"Yeah, you're right."

"So when can I see you again? I mean, like a real date," Bart quizzed.

"Bart, I should tell you something: I don't date dudes. I might hit it with a hardhead every now and then, but I don't date," I said firmly.

"Cool, then when can we 'hit it' again?"

"Leave me your number and I'll get back with you," I said. Bart walked over toward my phone, where I kept a notepad and a pen, and wrote something down. He took a piece of paper and pen and handed it to me, asking, "Can I have your phone number?"

"I'll give you a call. You see, my shit is on the down low. I'm dating a female pretty seriously," I lied.

"I don't date bisexual men," Bart said.

"Then we're on the same page," I said.

"But sometimes I make exceptions when they look like you," he said.

"Hey, let's just take it slow and see if we gel. But you'll have your chances," I said as I walked toward the bedroom. I went to my closet and pulled out a dress shirt and began to put it on. I figured if old dude saw me getting ready for work he would finish dressing himself and hit the road.

Bart walked into the bedroom and watched me dress for a moment. Then he said softly, "I have my own place, and you can come see me anytime." This was beginning to feel too deep for me, so I decided to lighten things up.

"Dude, Bart, I only give the fellows three coupons. You've really used up two, but I am willing to count last night as one." I laughed.

"Coupons? I don't understand."

"Three times to ride the jimmie, and then I move on."

"Is there any way I can earn some bonus coupons?" He grinned.

"What do you mean?"

"If I want to see you more than three times? I think you had a good time last night. That was just the beginning. It gets better," Bart said.

"I don't think so. Every time I break my own rules, trouble follows. So for now I think we better just say you got two coupons remaining. Besides, I mean, a good-looking brotha like yourself can have your pick of the dudes and bitches," I said.

"Don't you remember what I told you last night? I don't date women," Bart said.

"Never?"

"Never. So what about the job? If you think I'm so good-looking, why don't you make sure I get the modeling job?" Bart said.

"I'll talk with some people," I said.

"Judging by the size of your office, it looks like you got the juice," Bart said.

"I got the juice." I started to make it clear that I wasn't promising him the modeling gig. Damn, if I hired everybody I fucked, we'd be out of business.

"So I got the job," Bart said confidently.

"If you say so. It's a good thing to think positive."

"Make sure you tell your marketing director Sherrie that. I could really use the work," Bart said.

"I'll do that. Hey, I got to get ready to rock and roll," I said.

"I'll get dressed, but before I leave, do you mind if I use your phone to check my messages? I might be missing some calls from someone who knows my sex and love get better day by day." Bart laughed.

"Hey, I feel you. Knock yourself out."

The Red Carpet

I was glad to be home in New York, and Windsor had pre-pared my favorite dish: deviled eggs with a touch of caviar. As I walked into the kitchen, I noticed that she'd also fried some chicken and made cabbage laced with bacon strips, and chicken-flavored Rice-A-Roni. She'd even whipped up some skillet corn bread.

"Come on and have a seat, and let me fix you a plate," Windsor said.

"Windsor, you're not going to get me fat. I just bought a slammin' black silk charmeuse dress, and I have to be able to fit into it tonight! I'm going to a benefit at Carnegie Hall that Wyclef Jean is giving for his foundation. I heard a lot of divas will be there—Mary J., Macy Gray and Destiny's Child. So I got to look my best," I said as I walked over to the refrigerator and pulled out a bottle of water.

"Hmm," Windsor said as she drained the chicken oil into a can.

"So, Windsor, what are you going to do tonight?"

"Grade some papers and write in my journal," Windsor

replied, and then noticed that I was looking at her closely and asked me, "What are you thinking?"

"I just can't believe you're getting married and having a baby," I said in a soft whisper.

"All I know right now is that I'm having this baby," Windsor said as she placed our food on the table. While we were eating, Windsor told me how Wardell was suddenly having cold feet since he found out she was pregnant and that their conversations were short and strained. He had even asked Windsor to consider an abortion, which she refused to do.

"So what are you going to do? Raise your child in a broken home?" I asked as I took a bite of the piping-hot fried chicken leg.

"Yancey, the way I see it, it's better to be a product of a broken home than to live in one," Windsor said as she picked up a fork and nibbled on some rice.

"I hear you, girl. But you're a better woman than I am. I mean, having kids is hard enough with two people. And these kids today are demons. Shooting up each other. I hope you're going to send your child to private school and move to the suburbs."

"I think that's the big problem. Perceptions. I won't have any problem sending my child to an inner-city school. Those kids might get beat up and someone might take their lunch money, but at least their parents see them in the evening," Windsor said.

"I hadn't thought about that, and you make a good point."

"So how are you doing? I mean, I know you're all happy about your music career, but how is your soul?" Windsor asked as I thought about the improbable friendship Windsor and I shared. We were as different as lemons and watermelons. Even though it was relatively new, just about two years old, my friendship with her was something I valued. Before Windsor, I'd never had a close female friend.

"I don't know how my soul is doing, but my career, the most important thing to me, is doing just fine," I said.

"Have you talked to Basil?"

"I don't want to talk to Basil," I said quickly.

"Do you still love him?" Windsor asked, ignoring me.

"Why do you ask?"

"It must have been hard to leave him on your wedding day," she said. Windsor was so damn polite, she was still sticking to my version of the breakup, even though I was sure she knew better.

"I loved Basil, I think. He loved me more than I loved him, but it wasn't a totally lopsided love. Do you love Wardell more than he loves you?"

"I just love Wardell. I know he loves me, but who loves who more is a difficult question, especially since I only know how I love him," Windsor said.

"That's deep, Windsor. I've always focused on making someone love me more," I said as Windsor placed her hand on top of mine.

We sat in silence for a moment and then I said, "Windsor, there's a lot of stuff about Basil you and the public don't know. That boy has lots of secrets, and my new song might just tip off the world."

"What secrets does Basil have that the world needs to know?" Windsor asked.

I looked at Windsor with a cat-who-ate-the-canary grin and said, "If either one of us had a good-looking brother, we would be wise to keep him away from Basil."

"What are you talking about?"

"Let's put it this way. If Basil were still in high school, he'd fit right in at that school where you teach." I laughed.

"Are you telling me Basil's gay?"

"Not really all the way. I guess you could call him gay-lite."

"No, that's called bisexual. Which should surprise me, considering how fine and masculine he is, but teaching at Harvey Milk has taught me a lot about stereotypes. Still, I don't think that's something you need to tell the world. Basil has enough trouble, because no matter how gorgeous he is, he's still a black man. That's burden enough. Let him keep his secrets if he chooses."

"I hear ya talking, but his little secret might help my singing career get off to the right start," I said defiantly.

"Yancey! Why would you want to act so ugly? Great things are happening for you. Your voice will sell itself. Release the thought of revenge and you'll be blessed," Windsor said.

It was no wonder Windsor was pregnant—she was always acting like someone's mama. But I couldn't be too mad at her, since she did have a point. So I just looked down a moment and said, "I don't know, Windsor. His secret hurt me a lot, and I learned as a child not to let people mess over me. When they strike, you've got to strike back. Catch them unaware, after they've forgotten the pain they've caused."

Windsor took my hand in hers, looked into my eyes and said, "Whoever taught you that, Yancey, was flat-out wrong."

• • •

The traffic surrounding Carnegie Hall was hopelessly congested with limos and taxis, but I didn't care. I was floating on a magic carpet after witnessing my peers put on a show, each trying to outsing the others: Whitney Houston, Mary J. Blige, Macy, Beyoncé and her backups, Stevie Wonder, Marc Anthony and Eric Clapton.

But they were not the main reason I was floating. When I walked down the red carpet to enter the hall with Michel, photographers started screaming out my name, "Yancey B, would you stop for me, please?" "Who designed your dress?" "How does it feel to be the new pop diva?" "Why aren't you performing tonight?"

It was wonderful as I turned this way and then the other way, smiling all the time while flashes blinded my view. When Patrick Stinson from the *E!* channel pulled me off the red carpet for a live interview, I knew I had arrived. When he asked me about my song and if the lyrics were based on a personal experience, I looked at him, smiled and said, "Patrick, that's a great question, and I will answer it very soon, but right now I'm just here to support Wyclef and his kids." Who said beauty pageants don't serve a useful purpose?

When Wyclef himself invited me to a private after-party at Lotus, I politely declined, telling him I had an interview with Deborah Gregory of *Essence* the next morning and I wanted to be fresh. He gave me a kiss on the cheek and whispered, "Next time."

As I pulled up in front of my town house, a thin dusting of snow was beginning to cover the city.

"My name is Ruland; here's my card. It was nice driving you. Call me if you need me," he said.

"Thank you, Ruland, and I will," I said as I put my fur on and headed for my door.

Inside my house, it was dark as asphalt, and I figured Windsor was asleep. I was tempted to wake her up and tell her about all the stars I'd met, but instead I headed to the kitchen, when I heard the sounds of someone whimpering. I couldn't tell if it was a human or some type of animal like a cat. I became a bit uneasy, since I had never heard Windsor cry and she knew my rules about pets of any kind. When I turned on the light in the dining room, I was startled to see Windsor sitting in a chair, bent over and holding her stomach.

"Windsor! What are you doing sitting here in the dark?" I asked as I moved toward her.

"Yancey, I'm not feeling well. I think I need to go to the hospital," she said.

"What's the matter?"

"I'm spotting, and my stomach is so upset. Look at my hands," Windsor said as she moved her hands toward me. They were huge, obviously swollen.

"Do you want me to call your parents?"

"I need to go to the hospital. We can call them and Wardell from there," Windsor said. Her eyes in the dim light were shiny with tears.

"Let me call the driver," I said as I reached for the phone. I pulled out the card Ruland had given me and dialed his cell phone number. He picked up after a couple of rings.

"Ruland, this is Miss Braxton. You just dropped me off. I have an emergency. Where are you?"

"I'm crossing Madison Avenue. I can be back at your place in two minutes."

"Hurry," I said as I heard Windsor let out a huge moan, which sounded like she was in labor. But she couldn't be in labor if she was only four months pregnant. I hung up the phone and sat next to Windsor. I hugged her tightly and said, "Don't worry, Windsor, help is on the way."

Stray Boyz

A week had passed and I hadn't been able to catch up with Wylie, but I was dying to tell him about my date. I had to tell someone about my evening, even though I had promised Basil I wouldn't say a word. But didn't Basil know that the gay boy code of silence meant you wouldn't tell all of your friends? Just your top two, at the very least.

Wylie picked up the phone quickly, which meant he was probably on the other line.

"Who you talking to?" I asked.

"Well, hello to you, too, darling. I'm talking to LaVonya. Trying to find out the good tea before she publishes it in the paper. What's shaking?"

"I got something to tell you. Tell Ms. LaVonya it's a family emergency," I ordered. LaVonya Young was Wylie's resident fag hag and one of the city's most popular gossip columnists. She had her own radio show, and a syndicated column called "Lines from LaVonya" in which she would drop juicy one-liners without revealing the names. Once a month in her column in *Diva* magazine she would go into a little more detail but still no names. People would visit her Web site and post their guesses as to who LaVonya was talking about, but she would never confirm or deny. I liked LaVonya well enough, but I wasn't as close to her as Wylie. I knew better than to have a lot of women around me. Like that old saying, "No need to take sand to the beach."

"So what's the emergency, Bart?"

"I had the most amazing sexual experience of my life."

"I thought you had a couple of auditions today," Wylie said.

"I did. And that's where the story begins and ends."

I told Wylie about how I'd seduced the handsome Basil Henderson, blow by blow, as it were. Wylie would occasionally interrupt me by saying, "No, you didn't," and "Nurse Bart, you gonna make me throw this phone out the window."

"Are you going to see him again?" Wylie asked when I finally took a breath.

"Are grits groceries?"

"Last time I checked." Wylie laughed.

"It was amazing. I think I might be in love."

"I ain't mad a cha!"

"There is one small problem, though."

"What? He doesn't have the monster, does he?" Wylie asked. Monster was what some people called the HIV virus.

"No. I mean, I didn't ask him, but I'm sure he's clean. Basil thinks he's bisexual," I said. "I feel like I've seen him somewhere before."

"Maybe the bathhouse or the park, you think?"

"I doubt it. He doesn't seem to be the bathhouse/park type," I said.

"So he's one of those strays, can't decide if he wants to be straight or gay. Mark my word, very soon there's going to be more of them than us. Then we gonna be complaining like our sisters how black men are either in prison or can't make up their minds," Wylie said.

"I said he thinks he's bisexual. He's a top, but he liked me way too much to think he doesn't know which team he's on."

"Did you get the job?"

"What job?"

"The modeling job."

"You bet I got the job *and* a new man. I mean, Wylie, this may be the one! I feel that strongly about this."

"For real?"

"For real."

"But what if he is bisexual? You know he'll never settle down," Wylie warned.

"I can change him."

"Where have I heard that before?"

"Wylie, don't spoil this for me. Stop being a homo-hater." I despised it when Wylie got jealous.

"I'm sorry. Describe him once more, and go slow on the good parts," Wylie pleaded.

"Now, Wylie, sometimes a boy has to keep a little some-thing to himself. I can't have my best friend trying to go after my man." I laughed.

"Be that way. I guess I need to go to Stella's and see if I can't find me a dreamboy for the night," Wylie said.

"Good night and good luck," I said. Stella's was a midtown gay bar where Wylie and I went when we wanted certain one-night-stand sex. I smiled, because after meeting Basil I knew my nights at Stella's and cruising Mount Morris Park were coming to an end. No more nights of looking for Mr. Right or Mr. Right Now at the piers down in the Village. All the things I hated about being gay could end if I could get Basil to fall in love with me, and I was going to give it everything I had.

• • •

I was walking from my kitchen with a bowl of microwave popcorn when my phone rang. I figured it was Wylie trying to talk me into meeting him at Stella's, so I answered the phone, "I'm not going to go."

"Is this Bart?" an unfamiliar male voice asked.

"This is Bart. Who is this?"

"This is David. I met you at the Viceroy about a month ago. We went out and had a drink. I've called you a couple of times," David said. I remembered the tall and lanky man who I was certain was packing big beef, but when I grabbed between his legs all I felt was something the size of my thumb. Didn't he know that's why I wasn't returning his calls? Any self-respecting little-dick man knew not to step to me.

"Yeah, David. I've been busy," I said quickly.

"I was wondering if I could see you again," he asked softly.

"For what?"

"You seem like an interesting guy," he said.

"But you don't know me. What do you want to see me for?"

"I thought we had a good time. But I guess . . ."

"Listen, David, I'm sure you're a real nice guy, but you ain't packing enough for me to waste a minute of my time. And I'm dating a real man. Have a nice life," I said as I hung up and put a handful of popcorn in my mouth.

A Cold, Cold Wind

I almost cut myself shaving when I heard Yancey's voice sweep through my loft. I was in the bathroom getting ready for work when I heard Doug Banks announce, "This is the fastest-selling song in the country, 'Any Way the Wind Blows,' by Yancey B."

So old girl had changed her name and career path. The Yancey Braxton I knew wasn't going to be stopped until her name was listed, large and bright, on the marquee. The song was smooth, but I got nervous when I heard some of the lyrics, "You want him and not me." I better get a copy of this song quick.

When the song was over Doug asked Dee-Dee, his co-host, a question.

"So have you heard what this song is about?" Doug asked Dee-Dee.

"Yeah, it's about brothers on the down low." Dee-Dee laughed.

"But I wonder who she's talking about."

"I don't know, but it sounds like ole Yancey B got a score to settle," she joked.

"Well, you know she's going to be here in the studio real soon. Do you think she'll tell us?"

"If sister wants to sell some records, then she needs to do more than sing. She better talk." Dee-Dee giggled.

I turned the radio off, and tiny beads of sweat started to cover my forehead and neck. Unwanted memories of my last days with Yancey began to flood my mind. I grabbed a towel, wiped my face dry and then rushed to my phone. I dialed the office and then hung up. At first I wanted to know if my assistant, Kendra, who listened to *The Doug Banks Show* religiously, had heard the song, but then decided I'd rather find out when I got to the office. I still had Yancey's number on my speed dial. When a female voice picked up, I took a deep breath.

"Windsor, is that you?" I asked.

"Yes, this is Windsor. Who am I speaking with? Wait, I know this voice. Basil, how are you doing?" She sounded like the same old Windsor, optimistic and concerned about anyone she came in contact with.

"I'm fine. How are you?"

"I'm blessed and highly favored, even though I'm a little bit under the weather," Windsor said.

"What's wrong?"

"Got a little case of high blood pressure and then you add in I'm going to have a baby, well, the doctor has me on complete bed rest for a while, but my baby and me are going to be just fine," Windsor said.

"So when's the big day?"

"Which one?" Windsor asked.

"When's your baby due?" I asked, suddenly thinking about Rosa and wondering how her pregnancy was coming along. Damn, I didn't need to be thinking about Rosa and her problems with Yancey and her song worrying the crap out of me.

"At the end of June or the first part of July," Windsor said. She didn't sound like she was seriously ill.

"I didn't know you and Yancey were still roommates," I said, forcing myself to sound unbothered and friendly.

"Well, not exactly. I've been house-sitting for Yancey," Windsor said.

"That's why I'm calling. I just heard her song on the radio. Doug Banks and Dee-Dee said it's zooming up the charts."

"Yeah, it's doing great!"

"Do you know how I can get in contact with Yancey? I want to congratulate her," I said, wondering if Windsor could detect the desperation in my voice.

"That's so sweet of you. You can reach her right here. Does she have your number?" Windsor asked.

"Tell her it's the same," I said.

"I think maybe you should give it to me again. Yancey asked me to throw out a lot of stuff when she went to Los Angeles," Windsor said.

"So she's been hanging out in Los Angeles," I said. Now I knew why I hadn't run into Yancey or heard from her since our aborted wedding.

"Yeah, she's been doing great out there. So give me the numbers, and I'll make sure she gets them."

"Thanks, Windsor," I said as I gave her my home, cell and office numbers.

When I got to work, I sent Kendra over to Tower Records to get a copy of Yancey's CD. I thought about going and purchasing it myself, but I had several contracts I needed to review by noon.

Kendra returned all excited, telling me about how much she liked the song and how Yancey B had a huge display in the record store.

"When did you first hear the song?"

"While I was listening to it at Tower, I realized this was the song one of my girlfriends had been talking about," Kendra said.

"So the song's pretty popular? I'm going to pop it in and check it out. Hold my calls."

I slid the CD into my stereo and gazed at the cover. Yancey looked damn good sporting a gold halter top and skintight pants and serving much attitude. I hit the Play button, and Yancey's voice filled my office:

"You said I was your lady
As sweet as candy baby, and I fell for you
But then one day I come home
To find you're not alone
This can't be true . . . it can't be true
You were in the arms of another man
That was more than I could stand
I had to let you go."

I was relieved after the first verse, because I realized it was just a song. Yancey couldn't be talking about our relationship, since she never even caught me looking cross-eyed at another man. A long time ago, I'd been caught in an awkward position with a dude, and I'd learned a lesson. I continued to listen.

> *"I can see your love goes*
> *Any way the wind blows*
> *Even though I know I have to*
> *I don't want to be without you*
> *I can see your love flows*
> *Any way the wind blows*
> *It's such a dangerous breeze*
> *You want him and not me"*

I was falling into the groove of the song when I heard someone knock on my door. I got up from my chair and hit the Pause button on the CD player and said, "Come on in."

"'Sup, buddy," Nico said as he walked into my office. He was one of the best-dressed dudes I knew. Nico had on an off-white French-cuffed shirt, with a mustard-yellow tie, navy blue pleated slacks and reptile loafers. He'd been lifting weights with me a lot and had transformed his basketball body into a solid muscular look, and developed a thick neck and broad shoulders. Now Nico was so into lifting that he made sure there was always a real gym near his hotel when he traveled. Once when we were in Florida together, visiting prospective clients at Florida State, he dragged me to a gym after ten o'clock. I had created a gym monster.

"'Sup, Nico," I said as I watched Nico walk over to my desk and pick up Yancey's empty CD case.

"Damn, dude, who is this?" Nico asked as he moved the case close to his eyes to inspect it more closely. "She kinda looks like that singer Pebbles from back in the day."

"You don't know who that is?"

"She looks familiar and tasty," Nico said, as he licked his lips like he was ready to go "downtown."

"That's Yancey. The woman I was engaged to," I said as I took the case out of his hand before he started to lick it. I could see I was correct in not introducing Yancey to Nico while we were dating. He wouldn't have thought twice about trying to hit on her. Nico was both a baller and a playa hater. I had invited him to the wedding, but Nico told me he couldn't bear to attend a ceremony celebrating a playa giving up his freedom.

"Damn, B, now I see how this honey almost got you to turn in your playa card. I bet she was pissed when you told her you wouldn't give up your freedom."

"It was a mutual decision. She wanted her career, and I still had some more hunney-hunting to do," I said with a slight smile. "What can I do for you?"

"Oh yeah, she made me forget my bizness. Who's the dude from CSU you just signed?"

"You talking about Daschle Thompson, right?"

"Yeah, that's him. Can I get his phone number? I'm trying to sign a basketball player over there, and I want to see if Daschle knows him," Nico said.

"Kendra has all Daschle's information. I'll reach out and tell him to expect your call."

"Thanks, Buddy," Nico said as he picked up the CD single-case and said to himself, "'Any Way the Wind Blows.'

I'm gonna have to check Yancey B out." When he looked back at me and saw the puzzled look on my face, he quickly said, "I mean, check out the CD. Got to support a sista who was almost like a member of the family."

"Yancey always appreciates support from her family," I said with a nervous grin.

• • •

Before I left the office for the evening, I got another e-mail from that crazy mofo out there trying to mess with me. I decided against blocking the messages, because I knew from the movie *The Godfather* that it was important to keep my enemies close. I opened the e-mail and read: *Why won't you answer my missives? I am serious. I don't want to have to post your name and picture on brothersontheDL.com—what would your business partners and clients think of that?*

I'm Ready for My Close-Up

I spent Monday in cold, sun-drenched New York, interviewing personal assistants at the Motown office near
Fifty-seventh and Seventh Avenue, and looking for a director. I saw about six candidates, most of whom had worked
for stars like Ashford and Simpson and Queen Latifah. The
most qualified was a young lady named Nancy, who had
worked for Diana Ross and Quincy Jones. She had excellent
references, but there was a slight problem. Nancy looked
like a model and had show business aspirations of her own. I
had a rule: Never trust a beautiful woman to cover my back,
especially one who carried her extra demo tapes in her purse
and wore "I'm a Stank Ho" blue jeans. In light of that, I'm
leaning toward this pleasingly plump sister, Amy, from the
Bronx. She's a little rough around the edges, but I think
she'll be fine for running the errands I hate, like picking up
laundry and buying my toiletries. I also needed someone to
help me with Windsor until she and her family decided
whether or not to try and move her back home.

I had insisted that Windsor stay with me in New York

until the baby arrived, but Windsor was worried about being in the way and not being able to pay rent since she wasn't teaching anymore. I told her not to worry, even though I was concerned she'd have another medical emergency. Wardell had assured me that if she got sick again, he would be in New York as soon as he could. I couldn't help but envy Windsor a little. She had a man who loved her so much that he would just drop everything to be by her side.

I shared a deli lunch of corned beef and chips with Michel, who seemed happy that I was in New York.

"So you think I'm going to like this director?" I asked Michel as he took a swig from his can of root beer.

"He's up and coming. And I worked with him on a Chanté Moore video—it was one of the best of her career," Michel said as he picked up the empty paper plate sitting in front of me. Our attempts to get two of the top directors, Billy Woodruff and Paul Hunter, had been unsuccessful. Both were booked for up to a year, and since they hadn't heard of Yancey B, both had passed. But that's okay. I intended to make them regret that decision when I got to my second or third video. By then I would have my choice of directors.

"Are you surprised by how well your first single is doing? I mean, I looked at some reports yesterday and it's the most requested song in ten markets," Michel said.

"I'm not a bit surprised. I'm just waiting for it to hit the top forty," I said confidently.

"It's well on the way," Michel said. "I mean to hit the charts after the first week is amazing for a new artist."

The phone in the conference room rang and Michel

picked up the receiver while I touched up my makeup. Just as I was closing my compact, there was a knock on the door.

"Come in," Michel said. The door opened, and in walked a man with an almond-brown leather coat, a hat and sunglasses. Hmm, I thought, who does this guy think he is? I'd only seen big stars wear sunglasses indoors.

"Are you Desmond Fowler?" Michel asked.

"I would be he," Desmond said. His voice was deep and strong, and he had a commanding presence.

"Have a seat. This is Motown's newest diva, Yancey Braxton, a.k.a. Yancey B, and I am Michel Rodriguez, head of A and R for our East Coast operations."

"Nice meeting you," Desmond said as he took off his jacket and hat. He had thin dreads the size of a new number-two pencil and honey-colored brown eyes. He was tall, I would say a little over six feet, with a lean build. He was handsome in an adult homeboy kind of way.

"Nice meeting you," I said as I extended my hand toward Desmond.

"Did you bring your reel?" Michel asked.

"Sure did," Desmond said as he reached into a leather duffle and pulled out a videocassette.

"Who have you worked with?" I asked.

"In terms of?" Desmond asked.

"What stars have you directed?" I asked trying to make what I thought was a simple question clearer.

"The only stars I believe in are in the sky. And I haven't worked with any of them. But if you're talking about people who sing and dance for a living, then I've worked with quite a few," Desmond said.

"Like who?" I asked.

"Eric Benet, Kenny Latimore, Peabo Bryson," Desmond said.

"Any female singers?" Michel asked.

"I just worked with Tamia."

"Ooh, I loved her last video," I gushed. "It was very sensuous."

"So you liked it? Thanks. I think that was some of my best work," Desmond said.

"Why don't you tell us about yourself," I said.

"What do you want to know besides the fact that I'm a damn good director? Naw, make that a slamming director," Desmond said confidently.

"You don't have a resume?" I asked.

"Everything you need to know is on that tape," Desmond said.

"Where did you get your film training?" Michel asked.

"I went to undergrad at the University of Minnesota and went to film school at NYU, but I dropped out."

"Do you mind my asking why?" Michel quizzed.

"I learned what I needed to know and then moved on."

"Have you listened to my music?" I asked.

"Yeah, and it was jive-tight."

I must have had a puzzled look on my face, because Desmond looked at me and smiled. "That means great. Your vocals and lyrics are real strong."

"Thank you." I smiled.

"You've seen the treatment for the video?" Michel asked.

"Yep, I read it."

"You know this might be controversial and we're on a

tight schedule. We need to shoot this in a week or two. Will that be a problem?"

"Not as long as you pay me and my staff overtime, and we shoot up in Harlem."

"Harlem? I don't think so," I said as I looked cross-eyed at Michel.

"Then I can't do it," Desmond said as he got up from his chair.

"Why do you have to do it in Harlem?" I asked.

"You must be from L.A.," Desmond said.

"Why do you say that?" I asked.

"'Cause Harlem is the joint these days. Besides, I have a wonderful relationship with a studio up there who can pull this shoot together fast. It's top-notch," Desmond said.

"Let's talk about the treatment," Michel said.

"Yeah. How do you see it?" I asked.

"Some of the stuff is cool. But this is your video and you should be the focal point, not the dudes. I mean, we need them to convey the song's story. I'd like to see you in something real sexy, but dressed down and revealing with your hair flowing. I would begin with a close-up of your face, with you singing the chorus without music, kinda like Whitney Houston did in 'I Will Always Love You.' Like this: 'I can see your love goes . . . any way the wind blows . . . even though I know I have to . . . I don't want to be without you . . . I can see your love flows . . . any way the wind blows . . .'" Desmond said as his words and singing melted together.

"You have a great voice," I said.

"I do all right for a director," he said.

"We still have to cast the men, and do you think we need dancers?"

"No dancers. Just this beautiful lady, the dudes, the sets and a little computer magic," Desmond said.

"The sets have already been prepared. That's why the Harlem studio might be a problem," Michel said.

"Not really. Let me check out whatever sets you got and if I decide to use them, I can get my guys to move up there in a minute. The other scenes we can do behind a white background and then use the computer to put in what we need. Simple, just like that," Desmond said as he snapped his fingers in the air.

"What casting agents would you recommend?" Michel asked.

"Jakki Brown is the best in New York, but you don't really need strong actors. You just need a couple of pretty boys in the background. So I would suggest using one of the modeling agencies like the Lyon Group or Ford. I want Yancey B out front singing her ass off, or should I say lips off, since she'll be lip-synching," Desmond said, and looked over at me just long enough to make me feel a little uncomfortable about the eye contact I'd made with him.

"So you want the focus on me," I said. I suddenly loved his vision, and maybe the Harlem studio would be less expensive. I didn't want to be one of those singers who ended up in bankruptcy court because I spent too much money on my video or my jewelry. I planned to walk right into places like Harry Winston and Versace and demand the same kind of goodies they give women like Whitney, Lil' Kim and Mary J. Blige.

"Yeah . . . yeah, Yancey B. I want you to show anguish and pain about losing your love to a dude. I want people to say, 'What kind of dumb mofo would leave such a beautiful woman?'" Desmond said thoughtfully.

I smiled and looked at Michel and said, "I think we've found our director."

• • •

I was getting ready to go home when Michel stopped me just as I was pushing the door buzzer. It was after hours, and the receptionist was gone.

"Hey, I got a package for you," he said.

"What is it?"

"Probably some fan mail. You better get used to it." Michel smiled.

I took the package from Michel, and the first thing I noticed was there was no return address. I shook the package gently, and it felt like it contained some type of cards or pictures. I tore open the package as I pushed through the glass door and walked toward the elevator. A few moments later the elevator arrived, and as I walked on, I dropped the contents of the package. Photographs of several pretty black girls fell out. How sweet, I thought. They were probably some of my young fans who wanted autographs, or maybe a stage mother who was trying to get video work for her daughters. But then I looked at the photos and noticed that none of the girls looked the same. One was very light-skinned, another a peanut butter brown, and the last was beautiful, with skin the color of coal.

The elevator reached the lobby, and I continued to study the photos. I looked inside the envelope for a note and saw a small yellow sheet of paper and pulled it out. As I walked out of the building, the harsh cold air hit my face with the force of a ceiling fan. A chill covered my entire body when I read the note: *Do you know which one of these girls doesn't have a mommy? Think about it. . . .*

• • •

I had just finished my bath and was trying to decide what I wanted for dinner when my phone rang. I was enjoying *How Glory Goes,* a CD by Audra MacDonald that I hated to admit I loved. That child could make magic with her voice.

"Hello, this is Yancey B," I said.

"Indeed it is," Ava, my estranged mother said in her usual flip manner. I hadn't spoken with her since the day after my aborted wedding. I was wondering what I'd done to deserve this phone call when I remember the photos I'd received earlier. Maybe she was calling to see if her childish pranks were rattling me, so I decided to act like nothing but great things were happening for me.

"Ava? I'm surprised to hear from you," I said in as cheery a voice as I could muster.

"I need to speak with you," she said, as I heard my phone beep.

"Hold on, I have a call coming in," I said quickly as I clicked over without giving Ava a chance to keep me on the line.

"Hello," I said.

"Yancey, this is Michel. Jut wanted you to know that we got B. Michael to design some great gowns for the video and the photo session with *Savoy,*" he said.

"Oh, that's great," I said as I took a seat on my bed and used the remote to turn the volume down on Audra's booming voice.

"Yeah, it was a real coup to get him to design for you. He's one of the hottest designers in town," Michel said.

"I know that's right. Were we able to book Sam Fine and Oscar James for my makeup and hair?"

"I think so, but let me double-check," Michel said.

"Please, I wouldn't want to do the video without them," I said.

"I'll have my assistant find out. I know we got Lloyd Boston to do the styling and Matthew Jordan Smith is going to do the promotional photos."

"Oh, that's wonderful. I can't believe you got them," I said. By now, Ava was probably good and hot, but I didn't care. I had my own business to tend to.

"Is there anything else I can do for you?"

"You guys are spoiling me, but I like it," I said.

"You're going to be a star, so nothing but the best for you."

"I like hearing that."

"I'll speak with you tomorrow. Have a relaxing evening," Michel said.

"Bye now. Thanks for everything," I said as I clicked back over to Ava.

"Are you still there?" I asked.

"I was getting ready to hang up! Have you lost your mind or something? Keeping me on hold that long. I got things to do," Ava said.

"It was important," I said.

"Who was it? The President of the United States or the Queen of England?" Ava scoffed.

"So how are you doing in California?" I asked, ignoring my mother's jab.

"Minding my business," Ava snapped, the tone of her voice changing quicker than a heartbeat.

"Glad to hear you got business. If you called to mess with me, then let's keep it short," I said, realizing that I hadn't missed our conversations one bit.

"I called to be nice. I saw you sing your little song on *Soul Train*. Have you been taking voice lessons or did they fix it up in the studio?" Ava asked.

"I need to go, and for your information that little record will soon be at the top of the charts," I said.

"Well, I guess anything is possible. I mean if Cher can have a number one song then I suppose you could too," Ava said.

"Look, I've got to run. I have a full day tomorrow. Give me a call when you want to act like a mother," I said.

"My, aren't we feeling bitchy? I called to be nice. I was thinking about coming to New York to help you out," Ava said.

"Help me out? What are you talking about?" I asked.

"It looks like the better judgment of the public ain't what it used to be and you might really make it big. You need someone to look out for your interests, and who better than me," Ava said.

"I already have a team in place," I said.

"But they're not family. I got some time. I need to make sure you don't make any mistakes."

"Ava, listen to me. I don't need your help. Stay out in Cali with your latest husband."

"Don't worry about my husband. You should be grateful to have a mother who knows the show biz ropes," Ava said.

"As long as you don't use those ropes to try and hang me," I said before putting down the phone.

Ain't Too Proud to Beg

Yancey was on my mind, and I was seeing her everywhere. Posters promoting her song were plastered all over the city. Every time I turned on the radio I heard her voice.

Today as I looked out the window, I could tell there was nothing good about this cold, gray Wednesday morning, so I might as well make it worse by calling Yancey again. It was a little after eight, so I knew Yancey was still enjoying her beauty sleep. I knew putting the call off wasn't going to solve my problems, so I picked up the phone and dialed Yancey's number.

After a couple of rings, Yancey picked up the phone. "Hello." The sleep made her voice sound deep and sexy.

"Yancey," I said softly.

"Basil?" Yancey said.

"Yep, it's me. So I guess you haven't forgotten my voice. How's Windsor doing?"

"What do you want? I know you didn't call over here to check on Windsor's health." The sexy voice was gone, replaced with a cool bitterness.

"I need to talk to you," I said.

"Why?"

"Yancey, will you just give me five minutes?" I asked.

"Tell me now," Yancey demanded.

"Yancey, just give me five minutes face-to-face. Can I come by around noon?"

"I won't be here," Yancey said.

"What about this evening, around seven?"

"I don't know. Let me call you. Is your office number still the same?"

"Yeah, do you still have it?"

"Why else would I ask you if it was the same, Basil? Have you gotten dumb all of a sudden?"

I didn't answer her question and decided I would try and lay on some charm. "Your song sounds great, and I've been seeing your posters everywhere. I guess you've made the big time," I said, choosing my words very carefully.

"Was there ever any doubt?"

"No, I guess not," I said, remembering that Yancey's extreme confidence was one of the things that attracted me to her.

"What do you want to talk about? My song?" Yancey asked. I guess she still knew me well. Same old Yancey.

"Just wait until you see me. I promise you, I only need five minutes."

"If I decide to see you, then that's all you're getting. I think we need to meet at a neutral site," Yancey said.

"What? Are you afraid to be alone with me?" I asked with my normal cocky tone.

"Not hardly," Yancey said coldly.

"Okay, I'll wait for your call, and if I'm on the phone, please tell my assistant to put you through," I said.

"That's *if* I call. Don't hold your breath," Yancey said as she slammed down the phone.

• • •

I'd just finished an intensive staff meeting, when Kendra walked into my office and said, "There's a Bart Dunbar on the phone. He says it's real important, and it's the fourth time he's called in the last two days."

"Thanks, Kendra, ask him to hold on," I said as I looked at the clock and realized that it was almost 7:30 P.M. Brison, Nico and I were trying to decide what to do about an offer made by PMK to purchase XJI. PMK was the largest sports management company in the USA. The financial package would make the three of us independently wealthy. Nico was in favor of selling, while Brison and I were wavering because we thought it would set a bad example if we sold out to the big boys just when we were making a dent in their business. PMK was offering us executive positions and we'd be able to keep our individual clients, but the thought of working for somebody just didn't sit well with Brison and me. We thought we'd left those days behind when we left professional sports.

Before I picked up the phone, I made sure my door was locked. I was a little pissed off that Bart was calling my office like some teenage girl enjoying her first major crush. I had the feeling this wasn't going to be a pleasant conversation, but I had to get this shit over with.

"Whatsup, dude?"

"You're not trying to slip away, are you?" Bart asked. As

far as I was concerned, homeboy had just crossed the invisible line I had warned him about after our first meeting. I didn't date men, and I certainly didn't like them calling my office during the day to chitchat.

"Dude, I can't talk right now. Let me get back to you," I said.

"But what about our plans?"

"Plans? What plans?"

"I got tickets for us to see *The Lion King*. I wanted to surprise you."

"Bart, I don't like surprises."

"Didn't you get the messages I left for you at your house?"

"I haven't been checking my messages. I've been tied up."

"I'd like to tie you up," Bart teased. There he was, crossing the line again.

"Bart, I'm sorry, but I'm not going to be able to make it. I have other plans," I said, suddenly feeling like letting Bart sample the beef could have been one of my biggest mistakes of the new millennium.

"Other plans that don't include me? You *are* trying to get away. Now, don't make me put you in a headlock, and you can take that any way you want to," Bart said in a playful tone.

"I'm sure you've got some other friends that would enjoy the show, and I'll pay for the ticket," I said.

"It's not about the money. It's about our debut," Bart said.

"Debut?"

"Yeah, as a couple," Bart said.

"Dude, how can I get this through your head?" I said in

a low, hushed tone. "We had a good time, but I told you I don't date hardheads."

"Yeah, I know, but I was hoping I could change your mind," Bart said.

"Bart, look, I need to run. I'll hit you back later," I said as I got off the phone quickly. After that conversation, I needed to hit the gym and work out some of my tension, then go and find me some new pussy.

Other Divas and CP Time

I had been rehearsing for a couple of hours for my performance at the Roxy when one of the backup singers got on my last nerve. Paul Ellis, the musical director hired by Motown, had hired three backup singers for my act, two females and one male. The male singer, Guy, a decent-looking brother with a honey-smooth tenor voice, and Terri, the regulation backup big mama with her gospel sound, were just fine. But this skinny bitch named Dove, with holes in almost every part of her body, was giving me fits. First of all, I wanted to ask her why her mother named her after a bar of soap, but I had more pressing issues on my mind.

Every time I was getting my groove on with my songs, Miss Dove would start singing over me, with riffs and notes that were *not* part of the arrangement. At first, I tried to be nice. I walked closer to the singers and sang with them. When I asked them if they knew their parts, they all nodded and smiled, but when we started to sing again, the only voice

I could hear was Miss Dove's. I motioned for Paul to stop the music, and Michel came over and asked me if everything was okay.

"No, it's not," I said firmly.

"What's the matter?" he asked.

"Dove's singing over me, and she's fucking everything up," I said.

"You think so?"

"Can't you hear her? She's singing stuff that's not even in my songs. I've asked her once to sing it the way I told her, but when we sing I can hear her trying to out sing me," I said as I folded my arms to let Michel know that I wasn't happy.

"But Dove is one of the top backup singers in the business. I think she's pretty close to getting her own deal," Michel said.

"Then let her sing that loud and that off-key with her own act. She's not messing up mine."

"Yancey, the Roxy performance is one week off. I don't know if we can get another singer at this late date."

"Then we'll have to make do with Guy and Terri. Fire that bitch right now," I demanded.

"Yancey, are you sure?"

"Fire her now!" I said as I stormed off the stage. When I got close to my dressing room, I heard the chatter of my assistant, Amy, who was already making a habit of being late. Sometimes it was ten minutes, and a couple of times it was two hours. She always had her cell phone attached to her ear, talking to either a girlfriend or her boyfriend, Jermaine.

"She's back. I got to go, Jermaine," I heard Amy whisper. As I walked in, I rolled my eyes to let her know I was not pleased.

"Hey, Yancey B. How's the rehearsal going?" Amy asked.

"Fine. Did you get the items I asked you to pick up?" I asked as I sat in front of the mirror.

"I got everything but the cold cream. I forgot what kind you wanted," Amy said.

"Noxzema! Why didn't you write it down like I told you?" I screamed.

"I forgot," Amy said. I looked through the bag of toiletries and didn't see the vitamins I'd asked Amy to purchase. "Where are my vitamins?"

Amy placed her hand to her mouth and giggled nervously. "I guess I forgot them too." Now I was steaming. I wasn't going to pay my hard-earned money to someone who couldn't follow simple instructions and operated on C.P. (colored people's) time. Amy needed to join Dove on the unemployment line.

"Do you know what you want for lunch?" Amy asked.

"No," I said, trying to figure out how to let Amy go.

"How about some shrimp fried rice?"

"Is that what you want?" I asked.

"Yeah, that sounds good."

I pulled a twenty-dollar bill from my purse and handed it to Amy. "Take this and go have yourself a nice long lunch. I don't want anything right now."

"Oh, that's so nice of you. I might go to Ollie's Noodle Shop. You sure you don't want anything?"

"Yes, I want something," I said coldly.

"What?"

"When you finish your lunch, don't come back. I don't want to see your face again."

"What cha mean? You firing me?"

"You got that right. And you don't even have to write that down," I said as I headed for the shower.

The Rodeo Kings . . . (or Queens)

I was kinda depressed because I hadn't heard from Basil since I invited him to *The Lion King*. When I called his office, he was always on the other line. When I called his house, the answering machine picked up. He was a little upset the first time I called him there and wanted to know how I had gotten his number. For some reason, I told him the truth. Well, my version of the truth. I told him his number showed up on my caller I.D. when I checked my messages the morning after we met. What I didn't tell him was that I'd checked my messages on purpose from his house to ensure that I'd have his digits.

Wylie noticed my love jones when I took him to *The Lion King* after Basil declined. A couple days later, Wylie invited me to dinner at one of our favorite restaurants, Maroon over on West Sixteenth Street, between Seventh and Eighth Avenues. We enjoyed spicy jerked chicken wings and stuffed pork chops and ended the meal with delicious red velvet cake.

After dinner we walked a few blocks over to Nineteenth

to G, a quiet bar where you could go to meet and greet or just share conversation with a good friend. Wylie ordered an apple martini for himself, and I got a lite beer.

"So are you falling in love with this stray?" Wylie asked after a few sips of his drink.

"Yep, I'm afraid so," I said.

"Why?" he asked. For a few moments I couldn't answer him. I'd spent the last three days wondering why I was even considering jumping off the cliff called love. I knew I could end up hitting rocks that would leave deep wounds. I already had enough scars from previous love affairs and my childhood. But what if Basil was the jackpot? Falling in love with him could be as soft as falling onto one million down pillows, providing perfect comfort.

The way I saw it, Basil was a triple-threat man. There was the power of his sex, and how I felt like he was branding me when we made love. His face, both handsome and beautiful, had a toughness and yet a feminine quality that was rare in masculine men. If his office and home were indications of his wealth, I was pretty sure he was financially stable. But I knew if I was honest with myself, I might be falling in love with him, because in him I saw all the things I've dreamed of for my own life. All the missing things. I couldn't share all this with Wylie without the risk of a lecture on the difference between love and lust.

"Bart, did you hear me?" Wylie asked. I found myself gazing into my beer and then looking around the circular wood bar at all the lonely faces.

"I'm sorry. I was just thinking," I said.

"Why do you think you love this Basil guy?" Wylie asked.

"Let's just say that since I met Basil the beat of my heart has increased, and it's made me believe that love can be found in New York City," I said.

Wylie looked at me and smiled sweetly and then motioned toward the bartender. After he ordered another round of drinks, he looked at me and said, "When you think of Basil, if your heart feels bigger, it could be love. If something else gets bigger . . . well, I don't have to tell you what that is. You've been to the rodeo before."

"Yeah, but this time I'm going to make sure the horse doesn't kick me off," I said.

The Dirty D.L.

I had just gotten home from hanging out at the Sportsline Gentleman's Club (a strip joint that Nico and I frequent). Nico was celebrating signing a new client, and I went to have a few drinks with him.

After a couple of private lap dances I felt like I needed a shower, so I came home and washed and scrubbed myself like I had spent the evening in a sewage tank. Either I was getting too old for this shit or I had too much on my mind. Maybe in the past I'd enjoyed strippers because they didn't require an emotional attachment.

When I got out of the shower, I wrapped a towel around my waist and rubbed some lotion on my chest. I pulled a beer out of the fridge and went into my study to check my e-mail. Another message from SWALZ: *Hey Sexyman, So you're going to ignore me? That's okay. Just wanted to give you a look at your profile on brothersontheDL.com. I think I hit it right on the head (pun intended): John Basil Henderson—Look for this heartbreaker anywhere around the country, but most likely in New York, Chicago, Miami and Atlanta. Tall (around 6'2") and still in the prime shape he was in while playing professional football. He's in his mid-thirties, though he could still pass for twenty-nine. Basil has mesmerizing cat-gray eyes, golden honey-brown skin. He is a card-carrying member of the PBP (pretty-boy pack), so his buddies, although hopelessly hetero, will be good-looking as well. Mr. Henderson is a great dresser, and a "baller" from the letter B. Likes women of all colors, though he tends to date the model-actress-airhead type. You won't catch him looking at men in public, because he's much too smart for that. Don't look for him in gay bars, parks or bathhouses, either. Basil has such a chameleon-like quality that he doesn't slip with hints of being a switch hitter. His oral skills are said to be among the best, but don't be fooled. You don't know where that tongue has been. If anyone has additional information, contact us on the DL.*

This shit was getting serious. Who was harassing me? I immediately typed in "brothersontheDL.com" and was deeply relieved to see "Site Not Found" flash across my screen.

Annie Get Your Switchblade

I was at the Scissors New York Salon and hating the fact that I didn't make enough money to have a hairdresser come to my home. Scissors was so popular for Broadway people and the like that it was always difficult to get an appointment, and sometimes the process of beautifying moved at a snail's pace. But it was well worth the wait once I got out of the chair and my mane would once again bounce and behave like the white girls' on TV.

I hated being under the dryer, because it prevented me from being in full eavesdrop mode. I loved hearing people talk about the business: What was happening behind the scenes. What shows were opening and closing. Who had a record deal or a workshop, who was doing who, and who was headed back home in defeat.

Since I knew I'd be tied up in the shop for a while, I brought along a book everyone was talking about, *The B.A.P. Handbook*. I was having a good old time reading about how we Black American Princesses should be treated until I came across the list of famous B.A.P.'s and didn't see my name. Who did these ladies think they were, not including a legitimate Broadway star? And now I'm a recording star! I was inclined to take this book back to Barnes & Noble and get my money back. So I put the book aside and pulled out a copy of the newspaper and began to flip the pages until I came across "Lines from LaVonya." I wondered whose life she was ruining today, when what did I see on the first line: *What up-and-coming R & B diva has a child about the same age she is claiming to be?*

Suddenly my face felt warm, and I rolled the paper up quickly and tossed it into the wastebasket. Who was LaVonya talking about? I was the only up-and-moving-very-fast diva. Could she know about Madison?

I decided I couldn't worry about LaVonya and her lack of journalism skills, so I pulled out a *People* magazine and made a mental note to get Motown to get me into this magazine, or at the very least *In Style.* I read a few of the album and movie reviews and continued to thumb through the magazine. Just as I was getting ready to put *People* back in my bag, I came across the headline "Diva with Diapers."

There was a large picture of a pretty black woman and a handsome man. He was holding two children who appeared to be the same age, and the woman was holding a newborn. The woman looked familiar, and when I pulled the magazine closer to my eyes I realized I did know her. It was Nicole Springer.

There was Nicole, smiling like she was on the top of the world and standing in front of an elegant two-story colonial home. The article said that Nicole and her husband, Jared, had had a difficult time conceiving a child and shortly after they adopted twins, Nicole got pregnant. And despite a difficult pregnancy, she had recently delivered a healthy baby boy. But that was not all. According to the article, Nicole was getting ready to return to Broadway in the lead role of the hit revival *Kiss Me Kate,* becoming the first African-American actress to play the female lead.

The article quoted Nicole as saying how happy she was about the miracle of birth and the miracle of faith. Well, I couldn't take any more of her happiness, so I closed the magazine. I wondered if she had been bedridden like Windsor. Had Nicole ever figured out that I was the cause of her sudden illness in Grand Rapids, Michigan, some years before? But most of all I wondered what it felt like to have the same man love you for so many years.

I actually felt a twinge of guilt over some of the things I had done to Nicole when I was her understudy in *Dreamgirls,* but it was very short-lived. Clearly, nothing I'd done had prevented her from fulfilling her life's dreams.

• • •

I had just gotten home from a strenuous day of rehearsals and meetings. I was getting ready to check on Windsor, when I heard several voices coming from her bedroom. I peeked in and saw Windsor and four other ladies. Two were sitting on her bed, one was sitting in a chair and a rather tall, pretty girl was standing up at the end of the bed. As I glanced at her, she looked at me like we knew each other.

"Yancey, come on in," Windsor said.

"How you doing?" I asked as I went over to her bed and gave Windsor a kiss on the cheek.

"Aw, I'm having a good day. My sorors stopped by for a visit, and we've been having a good old time catching up. As you all know, this is my famous roommate, Yancey B!" Windsor said as she motioned her hand gracefully in my direction.

"Hello, everyone," I said. Sometimes I felt competitive when I was surrounded by women. Not so with this crowd. Except for the tall girl, none of these ladies could ever be in the same limo with me.

"I'm Dionne."

"My name is Tara. I knew you at Howard," the one sitting on the bed said as she smiled.

"Lisa."

"And I'm Marlana," the tall one said with a deep, theatrical voice. "I also knew you at Howard, but you were a couple of classes in front of me." Marlana had long dark auburn hair, and she looked like she was on her way to a nightclub, since she was wearing a very expensive-looking leather blouse and matching pants.

"Oh. Well, nice meeting and seeing you ladies. I'm going to take a bath."

"Yancey, don't you remember me telling you about Marlana? She's a singer-dancer. Remember? I sent you her demo tape when you were out in Los Angeles."

"I don't think so. Are you working on something?" I asked Marlana as I turned toward her. I studied her face, and it was clear to me that she needed full makeup on a daily basis to achieve her look. Marlana was attractive, but she couldn't touch me.

"I just left the national tour of *Smokey Joe's Café*. I actually auditioned for *Chicago* when you were doing it on Broadway, but I didn't get the part. You know Broadway can't stand more than one or two black divas at a time."

"I'm sorry to hear that. Next time you're up for a show, give me a call and I'll see what I can do." I wanted to say *Diva?* Chile, please, don't make me knock some sense into you.

"Thanks, but I won't be doing Broadway anytime soon. I just turned down the lead in *Annie Get Your Gun,*" she said confidently.

"Why would you do that?" I asked. I bit my tongue to prevent myself from suggesting the producers would have to change the title to *Annie Get Your Switchblade,* with Marlana in the lead.

"I have a deal with Virgin Records. My single is going to drop in a couple of weeks," she said.

"Really? Good luck. This is a tough business. You ladies have fun," I said as I was leaving Windsor's room.

"Oh, Yancey, there's an envelope on the counter for you," Windsor said. "Dionne saw it outside and brought it in."

"Thanks."

I walked into the dining room and over toward the bar area, where Windsor usually left my packages and mail. The brown cardboard envelope didn't have a return address or a post mark, so I was a little bit leery about opening it.

I was sorry I did. Out fell two more photos of two little girls and another note. It read, *I've narrowed it down to two. Do you know which one is Madison yet?*

• • •

I opened my purse and took out a small mirror to check my makeup. I was getting frustrated. Michel and I had spent over six hours screening guys for my video. Almost fifty great-looking guys with bodies to match had responded to our casting call. But when we told them what they had to do in the video, all but one declined. You would have thought we were asking them to pierce a treasured body part. Even after we explained that viewers might not be able to see their faces, most declined. I wanted to tell them it was called "acting" for a reason. Yet most of these guys were models and probably didn't know the difference. In one scene we wanted them to appear shirtless and embrace another man, and in the other we wanted them to wear some sexy underwear and look lovingly at another man. What was the big deal? Nobody had asked them to kiss. And the few who were interested were way too unattractive to be on the same screen with me. I mean, we're talking bad skin, gold teeth, missing teeth and bleached blond kinky hair. One guy who had more bounce in his step than me had the nerve to decline for religious reasons. I wanted to say, "Honey, don't you think God knows about you?'

"Michel, didn't we tell the agents what we were look-ing for?"

"Sure did! But when they see a casting for a black man, they send anyone and everyone without really giving the guys the full story."

"I certainly don't appreciate their wasting my time."

"I hear ya. Do you want something else to drink, Yancey?" Michel asked.

"No, I'm cool." I said.

Michel was very attentive and always made me feel like I was a star who already had a number-one hit. When my song moved up only a few spots last week, I was concerned it'd reached its peak. Michel assured me that once we got the video in rotation on BET and VH-1, the single would shoot to the top.

Michel looked at his watch and said, "I'm going to see if this guy is waiting in the lobby. Sometimes models don't always follow instructions."

"Okay," I said as I pulled out a mint and popped it into my mouth. Just as Michel reached the door, a handsome man with skin the color of the crease in a cinnamon roll walked in. The first thing I noticed was his dazzlingly white teeth and full-bodied lips. I guess the men on the West Coast weren't the only ones bleaching their teeth.

"Is this the audition for the video?" he asked.

"It sure is. I was just coming to look for you," Michel said. "Come on in."

He walked confidently toward me and took a seat at the end of the table.

"Are you the singer?" he asked.

"Yeah, I'm Yancey B," I said as I extended my hand toward him.

"Nice meeting you. Are you the Yancey Braxton who was in *Dreamgirls* and *Chicago*?" he asked.

"That would be me," I said cheerfully. I already liked this man.

"Have you ever done a video before?" Michel asked.

"Yeah, I've done a few, but never as a principal. This is for a principal role, right?" he asked.

"Yes, it is," I confirmed.

"Tell me your name again," Michel asked as he looked at the yellow legal pad on which he was making notes about the guys we interviewed.

"Bart Dunbar," he said.

"Bart, yeah, that's right. You had a great comp card," Michel said.

"Thank you."

"Bart, before we ask to see your body, I want to make sure your agent told you what the video's about," I said.

"He did," Bart said quickly.

"So you don't have a problem embracing another man?" Michel asked.

"I do it as often as I can," Bart said as a huge smile crossed his face.

"So do you mind my asking if you're gay?" I asked.

"No, I don't mind, and the last time I checked I was." Bart giggled without looking at Michel or me, like he was enjoying his own private joke. I admired his honesty, but I couldn't help thinking, There goes another good-looking black man to the other side.

"So, Bart, do you mind standing up, taking off your shirt and dropping your pants to your knees? They did tell you to wear a swimsuit, right?" Michel inquired.

"No problem," Bart said. He stood up and very quickly pulled his sweater over his head and dropped his pants. Bart had a great body, with a double-barreled chest, small waist and nice ass. It reminded me a lot of Basil's body, except the skin and eyes were significantly different. Bart had serious eyes the color of warm walnuts, and he wore his hair cut close. He had on tangerine bikini swimming trunks that looked wonderful against his skin. Michel scribbled down a few notes and then looked over at me and whispered, "What do you think?"

"He works for me," I said.

"Great," Michel said as he looked up at Bart and said, "The job is yours if you want it. The shoot is going to take place next Thursday at a studio in Harlem."

"Hey, thanks a lot! I'm looking forward to it, and since I live in Harlem I won't have far to go," Bart said as he pulled up his pants and zipped them, then grabbed his sweater off the conference table.

"Thanks for your time, and I look forward to working with you," I said.

"Me too. My friends who are Broadway groupies aren't going to believe I'm working with Yancey Braxton," he said.

"Yancey B," I corrected.

"My bad, Miss Yancey B," he said with that smile that must melt many a young gay man's heart.

"I'll contact your agent and book you right away. I'll also have a final treatment messengered to your apartment," Michel said.

"Cool," Bart said as he tucked his sweater into his pants and grabbed his black leather bag from the floor. He shook Michel's hand and then looked at me and asked, "Can I have a hug?"

"Sure," I said as I gave my new leading man a simple embrace.

Seconds . . .

It was a little before midnight and I was getting ready to hit the sack, when my buzzer rang. I hit the intercom, and the doorman told me Bart Dunbar was downstairs. I had done a good job of avoiding his calls for almost a week, and even contemplated changing my digits. But I realized that wouldn't do any good, since he still had my office number.

At first I was upset that Bart would show up uninvited, but then I remembered how hot our first session had been and decided he was as welcome as a soul food delivery after a month of eating in Russia.

I quickly brushed my teeth and put on a pair of black boxer briefs, which were sheer in the right places. No need to be shy.

A few moments later, I heard the doorbell ring. I waited almost a minute and then opened the door. I couldn't appear like I was anxious to see him.

"Bart, whatsup?"

"Thanks for letting me up. I was in the neighborhood

and I thought I'd see what you were up to before I headed uptown."

"I was getting ready for bed, got a long day tomorrow," I said, trying to sound annoyed.

"Then my timing is perfect. Looks like you were expecting me." Bart smiled as his eyes moved up and down my body with bullet speed.

"Bart, if I didn't tell you the last time, I need to tell you: I don't like surprises."

"I'm sorry. I won't keep you long. Can I use your bathroom? I hate using the public ones," Bart said.

"Sure, in the master bedroom," I said as I pointed down the hallway.

"Did you get my messages?"

"Yeah, I've been real busy at work."

"I figured as much. I hope I haven't been calling too much. Don't want you to get a big head." Bart laughed. I didn't respond.

Bart removed his brown leather jacket and passed it to me. I draped the jacket on the back of my sofa, went into the kitchen and returned with two cans of ginger ale. Soft drinks at this time of night would prevent liquor-induced sex, and I'd be able to see just how good Bart was in bed. I had to admit Bart was looking good in tan cargo pants that were hanging off his ass with white underwear peeping over. I put on my Carl Thomas CD and took a seat on the sofa.

About five minutes later, Bart walked back into the living room and stood near the coffee table. I started to tell him to have a seat, but I could tell from the look in his eyes that the only place he wanted to sit was in my lap. I had twisted feelings about whether or not I was going to allow Bart to seduce me twice in one month. Then I remembered how he had swallowed the jimmie in one skilled move, and it started to pump in urgent beat. My magic wand was ready to wave.

"Sorry that took so long," he said as he looked around the living and dining area like he was seeing it for the first time.

"No problem. So how's the modeling business?"

"Slow. But I did just book a video with a girl singer, so you'll be seeing me on television real soon," Bart said as he noticed the can of ginger ale on the coffee table. "You got anything stronger?"

"Some wine and beer in the fridge. Make yourself at home," I said.

Bart walked toward the kitchen and asked, "So have you missed me?"

"Somebody missed you," I said as I started to massage my jimmie. A few moments later, Bart walked back in the room with a glass of red wine in his hand. He was looking a little too comfortable in my home, so I made up my mind to make this an oral quickie and send him packing.

"What are you doing over there?" Bart asked with a sexy smile. I didn't answer him, but I gave him a *let's get busy* look, which both males *and* females understood. Bart took a sip of his wine and then placed the glass on the table.

"So you did miss me." Bart smiled as he pulled his magenta turtleneck sweater over his head. He kicked off his light brown Timberland boots and then pulled his pants and underwear down with one quick motion. There he stood before me, butt-ass naked.

"You didn't answer my question. Did you miss me?" Bart said.

"It's all love," I said.

"So I got it like that," Bart said as he noticed his reflection in a mirror on the wall. He studied himself for a moment, touching the ripples on his stomach as he licked his lips. Then he turned back toward me and said, "Follow me." I stood up like I was a fraternity pledge following orders and watched Bart and his naked ass walk down the hallway into my dark bedroom. I checked the double-bolt lock on my door and then followed Bart's faint trace of cologne.

3-D: Doug, Dee Dee & the Diva

A little before seven-thirty, I stepped out of a limo on Park Avenue into a cold winter air that had a sweetness about it. I was on my way to an interview on the nationally syndicated *Doug Banks Morning Show*. I certainly wasn't happy about having to get up so early, but I knew the popular morning show would sell some more CDs. Before I got on the elevator, I stopped at a deli on the lobby floor and picked up a coffee and a buttered bagel.

Michel had offered to come with me, but I had convinced him that I could handle this on my own. I rode the packed elevator to the thirty-third floor without removing my dark glasses and ignored the stares of a couple of women who were either admiring my mink coat or looking at me in disgust. Either way it didn't matter. I had paid good money for my coat and was prepared to slap into next week anyone who said anything to me.

About fifteen minutes later, I was in the studio with Doug and Dee Dee after they had played "Any Way the Wind Blows" and invited callers in to talk with me. Doug and Dee Dee were really nice and told me how much they loved the song and how it had sparked a lot of debate with their callers.

"So is the song based on true life experience, Yancey B?" Dee Dee asked.

"I don't know, because it certainly isn't my life," I laughed. I decide to make light of the questions and hoped Dee Dee would ask me about the CD and my future plans.

"So, Yancey B, I guess you're saying that if the song is based on somebody, you're not talking?" Doug asked.

"I'm saving a few things for my memoirs," I joked.

"Lady, you're much too young to be talking about any memoirs," Doug said with a huge smile.

"Thank you, Doug."

"So are you dating anyone?" Dee Dee asked.

"Right now I'm dating my career."

"Have you ever dated a brother who was on the DL?" Doug asked.

"The DL? What's that?" I asked. I knew what he was talking about but I figured if Doug took time explaining to me on what the down low was, my time would be up.

Instead of Doug explaining, Dee Dee did the talking.

"Now Yancey B, come on, girl. Where are you from?" Dee Dee asked as she pulled a sheet from my press kit and stared at it.

"I'm from Tennessee, but I've spent the last four years in New York. You know I did Broadway before I started my recording career," I said.

"So you're telling me you've never met one of those good-looking brothers who pretend to be straight, wining and dining you, and then later you find out their best male friend is more than a friend?" Dee Dee asked.

I paused for a moment like I was really thinking about the question and then said, "No, I can't say that I have."

"Now Yancey B, come on now!" Dee Dee said in amazement.

Before I could respond, Doug asked me if I was surprised at how well the song was doing.

"I'm not a bit surprised. My record company, Motown had a great marketing plan and the music and lyrics are just great. Not just with the single, but the entire CD. Have you guys played 'I'm Not in Love'?"

"Yeah, and it's tight, but we don't get as many calls for that as we do for 'Any Way the Wind Blows,'" Doug said.

"I think that will change when people hear the entire CD," I said.

"Let's go to the phone lines and see what our listeners think. Good morning. You're talking with Yancey B, Dee Dee and Doug Banks," Doug said as he punched a blinking phone line.

"Look at all those lines light up," Dee Dee observed. "We haven't had this many calls since we had Janet Jackson in the studio."

I spent the next thirty minutes taking calls from all across the country. Everyone was telling me how much they loved the song and asking if I was going to tour their city. Several women told me that they'd bought several copies of the song and sent it to girlfriends who they thought were dating brothers on the down low. I thanked each of them and told them to go out and buy some copies for their male friends as well.

Everything was going smoothly until the last caller. "You've got a question for Yancey B?" Doug asked.

"Yeah I got a question for her. What about Madison?" a female voice asked in an unmistakable threatening tone.

"Madison?" Dee Dee quizzed. "Do you want to know if Yancey B is going to visit Madison, Wisconsin? Is that your question, caller?"

I drank the rest of my now-cold coffee and noticed Dee Dee and Doug exchanging puzzled looks. I suddenly felt like I couldn't breathe, and my heart felt like it wasn't going to take the next beat. There was also a pain pounding in my head and my body began to feel cold, so I pulled my mink back up to my shoulders.

"Caller, are you still there?" Doug asked.

"She knows what I mean," she said, and then we heard a dial tone in the dimly lit studio.

"I wondered what's her problem?" Dee Dee said as I breathed a sigh of relief and gave them both a weak smile.

When I left the studio and reached the lobby, my cell phone started ringing. The caller I.D. said "out of area" so I knew it wasn't Ava or Basil. I thought it might be the person who had just called the station, and I suddenly felt like I was ready to confront whoever was playing games with me. I clicked the *talk* button and screamed, "Who is this? Hello."

"Damn, baby, you get up on the wrong side of the bed? Do you miss me, baby?"

"Malik, why are you calling me so early?" I asked. I

looked at my watch and noticed it was a little before nine, which meant it was before sunrise on the West Coast.

"It's never too early to talk with my star," he said.

"What do you want?"

"I'm just wondering why I haven't heard from you. Haven't you been getting my calls? I even called Motown. Did you get that message?"

"No, I didn't. So you've been calling my cell. I don't have it on all the time," I lied. The truth was I was avoiding talking to Malik, hoping he would get the message that I didn't need him anymore in bed or out. I decided no one could manage Yancey better than Yancey. I wondered if he was behind the calls and photos but then realized he had no way of knowing I had a child. Even though Ava had made me aware that with a little bit of money a person could find out almost anything about anyone.

"Then give me the number at your house," Malik said.

"What?" I said as I walked out of the revolving doors into the cold winter air.

"Give me your number at home."

"Hello? Hello? I can't hear you. I'll call you later," I said as I hit the End button and smiled to myself at how easy it was to hang up on someone with a cell phone and blame it on the service.

Do You Hear What I Hear?

Icame home after waiting tables at the Viceroy, emptied my tips on my bed, and stripped down naked. I got on my knees and counted the night's take. Two hundred and fifty-six dollars, not bad for a Tuesday night, I thought. I took out my tip journal and wrote down "$126," in case I got audited by the IRS, then placed the money in the leather pouch I kept my money in until I made my weekly visit to the bank.

I looked at my answering machine and was a little disappointed the message light was not flashing. It had been several days since I'd heard Basil's voice, and I was determined to speak with him tonight even if I had to wait all night or make another surprise visit. I thought after my last visit I would hear from him more often. I had to hear him whisper "It's all love" once more. I couldn't remember the last time a man had said he loved me and I believed him.

I walked into my bathroom and turned on my shower. While I was waiting for the water to warm up, I lit a piece of jasmine incense and covered my face with Noxzema skin cream. I stepped into the shower and relaxed as the warm water ran like a river down my body. The water felt almost hypnotic. Five minutes later, I stepped out of the shower, drenched myself in baby oil and grabbed a yellow striped towel to wipe off my body. I wrapped the damp towel around my waist and walked into my bedroom. My apartment was quiet, almost peaceful, as I put my Mary J. Blige CD in my stereo system.

After a glass and a half of wine, I started thinking about love and being held by Basil's strong arms. I had to see him, so I muted Mary's voice and picked up my phone. Basil's number rang a couple of times and then I heard his deep, sexy voice. My heart started pounding with excitement, like I had just received a call telling me I had won the lotto.

"'Sup," Basil said.

"How you doing?" I asked nervously.

"'Sup, dude," Basil said.

"Is this too late to call?"

"I was kinda busy. Sorry I haven't returned any of your calls. Busy, you know," Basil said.

"Oh, that's cool. I've been busy too. You know, working and going on a lot of auditions," I lied.

"Cool. Can I get back with you later?"

I took a sip of wine and then said boldly, "I was hoping I could walk up on a good fucking tonight."

"I think we need to chill," Basil said.

"What did you say?" His voice had become so quiet I could barely hear him.

"We need to chill. We can get together sometime and maybe have a brew or two, but I'm back with my lady," he said calmly.

"What lady? You never mentioned any special lady. Besides, I don't care. I just want to see you."

"Let me call you when I get a minute," Basil said, and then he hung up the phone.

My face felt flush and the back of my neck felt tight. I gulped down the rest of my wine and suddenly had a headache. I was mad as fuck. How dare Basil just brush me off like I was some little bitch? I picked up the phone and hit the redial button. This time after a couple of rings, a soft female voice filled with sleep or sex picked up the phone and said, "Hello."

I hung up the phone, sank my body to the floor and muttered to myself, "Wrong move, Basil. Wrong fuckin' move."

Breakfast at Tiffany's

Tiffany was my latest overnight guest. I'd met her several nights before at Justin's while I was out hunting down some new pussy. I had planned to call her the night Bart showed up unannounced, but he'd given me what I needed at the time. But that would have to last for a while, because I was going back to the other side. It was time to start interviewing prospects for the mother of my children.

Tiffany played hard to get by telling me she didn't go home with men on the first night, but the second night was open for debate. There wasn't much of a debate, actually; I just called and asked her to come over, and she quickly obliged. All I cared about right now was the intense pleasure of chasing pussy, and the mystery and delight I felt at seeing another woman naked.

"Who was that?" Tiffany asked. "You must really like letting me answer your phone. Most men I know turn off their phones when I spend the night."

"Somebody who doesn't understand that no means no," I said as I thought about the three messages per day Bart had been leaving. Besides, every time I heard his voice, it sounded more and more familiar. I just couldn't figure out why.

"You're not gay or bisexual, are you?" Tiffany asked as she looked at me seriously while pulling the sheets over her orange-sized breasts like she was covering them from a hidden camera.

"Hell naw! That doesn't stop gay dudes from coming on to me. Some of those mofos are bold as shit. Like this guy. I did some business with him and now he keeps calling," I said, looking her dead in the eyes.

"You think just because you got a woman answering your phone that will stop him?" Tiffany asked.

"Maybe you could come over and ride this jimmie again, so we can videotape it and send him a copy," I teased. With all the talk of brothers who swung both ways, women still hadn't learned all the games. They didn't know that sometimes men brought shit out right up front so they would suddenly feel safe and secure and put their questions in the background. It was like talking on the phone with the old girlfriend while the new one lay beside you. Neither one would ever suspect shit else was going on.

"You're not serious, are you?" Tiffany asked as she gave me the sexy smile of a secure woman who suddenly felt like she had the upper hand.

"I'm kidding about videotaping us, but not about riding the jimmie," I said as I pulled the sheets away and started to suck her nipples and then between her legs. Tiffany began to moan like she was experiencing ecstasy for the first time. She hadn't felt nothing yet.

A Diva Duet

I swooped into Windsor's room looking pretty damn hot, if I do say so myself. I was wearing a peach-and-cream-colored silk dress, and my hair was in a French roll and I had done my makeup so it was as perfect as perfect can get without a plastic surgeon, or Sam Fine.

"Don't you look good," Windsor said. "Where are you going? To an opening or something?"

"I'm on my way to something very special." I smiled as I headed straight to Windsor's closet, pretending to look for something I thought I'd left in the closet before she moved in.

"What are you looking for?" Windsor asked.

"Oh, just something I stored in a box."

"I wish I could get up and help you find it," Windsor said.

"Don't worry. Everything will be just fine," I said.

I hadn't seen much of Windsor recently, because Motown had been working me like a field mule. But I didn't think Windsor had noticed, since her sorors and her church-lady friends were taking good care of her. They regularly brought her meals, flowers and books or magazines. Her two sorors

Marlana and Dionne came by almost every day. I wanted to tell Miss Marlana she couldn't get a career going attending to the sick and shut in, but I figured her talent was limited at best, and maybe by taking care of Windsor she would have something to fall back on, like being a full-time candy striper.

Windsor's parents and Wardell called three times a day every day. Her parents had even arranged to use their vacation time to take care of her during the last two months of her pregnancy. Then Wardell called and told me about his special plan that would change all that. Just as I located what I was looking for, I heard voices coming from the living room.

"Yancey, I think there's someone out there. Are you expecting company?" Windsor asked.

"Oh no, I must have left the television on. Look at this, Windsor, this is beautiful. Why don't you put this on," I suggested as I held up a beautiful ivory silk nightgown edged in lace.

"I can't put that on. It's a special gown Wardell bought for me. I've been saving it for our honeymoon. If that ever happens." Windsor sighed.

"Come on, put it on. Let's fluff you up," I said as I moved over to Windsor's bed and laid the gown against her face to show her how pretty it would look against her beautiful brown skin.

"Yancey, what's going on?" Windsor asked.

"Nothing. I just think if you put on something nice, it'll make you feel better. It always works for me," I said.

"I'm feeling fine," Windsor protested.

I didn't pay any attention to Windsor and marched right

over to her dressing table and grabbed her comb and brush so I could style her hair. I was so happy she had cut off her dreads and let her hair grow back into a more manageable style. About ten minutes later, Miss Windsor was looking pretty good.

Windsor didn't ever wear makeup, but I insisted, telling her we could pretend we were little girls playing dress-up. It had always been one of my childhood fantasies to have a sister to exchange makeup tips with. When I finished putting a little blush on Windsor's cheeks and mascara on her long thick lashes, I topped everything off with some plum-colored lip gloss. I gave her a mirror so she could admire my handiwork, and I think she was pleased, because she couldn't stop looking at herself. She was gazing so hard that she didn't even notice when Aunt Toukie walked in wearing a tacky lavender rayon suit and a Tina Turner wig.

"My . . . my, don't we look pretty," Aunt Toukie said. Windsor looked up, briefly startled, and I rushed over and whispered in Aunt Toukie's ear, "Now, don't forget this is a surprise."

"Aunt Toukie! What are you doing here?" Windsor asked.

"Thought I'd come up here to see you. I just bought me a new car from Mel Farr Motors. You know, the guy who does those funny commercials in the Superman suits. He gave me a great deal. Now, what did you ask me?" Aunt Toukie said as she sat down on the edge of Windsor's bed and kicked off one of the black patent leather pumps she was wearing.

"What are you doing here?" Windsor repeated.

"I told you. I bought me a new car and I wanted to put

the pedal to the metal, so I said to myself, 'Toukie, you need to go check on Windsor and see if she's still holding on to that baby,'" Aunt Toukie said as she patted Windsor's stomach. "So how you doing?"

"I'm doing fine. But why are you dressed up?"

"Don't you like my new hair? I thought, Shit, if Tina Turner can wear her hair in this style, then so can I. You know we around the same age," Aunt Toukie said.

"Aunt Toukie, can you excuse Windsor and me for a moment? I want to help her put this gown on," I said.

"Honey, I done seen Windsor naked many a time. She ain't got nothing new even if she is knocked up," Aunt Toukie said.

I figured it was no use arguing with her, so I let her help Windsor change while I went out into the living room to make sure everything was set. A few minutes later, I walked in with Windsor's cousin Bobo, Aunt Toukie's son, who broke out into song when he saw Windsor.

"Moving on up. To the East Side," Bobo sang. Aunt Toukie had told me Bobo's real name was Mouton and he had been like an older brother to Windsor. He was a tall, broad-shouldered man, with a plump face and the beginnings of a double chin. Bobo wore his head bald and had two gold earrings in each ear.

"Bobo, what are you doing here?" Windsor asked in a high-pitched voice that was almost like a scream.

"Had to come check out my cuz before she became a mommy. Cuz, you sho are living large up in here. If I was you, I'd set my ass up in bed all day and just have maids and butlers serving me caviar and shit," Bobo said.

"Just as long as it ain't no crack," Aunt Toukie said.

Bobo looked at his mother with a cross-eyed look on his face and said, "Mama, you know I don't mess with that shit no more."

"I guess not. You done smoked up all the crack in Michigan," Aunt Toukie said.

"You promised if I'd help you drive up here, you wouldn't bring up my past," Bobo said.

"I'm a mama, and I can break promises. Besides, I didn't say nuthin' to Windsor and Miss Yancey about how you spent a couple of weeks in the joint 'cause you didn't pay your child support."

"Bobo, you better take care of your kids," Windsor said.

"I try, cuz, but the job market is tight in Detroit. Even with all the casinos, it's still hard for a brotha."

"Especially when you think the jobs gonna come to you. You think you big time 'cause you spent a couple of years at Wayne State. You still didn't get your degree," Aunt Toukie said.

"I'm going back," Bobo said.

"You guys cut out your family mess," Windsor said.

"Okay, let's get to a few surprises we have for you," Aunt Toukie said.

"What surprises?" Windsor asked.

"Hold on," Aunt Toukie said as she went to the door and whispered, "Y'all come on in."

A few moments later, in walked Windsor's mother and father. They were dressed up nice. Her father was wearing a nice black wool suit with a white shirt and black tie. Windsor's mother looked beautiful in a lime-green silk suit and a kelly-green hat with different colored flowers covering it.

"Mama, Daddy. What are you doing here?" Windsor asked as I felt my own eyes filling with tears.

"We came to see our baby," Windsor's father said.

"But it was supposed to be next week," Windsor said.

"You want us to go back?" Mrs. Adams joked.

"No, no. I mean, I'm just so shocked," Windsor said.

"Well, we couldn't miss this," Mr. Adams said.

"Miss what?" Windsor asked. Suddenly the room became silent and no one answered. Mrs. Adams looked at her husband and then at her sister. Then she looked at me and smiled, and nodded at Bobo, who walked out of the room.

Windsor's room suddenly felt small and warm with all the people in it. It felt like this when her sorors and prayer circle friends visited.

"What's going on?" Windsor asked again. Still silence. Windsor looked around the room slowly, waiting for an answer, and then she looked at the door and in walked Bobo and a minister carrying a Bible.

"Reverend Winn! What are you doing here? Am I dreaming? Am I going to die? Did my doctor tell you something?" Windsor asked as she began shaking her head in disbelief.

"You better not die," a deep voice said. Everyone looked toward the door, and Wardell walked in with a huge smile on his face, carrying a bouquet of ivory tulips. He was dressed in a black pin-striped suit and black silk tie. He looked handsome, and when Windsor saw him she started crying a river of tears.

"Wardell, what are you doing here? Somebody needs

to tell me what's happening. What is Reverend Winn doing here? You know, he's the one who baptized me," Windsor said.

"Take it easy, Windsor," Wardell said as he sat on the bed next to Windsor. "I have to ask you something very important."

"Of course, you can ask me anything, Wardell."

"Will you marry me?"

"Don't be silly, of course I will. We're already engaged, and you know that's what I've always wanted."

"Today? Will you marry me today?"

All of a sudden, Windsor's face beamed like a row of track lighting. It finally dawned on her that we were all here for a wedding. *Her* wedding to Wardell. Until recently, planning a wedding, let alone attending one, was the last thing on my mind. But when Wardell called me and told me what he wanted to do, it sounded so romantic that I couldn't resist helping him plan it.

Since I was so busy promoting my album, I wasn't able to do much. But I had arranged for Windsor's parents and Reverend Winn to fly in and stay at the Trump Hotel in a corner suite. I had even invited several of Windsor's sorors and Sister Circle friends to join us after the brief ceremony.

After the minister had pronounced Windsor and Wardell husband and wife, Wardell cleared his throat and said he had something to say to Windsor. "Go ahead so we can eat and drink," Aunt Toukie said.

Wardell got down on one knee and said, "Windsor, I promise you a love that will never let you down. I know I can be a jackass sometimes, but I'm not too old to change.

You make me feel young. Vital. Like I can live forever as long as I have you in my life." I could see pearls of sweat on his forehead, but his voice was composed, graceful and steady like the professor he was. I looked at Windsor and her parents, who all had tears in their eyes, and then suddenly I felt tears well up in my eyes again. I was looking around for a handkerchief, and my eyes met Windsor's and she gave me the biggest smile I had ever seen. For the first time in my life, I felt like I was part of a family. Even though I didn't really know Mr. and Mrs. Adams, Wardell, Aunt Toukie and Bobo, I still felt like I belonged.

• • •

About a half hour later, Wardell, Marlana and Dionne wheeled in a cart with the most beautiful wedding cake I'd ever seen. It was three-tiered, and on top of the cake there was a kissing bride and groom. At their feet was a tiny little brown baby in a cradle. Candles were placed all around the bottom tier, and the mellow light reflected off the smiling faces of Windsor's family and friends, all standing around the cake looking happy and proud.

Marlana came over and whispered how happy she was that my record was doing so well, and I thanked her. Then she asked me if I was going to sing for Windsor and Wardell.

"I have a little something planned," I said softly.

"Would you like me to join you?" she asked boldly. I thought about it for a few seconds and gently touched her hand and said, "I don't do duets. I'm sure you understand."

"Of course. I just thought since Windsor loves the both of us to death it would make her so happy," Marlana said. I noticed she was wearing a sheer black formfitting dress and you could see her unspectacular undergarments. I wanted to tell her show business was about having a touch of class, not about seeing how stank you could be. But I didn't say anything, because Marlana seemed like the type who didn't follow instructions well. When I had called to tell her about the wedding, I told her to dress casual and not like she was headed to the hookers' ball.

"Trust me, Windsor can't be any happier than she is now," I said as I moved to talk to some of the other guests.

Wardell was pouring champagne for everyone and ginger ale for Windsor. Just as he handed me a glass, Windsor's father stepped forward to make a toast: "Here's to love and happiness. May Wardell and Windsor and that little one that's coming share a beautiful life together." We all clinked our glasses, and Windsor thanked her daddy for his kind words.

"One more little surprise for you, baby," Wardell said as he sat next to Windsor on the bed.

"Another surprise? Are y'all trying to kill me for real?"

"Yancey is going to sing—just for us."

I stepped forward and went from hostess to diva in a few seconds. I had to show Miss Marlana how a *real* diva took control. After I had sung a few bars of the Whitney Houston–Dolly Parton hit "I Will Always Love You," everyone broke into applause, as my melodic tones filled the room. I was flowing, and just as I was going for my note I heard Aunt Toukie guzzle some champagne and then belch.

Then, just as I got to the chorus, Aunt Toukie also broke into song. We sounded like a cross between an opera diva

and two cats fighting in the alley. I tried to ignore the inter-
ruption and kept singing, but Aunt Toukie was not to be
denied. Everyone looked at Aunt Toukie, but the screeching
continued. Every time I would sing a little louder, Aunt
Toukie got louder too. I assumed the champagne had taken
over her voice *and* good sense. Finally, Mr. Adams and Bobo
each took one of Aunt Toukie's arms and dragged her out of
the room. Just when I was hitting my final note, I heard the
door shut.

"And I, I, will always love you," I sang as I was hitting
the homestretch.

"And I will always love you-uuu," Aunt Toukie sang
from behind the door as her cat-screaming-off-key voice
echoed the chorus at the top of her lungs. She tried to hold
the final note with me but I was not having it. I held the
note for over fifteen seconds, when I suddenly heard cough-
ing and choking.

When I finished the last pure note, everyone clapped
and shouted, "Bravo! Bravo, diva! Encore!" Just as I was getting ready to take my bow, we heard a muffled "Thank you.
Thank you everyone," from behind the door.

Steam Heat

I went to Basil's office to let him know face-to-face he couldn't just treat me like a piece of bookstore trade. Not only was he not returning my calls, but when I went by his place, the doorman said he was not accepting guests.

I got to the office a little before 9 A.M., and as I passed a guy in the hall, I recognized a face I'd sworn I'd never forget. Suddenly, I realized how I knew Basil. About a year ago I had been in Tallahassee, Florida, for a rare out-of-town modeling assignment. After we finished the shoot, I went to a twenty-four-hour health club near the hotel called Run-N-Shot. I was surprised that such a small city would have a luxury twenty-four-hour health club, but Tallahassee is the state capital and a college town.

After a brief workout, I went into the steam room and saw these two men with hot-looking bodies sitting on the bottom level. They were busy talking and didn't notice me. I couldn't really see their faces, maybe because I was looking between their legs, even though they had towels covering the lower parts of their bodies. One of them stood up and removed his towel, and I could see that he was bottom heavy, booty, dick and legs of life. It was as though he was inviting me to make a move when he looked in my direction and quickly wrapped the towel back around his body.

I thought, shit, nobody knows me here, and I might as well see what trouble I can get into. So I got up from the wet bench, moved toward the two of them and deliberately dropped my towel. I bent over slowly to pick it up, but before I brought my body back to a standing position, I looked at the one who had dropped his towel and said, "Is there anything I can do for you while I'm down here?"

"What did you say?" he demanded. I knew I should have used that as my cue to move on, but I am never one to back down to a macho man, so I repeated myself. The next thing I knew, I felt his large foot crashing into my face, and I fell back on the floor. The two men then raced from the steam room.

I figured he didn't know how good I was, so I continued my steam. The night was young, and somebody else might walk in who could use my services. Moments later, a large white guy, fully dressed, entered the steam room with one of the guys and looked at him and said, "Is this the one?"

"Yeah, that's the faggot mutherfucker," he said.

"Come with me," the white guy demanded.

"Come with you for what?" I asked.

"Sir. Either come with me or else I will lock your fruity ass up in this steam room until the police come," he said. He looked at my accuser and said, "Sir, why don't you get dressed. I'll meet you up in the office so you can file a complaint."

To make a sad story short, I ended up being harassed, threatened and forced to sign a form that I would never enter a Run-N-Shot anywhere in the country. Those country mutherfuckers actually called the police, who warned me that sodomy was against local law and it was strictly enforced.

Basil, who gave the name John Henderson, wasn't around for the interrogation, but he told the manager and the policeman that I had made unwanted advances toward them. Nico Benson was the name and the face I couldn't forget because he stared at me in the tiny office like he wanted to spit in my face. He was the one who had tried to leave a footprint on my face. The *Dukes of Hazzard* police took down my driver's license number and offered it to Nico and Basil in case they decided to sue. They instructed me to make sure I had my ass on the first plane out of town the next morning or else.

Now that I'd figured out how I knew Basil, he'd better watch out. He didn't know who he was messing with. That gym incident had been the most humiliating experience of my adult life.

Fuck love, it's payback time.

Side B

Basil's Pride and Joy

I was looking over some scouting reports when Kendra buzzed me. I'd told her I didn't want to be disturbed, so I figured it was important.

"Yeah, Kendra," I said.

"I have your father on the line. I haven't told him you're in the office. Would you like for me to take a message?"

"No, put him through," I said as a huge smile crossed my face, and I laid the thick reports face-down on my desk. I picked up the phone and said, "I was thinking about you this morning. Whatsup, Pops?"

"I'm doing. How you doing?"

"Just trying to stay out of trouble. You know how the ladies can't leave yo boy alone." I teased.

"You always had your way with the ladies. I see you guys got a lot of snow. I keep telling you to move back down here full time," Pops said.

"I just might do that sooner or later. Some of the big muckety-mucks at PMK are trying to buy us, and it will make your son a very rich man," I said.

"Oh yeah? You already do pretty well. If you sell it to them, don't let it go for cheap. When you gonna get me my autographs?"

"What autographs?" I asked, trying to remember which one of my clients my Pops was a big fan of.

"Don't tell me you done forgot."

"Pops, come on, now. You know I'm getting up in age," I said, and laughed.

"Venus and Serena, the Williams sisters. You said you were gonna see what you could do," my father said.

"Oh yeah, but you know they're not my clients. I said I would check with one of their advisers." My Pops had been acting like a horny schoolboy ever since I took him to see Venus and Serena play in a tournament outside of Miami. He had complained the entire drive about not wanting to see no white folks hit no ball that dogs chased. That was until he saw Venus and Serena in tennis attire. The man hadn't been the same since.

"You do that, and make sure you have them put love and kisses," Pops said.

"So you going after the young now? Don't tell me I got to compete with you and all the other clowns," I said.

"Aw, it ain't gonna be no competition when they meet me. You better map out another plan," Pops teased.

"So you got it like that?"

"Yes, sir."

"How is everything else?"

"I can't complain. Life is good. I could stand another trip with my son, but I understand you busy with yo business and keeping track of the ladies."

"Where do you want to go?" I asked.

"How 'bout Vegas? Are there any fights coming up? I like that guy Sugar Shane Mosley. See if he's fighting. Or Roy Jones. I like him too," Pops said.

"Let me do some checking, and I'll get back with you," I said.

"Okay, son. Take care of yourself. Watch out for those women after yo money and your honey," Pops said.

I smiled at myself when I heard Pops say "honey," his term for male semen, and said, "I'll protect them both, Pops. I'll call you in a couple days."

"Take your time. I'll be here."

"You know I love ya, Pops."

"Yeah, I know," Pops said before hanging up.

I leaned back in my chair, savoring my relationship with and love for my Pops, when Kendra buzzed me and said she had a quick errand to run and that the phones would be unattended.

I clicked on the University of Miami football Web site to see what was going on with upcoming spring football, since I was intent on signing some more players from my alma mater. The Net had made getting information and statistics so much easier, and I printed out bios on several of the players I thought were definite pro prospects. I was making my way to the Florida State Web site when my phone rang.

"Basil Henderson," I said.

"Basil, this is Bart."

I silently mouthed "damn" to myself, then said quickly, "Bart, I'm real busy." I'd given Kendra explicit instructions to tell him I was out of the office if he called again, and now

I'd gone and got caught. Kendra had told me Bart had shown up at my office a couple of days before, asking about the modeling job, but said he raced out once Nico walked into the office. What was that about?

"I need to speak to you."

"Look, man, what don't you understand? First thing, stay away from my office. We had a good time, but that's all it was, a good time," I said. I couldn't believe I was having this type of conversation with a dude. Men, even gay men, knew how to separate love and sex, even if women couldn't. Well, maybe Yancey could, but she certainly wasn't your average female.

"So that's all I was, a good time?" Bart asked.

"We hit it a couple of times. That's it. From the beginning, I told you point-blank I don't date dudes."

"Then what about the modeling job?"

"What about it?"

"Am I going to get it?"

"I told you that's out of my hands," I said.

"So I was just a free fuck. You like messing with people's lives, don't you?" Bart responded sharply.

"Call it what you want."

"You said you loved me. How could you play me like that?"

What was this mofo talking about? I just shook my head and started focusing on some papers on my desk. I figured if I let Bart get out all of his emotional bullshit he would leave me the fuck alone.

"Are you still there?" he yelled.

"Look, mofo, don't holler at me. I never said I loved you. Damn, I don't even know you."

"The last time we were together you said it's 'all love.'"

"Dude, that's a brotherman greeting. But I don't guess you would know that, since you seem knee-deep in being gay."

"So you don't think you're gay?"

"Fuck no," I said, wondering why I dignified his question with a response. I couldn't figure out why I was still on the phone with this unbalanced mofo.

"Then you're either stupid or lying to yourself. Men like you are the ones who are an . . ."

I didn't allow Bart to finish his little tirade. I hung up the phone.

Lines from LaVonya

I dropped my backpack on my small kitchen counter, grabbed the phone and punched the speed dial to Wylie's office. I needed to piss, but speaking with Wylie was more important. He picked up after the first ring.

"This is Wylie."

"Wylie! I need you to do something for me," I said in a rushed voice. I was still fuming from my phone call with Basil, and I wasn't about to tell Wylie how he'd talked to me on the phone.

"What's the matter with you? It sounds like you been running."

"I was on the train coming back from a fitting for Yancey B's video, and I thought of a way to get back at that fuckin' Basil," I said.

"Honey, you need to just let that man be. He told you he was stray from the jump."

"Yeah, that's what you would do, but I'm gonna teach these so-called strays they can't play me like I'm some kind of drum. And I do know him from somewhere. I need LaVonya's number."

"Why?"

"I want to take her out for a drink."

"I thought you didn't have time for fag hags," Wylie said.

"Come on now, Wylie. I didn't say that. Besides, I need her to do something for me, and I'm going to do something for her," I said.

"So how did your fitting go?"

"Wylie, you're trying to change the subject. Give me the damn number."

"I don't have it. My assistant, Mollie, is downloading some information into my Palm Pilot," Wylie said.

"You should know her number by heart."

"I don't."

"Wylie, you're my friend, right?" I didn't know why Wylie was tripping, but I knew questioning our friendship could get him back on track.

"Bart, why would you doubt that? Of course I'm your friend."

"Then either give me LaVonya's home number, or you call her and tell her I want to take her out for drinks this evening."

"I'll have Mollie call you in five minutes with the information," Wylie said.

"Thanks."

"Bart, I'm beginning to worry about you. This guy might change his mind and give you another chance if you don't go off and do something stupid."

"You have a point there. But I've got to put a plan in

place to make sure he knows he can't treat me like shit. Not unless he's willing to put up with *Nightmare from Faggot Hell,* the movie, live and in person."

"Just promise me you'll be careful," Wylie pleaded.

"I'm always careful and correct," I said as I hung up the phone and ran to the bathroom.

• • •

I rushed to open the door of the Saloon restaurant, across the street from Lincoln Center. It was freezing cold, hinting that winter was going to stick around for a while. When I walked into the small annex of the restaurant, I saw LaVonya Young sitting on a bar stool.

I took off my coat and went over to LaVonya and gave her a hug and a kiss.

"Thanks for agreeing to see me," I said.

"No problem, boo. Whenever someone calls me and tells me he's got a story about sex and a famous man, I'm there," LaVonya said as she patted the empty bar stool next to her. "Here, have a seat."

"What are you drinking?" I asked LaVonya, as I took the stool next to her.

"Cappuccino. Ain't nothing like it in the winter," LaVonya said as she took another sip.

"Let me have what the lady is having," I said to a female bartender as I pointed to LaVonya's mug.

"So tell me," LaVonya said as she pulled out a narrow white tablet. I began to tell LaVonya my version: I met Basil, and after seducing me, he sent me out to pasture without the promise of a job, love or steady sex. LaVonya listened intently, and every now and then jotted down a few notes. When I stopped talking to take a sip of my cappuccino, LaVonya said, "Sounds like he spit you out like stale bubble gum."

LaVonya was a large woman with exquisite features and thoughtful brown eyes. She had a messy head of her own hair, plus a little weave. It was a little bit blond, brown and red, and the colors were slammed against each other. Her skin was pear brown, and LaVonya glowed like she had just been polished with some type of butter. She was wearing an expensive, snug, black gabardine suit with gold buttons and lots of jewelry. I couldn't tell if it was from Tiffany's or QVC.

After I finished my story, LaVonya looked at me and said, "You know, I'm going to have to get Mr. Henderson's version of the story. Is he out as a gay or bisexual man?"

"I don't think so, and I doubt if he'll tell you the truth or even talk to you," I said.

"Oh, he'll talk to me. Especially when I point out there is no future in frontin'. I couldn't wait to find out who you were talking about when you called, so I made Wylie tell me. I did a little research before I came to meet you, and Mr. Henderson was nominated for the Pro Football Hall of Fame. He didn't get in, but he'll be back up next year. He'll talk to anyone from the media who will get his name out there, and that includes a gossip columnist like me," LaVonya said.

"Before you speak with him, are you going to run one of your famous blind items?"

"I might do that," she said as she paused to take a sip of her drink. "So Mr. Henderson worked you over and still didn't give you the job that you went there for. Sounds like you ought to be talking to a lawyer too. It sure would make the story more juicy if I had a court proceeding I could be following as well."

"A lawyer? You think I could sue him?" Maybe the threat of a lawsuit could get me back in Basil's bed, I thought.

"You did trade sexual favors for a job you didn't get. Sure sounds like it to me. If I gave some pussy to a man who promised me a job and then he reneged, I'd be in a lawyer's office quicker than you can say money can't buy me love, but it can sure ease the pain," LaVonya said, laughing.

"Fuck pain, I need some money," I joked.

"So what do you think about bringing a suit against him? Even if it's thrown out, I could give you plenty of ink in my column. Who knows, some Hollywood producer might come around and make you an offer for your little story," LaVonya said with a broad smile.

"But a lawyer would cost money, and I don't have a lot of that," I said.

LaVonya picked up her large designer purse from the floor, pulled out a card and wrote something on the back. She passed the card to me and said, "Give this woman a call and tell her I sent you."

"What if she asks for money before she'll hear my case?" I asked.

LaVonya suddenly leaned in, lowered her voice and said, "Let me tell you a little back story to make sure she'll take your case. . . ."

Top Forty

I was on my way inside Tower Records at Sixty-fifth and Broadway to check out the first-day placement of my CD when my cell phone rang. "Blocked I.D." flashed across the console, but I clicked the phone on anyway.

"Hello," I said.

"Is this Yancey B?" a female voice said.

"This is Yancey," I said.

"Yancey, this is LaVonya, darling. How are you?"

"I'm fine. Do I know you, LaVonya?" I knew exactly who she was, but I didn't want to give her the satisfaction.

"Of course you do, darling. Remember? I covered your alleged wedding last year. I see you've bounced back in a big way. Way to go, girl," LaVonya said.

"What are you talking about?" I asked in an annoyed tone.

"Look at you. Making the media rounds. You're everywhere. Got a song climbing the charts, and it sounds like a tune of sweet revenge." LaVonya laughed. "I haven't checked lately—is your song in the top forty yet?"

"It's number thirty-six. My album's out today. What publication do you write for and how did you get my number?" I asked, still pretending I didn't know who she was.

"I know you've read me. I write 'Lines from LaVonya,' and I got your number from your publicist at Motown. Sounds like they love you over there."

"I've heard of you. You're a gossip columnist, right?" I said. I was relieved LaVonya was inquiring about my song rather than Madison.

"I'm a journalist. Listen: The reason I'm calling is because a little bird told me your new song, 'Any Way the Wind Blows,' is about somebody famous. Could it be that fine man who left you at the altar— Oh, excuse me, darling, I'm sorry, the man you left at the altar," LaVonya said. Her voice was so full of sister girl sarcasm, I knew LaVonya hadn't bought my wedding-day story. Now I was really worried and figured I needed to get off the phone before I said too much.

"LaVonya, why don't you call Austin over at Motown and set up a full interview. We can talk about the song then," I said as I rode the escalator up to the second floor of Tower in search of my CD display.

"I don't do full interviews, darling, unless it's a cover story for *Diva* or *People*. I'm much too busy. Just tell me if it's true and if the guy's name is Basil or John," LaVonya said.

"What did you say? I think I'm losing you," I said as I pushed the End button on my phone.

When Trouble Calls, You Betta Listen

B asil you need to look at this," Kendra said as she passed
me a large legal-sized piece of paper.

"What is it?" I asked as I took the papers from her hand.

"It's Daschle's credit application," she said, and smiled. I
had promised to co-sign a loan for Daschle to get himself a
car before the draft. I didn't like to do this, especially for
players who hadn't been drafted yet, but the big boys did it,
so on occasion for special players I would break my rule.

"What's that smile about?" I asked as I looked over the
neatly printed credit application. I knew from Daschle's limited correspondence that this wasn't his handwriting.

"Does Daschle have a girlfriend?" Kendra asked. "I
know you don't want to hear this, but Rosa called."

"Why do you ask, and who filled out this application?
This looks like your handwriting," I said, ignoring her mention of Rosa.

"It is." Kendra smiled. "He asked me to fill it out for
him, and I had a little extra time, so I didn't mind."

"You need to let that clown fill out his own applications. And be careful with him. He's a baller in training," I said.

"I'm not up on the latest jock lingo. What's a baller?" Kendra asked.

"You know, a good-looking dude with a woman in every city. Two or three in the big cities. Got money to spend and don't mind letting everybody know it," I said.

"You think that's how Daschle is going to end up?"

"I know a baller when I see one. I used to be one," I said, laughing, as Kendra walked out of my office looking slightly disappointed.

I was looking over Daschle's application and getting ready to have Kendra fax it to my banker, when she walked back into my office and said, "There's a LaVonya Johnson on line two. She's with the *Daily Press* and said she has a few questions about the Pro Football Hall of Fame."

"The Hall of Fame . . . huh. Didn't we just go through this? Maybe they've recounted the votes and I'm in." I laughed. "Put her through."

"You got it," Kendra said.

"Wait, Kendra. Here, send this over to Keith at my bank. And let this be the last time you fill out a credit application for a client," I teased. Over the two years Kendra had worked for me we'd developed a big brother/little sister relationship, which I found myself needing more and more since my own sister, Campbell, had moved to Pittsburgh.

"I hear ya talking," Kendra said as she closed the door to my office. I picked up the phone and pressed the button next to the flashing red light.

"This is Basil Henderson," I said.

"Mr. Henderson, thanks for taking my call. This is

LaVonya Young from the *Daily Press*. I had a few questions about the Pro Football Hall of Fame induction," she said.

"Sure, but you know I didn't get in this year. Next year will be my year," I said confidently.

"No, I didn't know that," she said.

"Are you a sportswriter? I thought I knew most of the female sportswriters in the country."

"No. Let's just say I am interested in the entertainment aspect of sports," LaVonya said.

"Okay. What do you want to know?"

"What do you think your chances are for getting inducted next year?"

"I'm real hopeful. I got the stats. A lot of guys don't get in the first year they're on the ballot. It's just an honor to be nominated my first year out. I was personally pulling for Lynn Swann. He was long overdue, and I was really psyched that he got in," I said.

"Lynn Swann? Who's he?"

"You haven't heard of Lynn Swann? He's just one of the greatest receivers, present company included, to ever play the game. Lynn played college ball at USC and pro ball with the Pittsburgh Steelers. He had been nominated for the Pro Football Hall of Fame a number of years in a row, but he never made the cut. This had to be his year," I said, wondering why I was spending my time talking to a reporter who obviously hadn't done her homework. Maybe I should keep this call short. She was probably a homely-looking female trying to use her position in the media to sneak up on a little sexing.

"I see. So how well do you know this Lynn Swann? Are you two close?"

"How well do I know him? To be truthful, I really don't know him, so you can't call us close. I've been introduced and we've chatted at a few Super Bowls, but I don't really know him," I said. I was trying to figure out how to get out of this conversation without cussing this woman out for wasting my time.

"Have you decided once you're inducted into the Hall of Fame who would introduce you?" LaVonya asked. Now she was asking some questions that meant something.

"My Pops and college coach," I said proudly.

"What about your teammates?"

"What about them?"

"Were any of them going to be in your wedding party?"

"My wedding party? What wedding?"

"You are the John Basil Henderson who was going to marry Yancey Braxton, aren't you?"

"Next question," I said.

"If you say so. Let me get back to the Hall of Fame. Do you think it would be a sign of progress if a bisexual man were to be inducted into the Hall of Fame?"

"What?"

"What if you're inducted into the Hall of Fame next year? Wouldn't it say that the world of professional sports isn't as homophobic as the media would lead us to believe?"

"Why are you asking me some bullshit like that?" The tone of my voice had switched from polite to that thin edge before I started calling people something nastier than mofo.

"You are bisexual, aren't you?"

"What? Who is this? Are you the one sending me those annoying e-mails?"

"Just answer the question, Mr. Henderson. I have sources that tell me they've been involved in a long-term relationship with you. A very handsome man, I might add."

"Bitch, this conversation is over," I said as I slammed down the phone. I was wondering who this crazy dame was, when I thought about Yancey and her song. Had Yancey put this lady up to calling me for free publicity? How else would she know about my connection with Yancey? Maybe I needed to get Yancey on the phone right now and remind her that I still had a recording of her and Ava plotting against me and other information, which neither of them would want to reach the public. If they expected me to continue to chill with the tapes, Yancey needed to keep singing and stop talking to the press about my life.

As I picked up the phone to give Yancey a call, Kendra walked into my office and said, "I've got a little problem."

"What's the problem?"

"Bart Dunbar is on the line. When I told him you were out, he said he'd hold until you got back. I asked to take a message, and he said it was a very important matter and he wasn't going to hang up no matter how long you were gone. He sounds serious," Kendra said.

I shook my head and told Kendra, "Don't worry, I'll take care of this. Why don't you go to lunch."

"Can I take a little extra time?" Kendra smiled.

"Don't push it," I said. After Kendra closed the door, I waited a few moments before I picked up the phone and said, "Bart, I told you to leave me the fuck alone!"

"Basil, I know, but I need to talk to you," he said.

"I ain't got time," I said.

"It's very important," he said in an anxious voice.

"What is it?"

"I need to see you in person. Can I come over to your place this evening?"

"No. Anything you need to tell me, do it now. I've told you, nothing else is happening between you and me."

"You might want to consider seeing me as soon as possible. I got a call from some lady asking questions about us," Bart said.

"Us? There is no 'us'! What lady are you talking about, and how in the fuck does anyone know 'bout you and me? Ain't shit going on between us," I said, suddenly wondering if Bart had anything to do with that bitch ass reporter. He was the *only* person who knew we'd dealt a couple of times, and since both incidents occurred at my house, there really wasn't any proof anything had gone on. I wondered if he was taping our phone conversation now.

"There is this woman named LaVonya or something, and a friend of mine told me she's a really powerful columnist. She told me she was doing a story on gay athletes," Bart said.

"Then that don't have shit to do with me," I said. As I was preparing to hang up the phone, I thought that if I was being taped I should cover my ass so I added, "I'm sorry you didn't get the modeling job, but I wasn't involved in the process. My office manager and my firm are pleased with the selection." Now let him use that tape, I thought as I hung up the phone.

Reunited

I was enjoying a glass of port, after a grueling day of interviews with *Ebony, Entertainment Weekly* and *Honey,* and it seemed all they wanted to talk about were the lyrics to "Any Way the Wind Blows." When the music critic from *Honey* asked if the song was based on a personal experience, I looked at her and said, "Darling, do I look like a woman any self-respecting man would leave for a man?" I was relieved when she laughed along with me and moved on to her next question.

The house was quiet, and I missed Windsor. After the wedding, she and Wardell had moved to Columbia, South Carolina, and we had talked a couple of times on the phone. We made plans for me to visit a couple of months after the baby was born if my schedule permitted. I didn't tell Windsor I was somewhat nervous about being around a newborn.

Things were going okay for me. No more pictures or phone calls from that mystery wacko, and my song moved up the charts to number twenty-three and the album debuted at thirty-one. Motown was putting together final plans for me to begin touring as soon as they found a suitable big-name male singer I could open up for.

I took the final sip of port and was on my way to the bar to pour another glass when the doorbell rang. I was listening to Erykah Badu's new album, *Mama's Gun,* because I wanted to see what the competition was doing, but I put Miss Badu on mute as I went to the door and looked out the peephole.

I saw a man with his back turned toward me, but with one glance I knew who it was. It was my ex-fiancé, John Basil Henderson. My body suddenly knotted up bone by bone. Why was I nervous? Should I open the door? I thought a few minutes, and when the doorbell rang again, I took a quick look at myself in the mirror and cracked open the door, keeping the chain lock on.

"Yancey," Basil said as he turned and faced me.

"What are you doing here?" I demanded.

"I need to talk to you," Basil said.

"Yeah, I know you do. But everyone wants to talk to me these days. You'll have to get in line," I said, sounding harsher than I felt. I knew he was bound to show up at some point.

"I just took a chance you might have some time," Basil said in a solemn and defenseless voice.

"I'm really tired. I had a long day," I said.

"All I need is a few minutes. Are you going to let me in?" Basil asked. There was an awkward silence for a couple of moments, and then I finally said, "Come in, but I'm putting your ass on the clock."

Basil walked in and began pulling off his cashmere jacket. He was wearing a sweater the color of ripened limes and draw-string black leather pants that fit his body like they were made for his ass and his alone. Damn, he smelled good, like he'd been lathered in soap and then glazed in a marvelous cologne. I couldn't help but notice the hard roundness of his biceps testing the strength of the sweater's fabric, and I wanted to push him out the door before I ripped off his clothing. Basil was the last great sex I had enjoyed, and I missed it badly.

There he was, standing in the foyer of my home with a hopeful smile on his face. A wave of mixed feelings took over my body. First was the powerful memory of our love affair and some of my own tender recollections. There were times I felt like the world was standing still and we were the only two people alive, when Basil would look into my eyes and tell me how much he loved me. Most times I believed him. I thought about how he used to shower me with flowers and beautiful gifts. But mostly I remembered our lovemaking and how we spent most nights sleeping like two Tiffany spoons. Yeah, Basil loved a beautiful ass; the only problem I had with that was it didn't seem to matter if it belonged to a girl or a boy. Then I started to remember the morning of our wedding, when his eyes looked so cold and he told me he could never marry someone like me. When I tried to hold him that day, his body felt like a block of ice. Now, just as my life had calmed down, and the wounds of rejection had healed, I'd allowed Basil to walk into my home like he belonged here.

"You look great," Basil said.

"Of course I look great. Did you expect me to turn into a broke-down stank ho 'cause you can't decide which side of the bread you like buttered?" I said while thinking, Give it to him, girl. Let him have it.

"Yancey, I could never look at you that way," Basil said.

"What's so important that you need to come over here and talk to me? You didn't even call first! In case you've forgotten, women don't like pop callers. So what do you want?" I had to get him out of my house fast before he started to ooze his dangerous arsenal of charm and sex appeal.

"This song of yours. Is this your way of getting back at me?"

I laughed out loud, like Rita Hayward in *Gilda,* making the object of her affection feel small.

"So you think I've been spending my precious time worrying about getting revenge on you! How dare you! Basil, let's get one thing straight, if I can use that word with you. When I left New York, I left *you* and all the shit that came with our *alleged* relationship behind," I said. "And you'd be wise to stick to my version of the story!"

"You know that's cold, but I feel you. People are talking about your song, and I just wanted to ask you not to use my name when you talk to the press," Basil said.

"Don't you worry about that. All the publicity is about my talent and me. My CD. My career. This is not about you. But I will say this. If somebody puts two and two together, I'm not going to lie. Matter of fact, some woman called me asking about you. So I can't sweep it under the rug, even if I wanted to." I started to break into singing the Carly Simon hit "You're So Vain." But I wasn't doing free concerts.

"What did you tell her? Was her name LaVonya?"

"Yes, and I guess you'll have to read the rest in the paper," I snapped.

"Yancey, you know that we could never get married. What I did was best for both of us. Let's just move on with our lives."

"I have done that. You're the one who seems worried about the past. What's the matter? Are you worried about a new girlfriend or a new boyfriend?"

"I'm not involved with anyone right now," Basil said quietly. I had to admit that he looked like a little boy who'd just lost his first puppy, but I couldn't resist delivering one more body blow.

"Can't decide whether to eat fish or beef?" I asked sarcastically.

"Do what you gotta do. If making me feel small makes you feel better, then knock yourself out. I was just hoping that we wouldn't have to share our past with the public," Basil said as he put on his jacket and walked out the door.

Don't It Make
My Gray Eyes Blue

I guess I shouldn't be surprised by the way Yancey treated me. After all, I had left her at the altar and beat her at her own game. What surprised me most as I hailed a taxi on Third Avenue was the touch of jealousy I felt when I thought about some other dude smashing Yancey on a regular basis. I knew somebody was hittin' it. I just didn't know who. Yancey could be every bit the Broadway star one moment and a sex kitten the next. One of the things I loved about her was that Yancey loved sex just as much as I did. Bart wouldn't have gotten anywhere with me if I'd still been with Yancey. The girl knew how to make my toes curl.

Yancey still looked damn good, even though she was trying to give off the impression that my visit surprised her. She looked fabulous with her hair whipped around her face like a gust of wind had placed it there. She reminded me of Raquel Welch on the movie poster for the flick she did with Jim Brown. Yancey is forever the actress and an undeniably sexy woman, and I did love her. Once. I guess now I was going to pay the price for falling in love with Yancey, with a large part of the public hearing the anatomy of a breakup blow by blow on the radio. Love sure can take a destructive slide when it ends, like lava from a volcano covering a bed of roses.

Maybe I should have been more forceful with Yancey rather than letting her do all the talking. I still had the master tape of Yancey and Ava scheming and plotting all sorts of stuff, and I kept copies in my safe-deposit box.

I wondered if Yancey had a change of heart about the child she'd had out of wedlock. With all the press she was receiving now, the news of a deserted child could negatively affect her career. I wondered if that bitch LaVonya knew about Yancey's daughter.

Didn't Yancey remember who I was? Maybe she needed to be reminded I wasn't the only one with threatening secrets. With the right embellishment, LaVonya might be more interested in a pop star who gave up a baby than who I was sleeping with.

• • •

As I was checking my messages, I was reminded of my other problem. Bart, the flip side of Yancey. He left a message: *You're going to be sorry for messing with me. Do you think you can just kick me to the curb like day old bread? I don't think so. You did it once before and I let it slide. I'm going to get me a lawyer and I'm suing you for sexual harassment, so I hope you got a good lawyer.*"

What was Bart, with his dumb ass talking about suing me for sexual harassment? Had he lost his mind? Could he be serious? I didn't harass him for shit. I thought about the last part of his message, about having a good lawyer.

I looked at my watch and then picked up my phone and called Raymond's office. I needed to find out if I had any reason to worry. I'd certainly never heard of a case of a man suing another man for sexual harassment, and I didn't want to be involved in the test case.

"Professor Tyler's office," a sweet-sounding voice said.

"Is he in?"

"May I tell him who's calling?"

"Basil Henderson," I said. A few moments later, Raymond was on the other line.

"How you doing? Two calls within the month. I can't believe this." Raymond laughed.

"You must be living right," I said.

"What's going on? I know you didn't call me just 'cause you were thinking about me," Raymond said.

"Why can't I do something nice?"

"Come on, Basil, whatsup?"

"Got a quick legal question. Can one man sue another man for sexual harassment?"

"Sure," Raymond said quickly and confidently.

"They can?"

"Sure. Who's suing you?"

"Who said it was me?"

"Oh, I understand. It's a friend," Raymond said in a knowing voice. I told him a real quick version of meeting Bart, our two-night stand, and how when he wanted to get serious I'd given him the old heave-ho.

"I don't think he can sue you. Depends on what the

New York law is. Now, if he was working for you he might have a chance, but I don't think you have to worry since he wasn't an employee," Raymond said.

"Thanks. That's good to know," I said as I breathed a sigh of relief.

"It doesn't mean you're out of the woods. We live in a country where people can still file a lawsuit if they feel like they've been wronged. There's no law against doing that. The courts are filled with frivolous lawsuits. If he finds a lawyer who's willing to take his case, with or without merit, you could find yourself in court. Look, I don't think you should worry. I got to run. I have a class to teach. Keep me posted," Raymond said.

"I'll do that. Thanks, Raymond."

"No problem. Be good."

"Always," I mumbled before I hung up the phone.

The Lawyer and the Liar

Now, Mr. Dunbar, who did you say recommended me?" Gail Dennis asked as she looked over some notes from her large glass desk.

"LaVonya Young. You know, she writes the column 'Lines from LaVonya.' She said you were one of the best sexual-harassment attorneys in the country," I said.

"Oh yeah, LaVonya. How could I forget her," Gail mumbled.

"So will you take my case?" I asked. Gail remained silent as she leaned back in her chair, studying me while twisting a silver pen in her hand. She was an above-average-looking white woman. She was tiny, with reddish blond hair, high cheekbones and a prominent chin. Gail's makeup was perfect and pale and brought attention to her piercing blue eyes.

"I don't really do a lot of sexual-harassment cases. My notes say you're a model and a waiter. Who do you want to sue?"

"John Basil Henderson."

"Then why are you suing his firm, XJI?"

"Didn't your assistant or whoever I talked to tell you?" I wanted to know why whoever I had talked with was wasting my time.

"Oh yeah, it's all here in the notes. But I want to hear what you have to say," Gail said.

"Let me see, where should I start?"

"Why not from the beginning."

"Okay," I said. Right when I was getting ready to start my story, Gail spoke again. "I'm going to tape this. Is that a problem?"

"No."

"Let's get started."

Instead of telling Gail what had happened, the lies began pouring out of me, as they had in my earlier conversation with Gail's assistant.

I told Gail how I had been promised the job of being a part of XJI's ad campaign if I serviced John Basil Henderson.

"What do you mean, service?" Gail interrupted.

I looked at Gail with a puzzled stare and said, "Suck his dick, sit on his dick. Whatever he wanted me to do."

"So you are homosexual?"

"You would be correct with that assumption," I said.

"So you didn't get the job. Were you told why?"

"He gave me some bullshit excuse about how the other partners and office staff had picked someone else. This could have been my big break. You know, like Tyson getting that Ralph Lauren campaign."

"Who's Tyson?"

"It's not important," I said. I wanted to tell her how it pisses me off when white folks don't know shit about African Americans. I had stopped watching one of my favorite shows, *Who Wants to Be a Millionaire,* because white contestants didn't know anything about us. Now I was sitting in front of someone who was displaying the same type of ignorance and I needed her help.

"Okay, go on. Wait, was this relationship you had with Mr. Henderson consensual?"

"Consensual?"

"Did you agree to have sex with him before or after he promised you the job?"

"I didn't want to have sex with him, but things were tight and I needed the job. And it seemed that if the only way I could get it was to get on my knees, then that's what I was going to do," I said with bitterness in my voice.

"You know, male-on-male cases are rare and difficult. I don't know if I'm the right person," Gail said.

I wanted to tell Gail she was the only person. She didn't know that LaVonya had told me a little bit about her background and why she might be interested in taking my case. Apparently Gail had been married to one of the top players in the NBA. They were one of the city's glamorous couples, and their wedding had appeared in *Town and Country.* Gail was called out of town suddenly for a business trip, and when her flight was canceled, she returned home to find her handsome husband with not one, but two of the building staff (the doorman and an electrician) entertaining her husband in their bed. Suffice it to say, Gail was not a big fan of bisexual men. She owed LaVonya a favor for when LaVonya had agreed not to print Gail's story in one of her famous blind items. I'd promised LaVonya juicy details about the talented Mr. Henderson once the lawsuit was filed. I'd lied and told her Basil had given me the names of several other high-profile athletes and entertainers who swung both ways.

"I know it's going to be tough. But men like John Basil Henderson must be stopped," I said firmly.

"John Basil Henderson," Gail said out loud while look-ing out her huge picture window. "Why does that name sound familiar? Did he play basketball?"

"I think he played football." I was certain Gail was won-dering if Basil had "hit it" with her ex. Maybe that would convince her to take the case.

"Did you play sports?"

"Powder-puff football," I joked.

"So you know this will attract the attention of the media?" she asked. I wanted to say if we're lucky, but instead I said, "I have truth on my side, so that's not a problem for me."

"Are you prepared to put me on retainer?"

"LaVonya said you might cut me a break. I mean, if you take my case," I said.

"Let me think about this. It might be hard to sue the firm, or even Mr. Henderson. You weren't really an employee, and it will come down to your word against his," Gail said.

"What if I have proof?"

"Proof? What kind of proof?"

"Say I got him to admit what happened to us on tape?"

"Are you still in contact with him?"

"No, but I have his number. I know his reputation is important to him, and he might be willing to settle if he's approached by the right person, like a high-powered attorney."

"I don't want to be a part of anything like that, and you might find yourself looking for an attorney to defend you against an extortion charge. I am advising you to discontinue any communication with this man. I will get back to you within twenty-four hours," Gail said as she stood up, closed her binder and extended her thin hand. I could feel her wavering and I had to bring her back over to my side.

"We can't let these men who call themselves 'bi,' continue to destroy the lives of people who are comfortable with their sexuality. Somebody has to pay," I said as I shook her hand firmly. The sudden change in Gail's stern demeanor gave me hope that she agreed.

Diva Dearest

I was getting ready to head up to Harlem for a run-through of my video when my doorbell rang. I figured it was the car service, so I opened the door without looking out the peephole. This was the second mistake I'd made since I returned to New York, the first was opening the door for Basil. Now standing at the door, wrapped in fur from head to toe, was my mother, Ava Parker Middlebrooks. When I didn't hear from her again after her phone call, I figured she would get the message that I didn't have time for her. No such luck. A deep disappointment bubbled up in my stomach. Ava's visit was about as welcome as an early-morning snowstorm, but at least snow eventually melted.

"Ava, what are you doing here?" I stuttered.

"You need to get a two-way pager. Everybody who's anybody has one," Ava said.

"What are you doing in New York?"

"I got business here. Need I remind you that I have a big investment in this little career of yours? All the money I've spent on singing, dancing lessons, not to mention gowns for pageants where you always came in second. It's payback time. I thought I'd drop in and surprise you. It's all decided: *I'm going to manage your career*," Ava said as she walked into my town house, removing her hat and coat and dropping them on an empty chair.

"I already have a manager, and Motown handles all my other needs," I said.

"I'm sure whoever they got, I'm better, so just fire them," Ava said flatly.

"I'm on my way out. I thought you were the car service," I said, figuring it was best just to ignore Ava's ranting.

"Car service . . . oh. I guess you're back in the money," Ava said as she sat on the sofa. She was wearing a too-tight black leather skirt and rust-colored scoop-neck blouse. Ava simply refused to dress her age.

"My record company is picking up the bills," I said. I didn't want Ava to think I had any extra money lying around.

"So it's *your* record company now. Funny how I missed that announcement in the trades," Ava said.

"You know what I mean."

"Yeah, I do," Ava said as she patted the sofa cushion. "Come sit down. Let's catch up."

"I can't talk now. I've got to run," I said as I went to the door and looked out, praying that I would see a limo outside with my name in the window. When I didn't, I went over and sat next to Ava.

"So don't you want to know what I've been up to? So much has happened since that sad, sad wedding day of yours. I've been doing a lot of singing engagements in Spain, and I'm thinking about starting my own record company. I have an agent who sent my demo to Hidden Beach Records—that's Michael Jordan's record company. I tell you, if I could get rid of all those secretaries and executive assistants and talk to Michael myself, I know I could get myself a deal. But at least with my own label I don't have to take shit from anybody else. I think I'll release my CD in Europe first and then bring it over here to the States. Who knows? You and I could be the first mother-and-daughter on the charts at the same time," Ava said. She liked to fill the air with her own voice; it didn't matter that no one cared or listened to a word she had to say.

"That's nice," I muttered as I looked at my watch and wondered where my driver was.

"So tell me. Have you heard from that sick ex-boyfriend of yours?"

"Who?" I asked. I knew she was talking about Basil. Ava gave me an *are you stupid?* look and said, "Yancey, don't play with me. You know I'm talking about Basil."

"He called, but I haven't spoken to him," I lied.

"What did he want?"

"I guess he called to congratulate me on my success. My song is the talk of the country," I said proudly.

"Child, you better get the getting while the getting is good, 'cause there ain't no real singers out there. I mean, Britney Spears and that group Destiny's Dolls. Those girls are something else! I mean, what kind of parents are raising these children?" Ava asked as she looked around my apartment.

"I think it's great that Destiny's Child has parents who are so involved in their careers. And if record sales are any indication, they're doing a pretty good job," I said. Ava rolled her eyes at me and then glanced around the room. I could tell from the look on her face that her next topic of conversation would include a few body blows to my budding recording career. To avoid that, I got up from the sofa and went over to my desk and pulled out one of my early reviews from *Entertainment Weekly.*

I stood near my dining table and said, "Listen to this," as I began to read the review. "Motown's Yancey B has a hit on her hands the first time out. With great lyrics matched with lovely melodies, the results are exquisitely brilliant. An album that tells a story with each song. Yancey B's Broadway-trained voice, with a little bit of soul and pop, shines on the first single, 'Any Way the Wind Blows,' and with this beautiful voice Yancey B is going only one way. Straight to number one. Grade: A+."

"Did you write that?" Ava asked coldly.

"No, I didn't. That's from *Entertainment Weekly,*" I said proudly.

"Do you have anything to drink? My throat is parched," Ava said as she gently touched her neck.

"What would you like?"

"Water or wine. I don't imagine you have any snacks around," Ava said. I walked into the kitchen and pulled out a bottle of water and silently congratulated myself on my self-restraint. I wanted to tell Ava to get her ass out, but I was not going to let her ruin my day. I walked back into the living and placed the bottle of water on a coaster.

"What, no glass? Who do you think I am?" I turned toward the kitchen to get a glass when she said, "That's all right. I can drink it out of the bottle."

Ava drank almost half of the water and set it back on the table. Suddenly her voice changed, taking on the dramatic manner she used to describe her latest schemes. "Yancey darling, I have figured out a plan to make you even bigger than most limited-talent girls ever get. We might have to eliminate a few with *Enquirer*-like scandals."

"I'm not interested," I said firmly.

"What! Are you crazy? One hit doesn't make a star."

Just as I was getting ready to tell Ava where she could go, the doorbell rang. I rushed to the door and looked out the peephole. An older white man stood there holding a sign with my name on it. I quickly opened the door like I was trying to escape from prison.

"I'm here for Miss Yancey Braxton," he said.

"I'm Miss Braxton. I'll be with you in a few seconds. Come on in," I said. I usually didn't invite drivers into my home, but I figured it would be one way to get Ava out of my house, since I knew she didn't associate with hired help.

"So I guess you're kicking me out?" Ava said as she got up from the sofa. I reached in the hall closet and grabbed my leather jacket. I grabbed my bag and gave Ava one of the fake smiles I'd learned from her, then said, "Good seeing you. I'm off to shoot my video."

"I'll have my driver follow you. Maybe I can give you a few pointers. You know what, maybe we should consider being a duo like the Junes. I mean the Judds. No, scratch that, it means I would have to admit to being a mother," Ava said wistfully. "But I can still help with your first video."

"Sorry, the director insists on a closed set. Make sure you lock the door when you leave." As I followed the driver out the door, I heard Ava say, "Call me when you change your mind. I'll be at the Plaza."

Beauty Bonding

Miss Yancey B walked into the studio looking fabulous. If I were into women, then Yancey would be the kinda bitch I'd date. Beautiful, talented and in control. I bet she had all kinds of good-looking men sniffing behind her for just a little taste of her sugar.

"Bart, how are you, sweetheart?" Yancey said as she gave me a peck on the cheek like we had known each other for years. I was glad I had worn my suede pants and a form-fitting beige turtleneck. I wanted to show her I knew how to dress for success.

"I'm fine, Yancey. You look great," I said.

"Thank you. Where is everybody?" she asked as she took off her short leather jacket and looked around the studio.

"The director is back there," I said as I pointed to a small room with light pouring out into the large, dark studio.

"Oh, Desmond's here," Yancey said as her eyes lit up with an *I want to know you better* look.

"Yep, he's here. Doesn't talk much, though," I said.

"Do you think he's on your team or mine?" Yancey asked.

"Depends which team you're on, Miss Yancey," I said. "Do you like boys or girls?"

"Oh, I guess you could say we're on the same team. I like men. I don't care how good a girl is, she ain't getting near this," Yancey said as she outlined her chest and hip area.

"I think he's for you," I said.

"You think so?"

"Yeah, the old gaydar didn't pick up any signals, but he is a cutie," I said.

"I like you, Bart," Yancey said as she put her hands softly on my shoulders. "You keep me feeling like this and I might have to take you on tour with me."

"Cool! So you're touring?"

"Yeah, I think we're going to wait until we drop the second single. They tried to hook me up with a male singer to tour with. But they want me to audition. And I am over that," Yancey said.

"I heard that. Do you miss Los Angeles?"

"Child, pleeze, with all those fake-ass people? No, I don't miss it a bit," Yancey said.

"But I know movies have to be in your future," I said.

"Yeah, but a lot of films are shot here in New York and in Toronto. Los Angeles has become so expensive," Yancey said.

"What kind of roles do you want? I see you as the Sanaa Lathan/Nia Long type," I said.

"They should see themselves as *my* type." Yancey laughed. "I want the kind of roles Jennifer Lopez is getting. I hear that heifer is getting nine million dollars a film. If they want to give away that kinda money, I wish they'd give it to somebody who can act, like Angela Bassett or me."

"Ain't that some shit. I mean, how many awards, nominations has she gotten? When Miss Angela, Vivica, Lela and all them *Waiting to Exhale* girls have to beg for roles, you *know* the business world ain't fair," I said.

"I hear you. Doesn't it just drive you crazy when everyone talks about J-Lo as a woman of color? Do you think if the studio'd considered her a woman of color she'd be doing love scenes with George Clooney?" Yancey asked.

"I feel you! Even though I think he has a little case of jungle fever," I said with a grin.

"I'm not a bit surprised." Yancey smiled.

"Don't you think it's funny that Hollywood is supposed to be so liberal, yet there ain't never gonna be a superstar black woman actress, much less a black gay male actor?"

"I hadn't thought about that. I guess if you're black and gay and you're an actor, then you better keep your mouth shut," Yancey said.

"And trust me, there are plenty of black gay male actors. They act when they're on the screen and when they're off. Showing up with their fake girlfriends and wives," I said. I was getting my dandruff up. It happened every time I thought about all the black men who were afraid to tell the truth about who they really were.

"You got any names?" Yancey said as she rubbed her hands with glee.

"I might drop a few when I get to know you better. I

don't know, though, you might be working undercover for the *Enquirer* or something," I said, and laughed.

"I probably know more names than you," Yancey said. Just as I was getting ready to see if I could pump any information out of her, my cell phone rang.

"Excuse me," I said as I flipped open my phone and moved a few yards from Yancey.

"Hello," I said.

"Bart, this is LaVonya. I just wanted to make sure you read my column tomorrow. There will be something on you and Basil."

"I can't talk right now. I am working," I said.

"When will you be finished?"

"I don't know. What's it going to say?"

"Wait and see."

"I'll do that," I said. Just as I was getting ready to hang up, my other line beeped. "I'll call you back."

"No need, darling," LaVonya said.

I clicked over to the other line and said, "Hello."

"Bart, this is Gail Dennis. I've decided to take your case and will be filing the lawsuit in a couple of days," Gail said.

"Thank you. That's great news. How much money do you think we can get?"

"Let's just file the suit and see how he responds. One other thing: If I'm going to handle your case, I'm going to insist that you deal only with me. I don't want to try this case in the media. Which means no 'Lines from LaVonya.' Do you understand?"

"I understand. Look, I'm in the middle of something. I'll call you back later this afternoon," I said.

"Fine. If I'm not in, have my assistant track me down," Gail said.

"I will," I said as I clicked my cell phone closed.

I walked back to the center of the studio, where Yancey was now chatting with Desmond and another very attractive man. He was light-skinned, with hazel eyes and perfect white teeth. He had a lean, muscular build and a nice bulge I couldn't help but notice in his tight-fitting jeans.

"Bart, good seeing you. This is Evanston, your love interest in the video," Desmond said.

"Nice meeting you," I said as I shook Evanston's hand. He had a firm handshake. Yancey looked at the two of us and smiled to herself.

"Same here," Evanston said.

"Okay, let's get started," Desmond said as he and Yancey started walking toward the set. Evanston followed them, and I trailed behind, thinking, Maybe I won't miss Basil so much, after all.

May I Serve You?

It was Monday or, as it was better known, BPN (Black People's Night) on the UPN (U People's Network). The only night of the week when you see brothers and sisters making fools of themselves like the white boys and girls do each and every night. I was drinking an orange soda and waiting for dinner from my favorite Italian restaurant in my neighborhood. When the doorman buzzed, I told him to send the delivery up.

A few minutes later, when I opened the door, I saw a tall, square black woman with unfriendly eyes. Before I could say hello or figure out why she was standing at my door without my food, she said, "John Basil Henderson," in a very firm and authoritative voice.

"Yes."

"You have now been served," she said as she placed an official-looking document in my hand and disappeared before I could say "What the fuck?" I quickly opened the envelope, although I knew full well that punk-ass Bart had followed through with his threats.

As I read the document, a wave of anger welled up in me, especially when I read the words "sexual harassment and assault." Every muscle in my body became tense, and I felt a slow explosion coming on.

My first reaction was to call Bart, or better yet, to head up to Harlem and kick his ass. Then I remembered Raymond's offer to help, so I picked up the phone and hit the speed dial. After a few rings, a dude, not Raymond, answered the phone.

"Hello."

"Is attorney Raymond Tyler in?" I asked, letting whoever had answered his line know that this was a business call.

"Can I tell him who's calling?"

"Basil Henderson," I said firmly. A few seconds later, Raymond picked up the phone.

"Basil, what's going on?"

"Can you talk?" I asked. I wondered if his partner, or whoever that was, was standing near him, hovering over and listening to one side of our conversation.

"Sure."

"That mofo sued me," I said.

"Who?"

"Bart, the guy we talked about. I was just served with a lawsuit," I said.

"What is he suing you for?"

"I haven't read the entire document, but it says something about harassment and assault," I said.

"Do you have a fax machine?" Raymond asked.

"Not at home, but we have several at the office," I said.

"Then I need you to go up to your office and send me the

entire document tonight. I'll look it over and give you a call later tomorrow. I'll also contact his lawyer," Raymond said.

"You know, this shit pisses me off. All I want to do is haul my ass up to his apartment and cram this document down his throat," I said.

"Basil, I know you're upset, but you need to chill. Listen to me. If you want me to help you with this, then just take the document and send it to me. I'll take care of this, but I'm not going to handle any criminal assault cases because you lost your temper. Don't think that every time your sex gets you in trouble, your fists can get you out."

I thought about what Raymond was saying, and after a few moments, I said, "I feel you. Give me your fax number, and you'll have the papers in an hour."

· · ·

Three days had passed and I still hadn't heard from Raymond, and I was getting nervous, so I asked Kendra to get him on the phone. A few minutes later, she knocked on the door and said, "I have Mr. Tyler on the phone." I wondered for a few seconds why Kendra had knocked on my door instead of using the intercom, but I couldn't spend a lot of time thinking about that with Raymond on the line.

"Raymond. Why haven't I heard from you?"

"Sorry, but I've been real busy working on this case. I had to look up the New York employment law, because Bart's basically saying he didn't get the job because he wouldn't continue to sleep with you," Raymond said.

"Please tell me you're kidding. That lying sonofabitch! I can't believe this shit," I said.

"Look, Basil, I really think you can beat this. It might not even make it to a judge, but that's a chance you might have to take. I talked to his lawyer, and she sounds like she's ready to deal. It might make sense just to make an offer and move on," Raymond said.

"How much?"

"Did you check with your insurance company?"

"No, I don't want anybody in my business. I could move some money around and pay him from my own funds. What do you think we should offer?"

"I might start with twenty-five thousand and be willing to go to low, and I do mean low, six figures," Raymond said.

"Are you kidding? This is bullshit. All of this for a piece of ass," I said.

"In this case, a very expensive piece of ass," Raymond said.

"You ain't never lied, but I need to get this situation taken care of. I'm worried about this stuff getting in the press or my partners finding out. So do your thang," I said.

"I'll call his lawyer this afternoon and make an offer. It might take a couple of days, because I'm sure she will make a counteroffer and we'll go back and forth for a day or two."

"Just keep me posted," I said.

"Basil, can I ask you something?" Raymond said. His voice had switched from very businesslike to a sensitive and caring tone.

"Sure."

"Is it worth this much just to avoid saying what's true about your life?"

"It's worth millions for me to protect my reputation and my family," I said firmly.

"Then you better go sign some more number-one picks, because if you keep doing this stuff, your money is going to disappear quicker than dot.com stock," Raymond said.

"Listen to me, Raymond. Do whatever it takes. Make this go away."

"I'll do what I can."

Bart's Big Break

I had just gotten home from working a lunch shift when the phone rang. I was going to let the answering machine pick up the call and go ahead with my shower, when I saw "Plaza Hotel" flash on the caller I.D. I didn't know anyone at the Plaza, so I was curious and picked up the phone before the answering machine took over.

"Hello."

"May I speak with Bart Dunbar?" a sophisticated female voice asked.

"Who's calling?" I asked.

"Is this Bart?"

"Like I said, who's calling?" I repeated in an annoyed tone.

"Bart. You don't know me, but we know someone in common," she said.

"Look, I am too old to be playing high school games on the phone. State your business, or else I'm hanging up this phone."

"I understand you've had a little run-in with one John

Basil Henderson. I have some information that might help your case," she said. Now I was really curious—why would someone be calling me about Basil?

"And do you have a name?"

"I do. Are you interested in my information?"

"Only if I know to whom I'm speaking," I said. She sounded so proper and full of herself I wanted to slam the phone down, but instead I decided to play it her way.

"My name is Ava Parker Middlebrooks, and I obtained your number from LaVonya Young. I first read about you on her Web site, www.linesfromlavonya.com, and it's in the paper today. I know LaVonya from my New York days. I gave her a call and told her I wanted to help you out," Ava said.

"I haven't seen today's paper. What does it say?"

"Let me read it to you," Ava said. She cleared her throat and then started to read: "'What former all-star football player is being sued by a male model for sexual harassment?'"

"So LaVonya came through. Now how can you help me out?"

"Well, not only do I have confidential information about Mr. Henderson, but I understand from LaVonya that you have a great lawyer who's gonna make him pay. The trial will be the talk of the sports world. I think you're going to be famous."

"I hope so. But how is the information going to help me? If he makes an offer and I take it, then there won't be a case," I said.

"Oh no, Bart. There's *got* to be a case. I mean, think of what this asshole did to you and so many others. Next thing you know, he'll be in the Pro Football Hall of Fame with some fake wife and the world will never know what kind of sick man he is," Ava said.

"He musta fucked you over good, sister. I mean, I can feel the venom coming through the phone line. Tell me what happened," I said.

"No, darling, he didn't fuck me physically, but he tried to fuck me personally. And from what LaVonya tells me, you're a young man who don't take shit from anybody. Well, I am that kinda woman. I vowed I would get Basil Henderson back, so I was utterly delighted when I heard about your little escapade."

Ava spent the next ten minutes telling me how Basil had left her younger sister at the altar after she had spent more than $200,000 for a big wedding. She went on to tell me how Basil had been seeing a shrink to cure his lust for men and how he was secretly in love with a man. This pissed me off, since he'd told me he didn't date dudes. I guess that didn't include falling in love.

"How does your sister feel about you sharing this information?" I asked.

"She doesn't know. She was so depressed that I had to put her in a home," Ava said.

"Still . . . I don't understand how this is going to help my case," I said.

"You want him to pay, right?"

"Yeah."

"You want him to be embarrassed, right?"

"Yeah."

"Then you have to proceed with the case, even if you don't win or the suit is dismissed. Think of the public relations nightmare it will be for Mister Big-Time Football Star and that company of his."

"I hear ya, but my lawyer and I are suing for six figures. Now, I don't know about you, but for a struggling model and waiter, six figures is still a lot of money," I said.

"What if I matched whatever he offers? I know he's going to try and settle out of court. He doesn't want to face the possibility of a very public trial. Would you be willing to continue this fight, if not for yourself, then for a heart-broken sister?" she said. Her voice was cracking, and she sounded like she was about to start crying.

I looked at my phone like I couldn't be hearing this woman correctly. Had she just offered me a hundred grand just to keep harassing Basil?

"You would do that?"

"Are you interested?"

"What are you going to do? Just write me a check? Naw, scratch that, I ain't taking no check from somebody I don't know. I don't care if you live in Beverly Hills or Monte Carlo," I said firmly.

"But I don't expect you to take a check. What if I showed you I can be trusted?"

"How are you going to do that?"

"What's your address?" Ava asked.

I gave her my address without even thinking what I was doing. What if she was a crazy stalker or, even worse, some kind of double agent working for Basil to set my ass up?

Maybe they were planning to kill me or something to keep my mouth shut. Maybe I was watching too much Court TV.

"So you live up in Harlem, huh?" Ava asked.

"Yeah, I do."

"I heard the real estate market is going crazy. LaVonya said white folks are buying up everything. I might need to come up there and make a few investments myself," Ava said in a casual voice, like two old friends talking.

"So what are you going to do?" I asked.

"Please, just don't do anything until you hear from me?"

"I'm not making any promises to a lady with a nice voice," I argued.

"Bart, listen to me. Wait until tomorrow morning. Make sure you're home around ten," Ava instructed.

"That's my gym time," I protested.

"Honey, if you help me with my plans . . . you will have enough money to build your own gym." Ava laughed.

"I like the sound of that," I said, letting my guard down slightly.

"Then you'll give me at least forty-eight hours?"

"You said tomorrow morning. Now you're saying forty-eight hours. What kind of game are you trying to run?"

"No, listen to me. Tomorrow morning is when the partnership of Ava and Bart begins. I need forty-eight hours to be able to meet my new partner face-to-face," Ava said.

"Show me you mean business and then we'll talk," I said. Suddenly realizing I had already said too much, I hung up the phone.

• • •

I was enjoying a cup of coffee in my kitchen after a restless night's sleep. I had spent the night thinking about the phone call from Ava and if she was serious or just talking smack. I got the answer a few minutes later when there was a knock at my door.

"Are you Bart Dunbar?" Aren't all overnight delivery-men good-looking? I thought.

"Yep, I'm Bart Dunbar."

"Sign here," he instructed. I signed his clipboard and he handed me an envelope, which I ripped open while closing the door.

After I picked my face up off the floor, I raced to the phone and dialed Wylie's office.

"Wylie Woolfolk's office," Mollie said in her perky white-girl voice.

"Hey, Mollie. Is he in?"

"Bart? Sure, let me see." A few seconds later, Wylie picked up the phone.

"What's up, diva?"

"Please tell me you don't have plans this evening," I pleaded.

"I don't. What's going on?"

"I want to take you to dinner. Your choice, and it can be the best restaurant in town. Jean Georges, Club 21, you name it," I said proudly.

"Did you land some kind of Ralph Lauren campaign or something? I didn't know you were up for major work. You keeping secrets?"

"No, it's not a campaign. All my booker has been send-ing me on are video go-sees. But something wonderful happened just a few minutes ago. I opened the door, and this FedEx man had an envelope for me. I opened it and out fell a hundred crisp hundred-dollar bills. Who said there were no more fairy godmothers?" I laughed.

"Where did the money come from?"

I told Wylie about the call from Ava and how she wanted to help me with my case against Basil.

"Did she say why this was important to her? Have you met her?"

"No, but I think I will."

"Have you told your lawyer about this?"

"No! It ain't her business if I'm getting a little cash on the side."

"Baby, you better be careful. You don't really know nothing about this lady and what she really wants you to do," Wylie advised.

"I don't care what she wants me to do if she's got money to throw around like this. I mean, within reason I don't care. I think she's some woman he fucked and left high and dry. She said it was somebody else, but I don't believe her."

"How did she find you?"

"Who else? Miss LaVonya."

"Did you call LaVonya and make sure she knows this lady?"

"Wylie, what part of 'I don't give a shit' don't you understand? I'll worry about LaVonya later. Let's celebrate. Let me treat *you* for a change," I said.

"Sounds good. I will call you in a couple of hours when my taste buds tell me where I want to go. Maybe Mollie has heard of something good and trendy," Wylie said.

"Okay. If I'm not here, leave me a message. I'm going to buy me a DVD player and some DVDs."

"Don't spend it all in one place."

"Don't worry. But I do need to make sure this money is real. If you don't hear from me this evening, start checking the jails," I said, and laughed.

"I will, but I'll give you a week or two to make some new friends," Wylie teased before saying goodbye.

Desmond the Delicious

Desmond, it's just brilliant," I said as I clapped my hands with a childlike glee. I had just finished watching for the third time the final cut of my "Any Way the Wind Blows" video.

"Yeah, we did good, didn't we?" Desmond asked as he rubbed his chin.

"Come on. We have to celebrate," I said as I took his hand and led him toward my dining room.

"Where are you taking me, Yancey?"

"We're going to get some champagne. We can't celebrate without champagne," I said.

I took Desmond into the kitchen, and I pulled out a moderately priced bottle of champagne. I was saving the good stuff for my first platinum single or CD, whichever came first.

We then went into the bar area, where I kept my good crystal flutes. I poured two glasses of champagne, and Desmond offered a toast: "To a number-one record and video. The first of many." Desmond then sat on the bar stool.

"Cheers," I said with a smile, still standing and trying to decide if I should move closer.

"So you're really pleased?"

"I can't tell you how pleased I am. I loved how you worked all my scenes and my wardrobe changes. I loved how you'd flash to the guys and then back to me! And how did you get that snow scene in? That was fabulous with the fur coat. I felt like Vanessa Williams in her 'Save the Best for Last' video," I said.

"You know, almost anything can be done with computers now," Desmond said as he took a sip of the champagne.

"I can't wait to see it on BET, VH-1 and MTV!" I said.

"I think they're going to start running it immediately. I mean, the song is burning up the charts. What number is it now?"

"Number seventeen with a bullet," I said proudly.

"This video will help, but I think they should have done it a little sooner."

"Yeah, but then I wouldn't have had the chance of doing it here in New York and meeting—I mean working—with you," I said. "Besides, I'm sure most record companies take their time with new artists."

"It's been on the real working with you. Yancey, you're a talented and beautiful lady," Desmond said.

"Thank you," I said, blushing. I took another sip of my drink and gazed at Desmond, who was wearing a sweater the color of a faded blue summer sky and tan slacks. This was the first time we'd been alone, and it felt good.

"It really helps that you can act. A lot of these music divas can't act or lip-synch, and it makes my job tough," Desmond said.

"I am thankful for my Broadway training. I know how to show emotion, and I don't have a problem singing live," I said.

"I have a secret," Desmond said as he leaned closer to me. There was something wonderfully sexy about the way Desmond smelled, like a wisp of cologne mixed with the clean fragrance of soap.

"Tell me a secret," I said as I welcomed Desmond into my personal space.

"I've never been to a real Broadway show," Desmond whispered.

"I can't believe that! How can you be a great director if you haven't seen a Broadway show?" I asked with a broad smile.

"Just haven't got around to it. I will one day, maybe. I was never really interested in directing for the stage, so I spend a lot of time watching films. Both old and new."

"Who's your favorite director?"

"I love Orson Welles, and *Boyz N the Hood* was the best movie I've ever seen, and of course, Spike never really disappoints. I mean, have you seen *Bamboozled*?"

"No. Is it good?"

"Brilliant. I have the video. I'll loan it to you. Even though I don't know when you'll have time to see it. I mean, it sounds like your record company is keeping you pretty busy."

"Yeah, that's right. But if you say it's good, then I'll make time. So what's next for you?"

"You mean this evening?" he asked as a smile danced on his lips.

"No!" I said, wondering if he was thinking what I was thinking. "I was talking about the future. You plan on giving Spike and John Singleton some comp, I bet."

"Yeah, I'm going to do features one day, but I just want to do the best work I can and not worry about the others," Desmond said confidently.

"So how does your better half handle your schedule? Being a director is very time-consuming."

Desmond released a hearty laugh as he slapped his knee. "Yancey . . . come on, now! You're an actress. I know you can think of a better way to ask me if I'm married or serious about someone!"

I smiled at Desmond, even though I was a little embarrassed that I'd been caught. I drank the rest of my champagne before responding.

"So are you dating anyone?"

"Not now."

"So you like being alone?"

"Alone doesn't always mean lonely," Desmond said as he stood, stretching, as if he was about to leave. But before he did, I needed answers to a few important questions.

"There is no polite way to ask you this, so I'll just spit it out. Have you ever slept with a man?"

Desmond didn't hesitate and said firmly, "Of course I have."

I felt a twinge of sadness and disappointment bubble up within me, but I was glad that Desmond was honest. When I looked over at him, there was an amused expression on his face. We were both silent for a moment, and then he broke into a wide smile.

"Yancey, come on, girl. Relax. When I say I've slept with a man, I mean my bloodline. My brothers. There were four of us, and we shared a room growing up. Why didn't you just ask me if I was gay or bisexual?"

"I didn't want to offend you," I said softly.

"I wouldn't be offended. And the answer to that question is no. Ain't nothing wrong with it, but the person I intend to have as my life's heartbeat will be a woman," Desmond said.

"So you're just messing with me. You've got a sick sense of humor," I said with a grin.

"So I guess the rumors are true," Desmond said.

"What rumors?"

"That the song 'Any Way' is about you and some dude you used to be tight with."

"Where did you hear that?"

"People talk. I mean, I've heard a couple of DJs talking about it after they play the song. Controversy is good for a product."

"Let people talk," I said. I didn't like the fact people were talking about my past. Besides, if they were going to talk about me, I preferred that they gossiped with *my* version of events.

"So is it true?"

"No," I said calmly.

"So what other questions do you have for me?"

I was thinking about what else I needed to know before

I allowed the little surge of excitement I had been feeling to return. The phone rang.

"Excuse me," I said as I gently touched the top of Desmond's hand. I went into the kitchen and picked up the cordless phone. "Hello."

"Yancey, have you seen the paper today?"

"Hello, Ava. No, I haven't." Perfect timing, as always, Mother.

"Then you need to tell me why you're protecting that asshole Basil."

"What are you talking about?"

"Read it! It's right there in 'Lines from LaVonya.' Let me read it to you. 'What pop star is getting revenge with her music and why won't she talk about it?'" Ava said.

"Look, Ava, I don't know if that's about me. I didn't tell that LaVonya lady anything. I don't know if any of my friends read her anyway," I said.

"Oh, I guess you're too big-time now. I guess you only read Liz Smith and Cindy Adams," Ava said in that I'm-going-to-drive-you-crazy-until-I-make-my-point voice I had heard too many times.

"Look, I've got a guest. How long are you going to be in town?"

"I don't know. Maybe until you realize you need me to help your career. Any good manager would tell you that you can use this little tidbit to your advantage. Might help that little record of yours."

"My single is doing just fine. Thank you very much," I said quickly.

"I'll thank you when you pay me my money back. That's the only thank you I'll give out. And I'm not talking about my commission for managing you."

"How many times do I have to tell you that I already have a manager?"

"Then tell me, who?"

I started to name one of the big firms like ICM or tell Ava that I had gone back to my former agent, Lois Drew. But I suddenly thought of the one person who would mess with Ava's mind and I said, "Basil represents me now."

"What!" Ava screamed. "Now I know you've lost your mind! What does he know about the business? Why are you even talking to him after what he did to you?"

"Ava, I don't need to explain any of my business decisions to you, but I will say this: Basil will do a great job for me. He co-owns one of the premier sports agencies in the business and now he's getting into entertainment. I have to go," I said as I hung up the phone. Before I could exit the room, the phone rang again.

"Hello."

"Listen here, missy, don't you ever hang up the phone in my face. I want my money for your aborted wedding, and I want it now. Should I call Basil, since he's your manager, and get a check?"

"Don't you call Basil for nothing! As soon as I get my first royalty check you'll get your money."

"You two are fucking with the wrong diva. If I don't get my money soon, you'll both be sorry."

"Goodbye, Ava," I said as I placed the phone back into

its cradle. I walked back into the dining room and was greeted by the sound of my own voice. The ballad "I'm Not in Love" was playing, and I must say it sounded perfect.

Desmond smiled at me and said, "I hope you don't mind. But I had a sudden urge to hear a beautiful lady do her thang."

I wanted to cry at Desmond's kind gesture, but instead I walked slowly toward him. Desmond opened his arms, pulled me close like he wanted to protect me from the world, and slowly we started to dance.

The Liars Who Lunch

Iwas sitting at the bar at B. Smith's in midtown having my second club soda, when a woman looking like Pam Grier's older sister walked in the place like she owned it. She paused, looked around and then strutted over toward me like she was walking the catwalk.

"Are you Bart Dunbar?" she asked.

"Yeah, I'm Bart," I said as I lifted myself from the barstool and extended my hand.

"Oh, honey, give me a hug. I'm Ava Middlebrooks, your partner in revenge," Ava said as she hugged me.

"Nice meeting you, and thanks again for the little care package," I said as I pulled away from Ava.

"Come on, let's get a seat. I made a reservation and asked them to give us something private so we can talk without somebody hanging on our every word. You know, LaVonya and her gossip friends get a lot of their information from waiters and busboys," Ava said.

A model-thin Asian hostess led us to a table in the back of the pale pink restaurant. Ava pulled off her aqua silk scarf and stood with her back to me. It took me a few seconds to realize she expected me to help her out of her fur coat. This woman was playing her diva act to the hilt, I thought as I removed the coat from her shoulders. Ava was dressed in an elegant raspberry sorbet-colored sweater dress that looked like mohair or cashmere, and her body looked fabulous for a middle-aged woman. She was also wearing a lot of expensive-looking jewelry. At least, it looked expensive. Could have been Joan Rivers jewelry for all I knew. The waiter pulled out a chair for Ava, who sat down like she was a graduate of Miss Porter's.

"Would you like me to check your coat?" the waiter asked.

"No, baby. It's fine right here next to me." Ava smiled.

"Can I get you something to drink?"

"Yes, darling," Ava said, and then she looked at me. "I never get tired of saying this," she whispered. Then she turned toward the waiter and ordered, "Bring us a bottle of your finest champagne, darling young man," as she released an infectious laugh.

"I don't know if I should be drinking in the middle of the day. I have a couple of callbacks this afternoon," I said.

"Callbacks. Oh, how I love that word. Are you an actor, darling?"

"Not really. I do some videos, and if I'm lucky, a commercial every so often. I hope you didn't think I was being shady when you called me. There are so many crazies out there. I have to watch my back," I said.

"No, I didn't even think about it."

"That's good to hear."

"So you're a model slash video hunk? You *are* a good-looking, man. I see why that Basil was after you. You need to consider letting me manage you once we finish with Basil," Ava said as she picked a piece of sourdough bread from the table's wicker basket. She delicately took the proper knife and spread butter on the edge of the bread.

"So you're a personal manager?"

"Yes, but I only take select clients. Ava only deals with the best."

"Did I thank you for the little care package?" I asked as I pulled a sesame seed breadstick from the basket and took a small bite.

"Honey, that's only the beginning." Ava smiled. "And yes, you did."

"So you must really hate Basil," I said.

"*Hate* is such a harsh word. Let's just say nobody fucks with Madame Ava's family and just walks away without scars. I have always been one of those girls who'd put my gym shorts on under my dress, Vaseline my face and go kick ass. Despite how glamorous I am now, that young girl is still a part of me. And she makes sure nobody messes with Mommy," Ava said as she took a sip of water.

"I hear ya. I know about that inner-child shit. So how do you know LaVonya?"

"LaVonya is one of those people I call 'air-kiss girl-friends.' You know, we give each other kisses when we see each other, but we don't really have long conversations unless we need something. She uses me, and I use her. Sounds like a marriage, doesn't it, Bart?"

"I guess so." I had never heard anybody talk about

LaVonya this way. Most folks were scared to rub LaVonya the wrong way. I guess Madame Ava wasn't most folks.

"So tell me, how did you meet Basil?"

Just as I was getting ready to tell Ava my version of our meeting, the waiter came over with his pad in hand. "What would you like to have?"

Ava glanced at the menu and said, "I'll start with a nice green salad with oil and vinegar, and I'll have the the slow-baked salmon."

"And what can I get for you, sir?"

"For starters, the smoked salmon on scallion pancake, and the New York strip, medium well. I like it pink," I said, thinking how wonderful it was to have someone wait on me for a change.

After the waiter left, Ava asked me again about Basil.

"I don't know how much I should say, since my case is still pending. Let's just say I made it hard for him to resist the generous charms and gifts from my gene pool," I said.

"Are your parents alive?"

"I don't talk about my parents," I snapped. Why would she ask such a thing? I wondered what she was getting at.

Ava touched my hand gently and said, "Touchy . . . touchy. That's okay, darling. I don't talk about mine either. You can pick your nose, but not your family. I just want to make sure I'm not dealing with some psycho like Basil. I should send you a copy of the report I had run on him when he was trying to marry my dau—oh, I mean sister."

"What kind of report?"

"I hired a private investigator who tracked down all kinds of juicy information on him. Honey, that PI even got his shrink to talk!" Ava said, smiling like a woman proud of what she'd done.

"Damn, you don't play. I got to make sure I don't cross you," I said.

I took a sip of my water as Ava smiled and said, "A very wise choice, Bart. I think we'll get along fine. So tell me, is Bart really that good in bed?"

For a moment I said nothing, and when Ava remained silent I finally said, "He'll never hear complaints from me," as a smile crossed my lips at the memory of Basil's body covering mine like a canvas.

The champagne was served, and Ava toasted me by saying, "Here's to new friends and sweet revenge."

"Cheers," I said as our champagne flutes clinked with the tone of a sinister symphony about to start.

• • •

After I got the money from Ava, I quit my waiter job at the Viceroy and spent my first day as a man of leisure on my new sofa flipping between *Judge Judy* and *Oprah*. When the phone rang, I picked it up and said, "Speak." I was feeling my B-boy genes.

"Bart Dunbar, please."

"This is Bart."

"I have Gail Dennis. Please hold on."

I put the television on mute, and a few seconds later Gail came on the phone.

"I have some good news," she said.

"I'm listening."

"Mr. Henderson's lawyers have made an offer."

"That was quick," I said.

"Yes, I guess they want to wrap this up as quickly as possible. Do you want to know what they offered?" Gail said. Her voice sounded like it was bursting with excitement.

"How much I am getting?"

"They've offered twenty-five thousand dollars, which I think is wonderful," Gail said.

"Is that all?" I said. I was thinking after taxes and legal fees I wouldn't have shit. At least Ava's money might be tax-free if I could convince her to pay me in cash.

"I think it's a fair offer," Gail said.

"You obviously don't have bills to pay. And if I accept this offer, then that means he just walks away without anyone knowing what he did," I said.

"That's right. His lawyer has inserted a clause in your acceptance that you can't talk about the suit or your relationship with Mr. Henderson. Ever!"

"Then fuck that. I want people to know about him," I said. I thought I had lost enough men to women and Jesus. I was thinking about Brandon and this bumpkin named Dale I'd dated for a minute until he started trying to save me after fucking. He was so weird with his scripture-quoting ass. I let him stick around for a couple months longer than I should have because he had one of those "amaze-a-grow" dicks. The kind that on first sight looked like a link sausage but grew into a foot-long hot dog.

"Mr. Dunbar, as your attorney, I am strongly advising that you accept this offer," Gail said firmly. I started to remind her that I was running this show and I didn't want to be forced to tell LaVonya that she was being uncooperative.

"I don't think so. I either want to go to trial or get more money." I needed a trial if I was going to get enough attention to maybe write a book or at the very least be interviewed by Montel Williams—or maybe even Oprah if I played the game right. I could imagine myself putting Oprah on hold while I took calls from Bryant Gumbel and Barbara Walters.

"Then I think you're going to have to find other representation. Plus you didn't follow my instructions about not talking to the press. Good day," Gail said as she hung up the phone. I muttered "arrogant bitch" to myself as I switched the television back to *Judge Judy*.

Then it occurred to me. Why did I need another lawyer when I had Ava?

Show Me Love . . . Please

It was a little past midnight. I was lying naked on my bed, sprawled out like a billboard hovering over Times Square. I'd spent the evening having drinks with Brison and Nico at Nell's on Fourteenth Street, discussing a more lucrative offer from PMK. I was starting to think maybe we should sell the firm and I could move back to Florida or maybe even California. My youth was running out, and if I was ever going to live in LaLa Land, I needed to do it while I was still able to enjoy all the hunnies.

February had been a jacked-up month for me. Yancey's song was everywhere. And everyone was trying to figure out who she was singing about. Nico told me females were now asking brothers, "Are you a Yancey B Boy?" when you tried to pick them up at bars. Brison told us how his wife had seen something in a gossip column about a model suing an ex-football star, and I acted as shocked as Nico. Throw in Bart's dumb-ass lawsuit and February was anything but the month of love for me. The only good thing was that the Internet asshole had stopped sending me messages.

I got out of the bed to put on my Faith Evans CD, when I noticed that I had five messages on my answering machine. Before I'd left the office I'd checked and I didn't have any.

The first message was from my nephew Cade, telling me how much he loved me. Next was my Pops, asking about his autographs from the Williams sisters and the Vegas trip. Then a call from Tiffany. I guess she hadn't realized yet she was a one-night stand. The fourth call freaked me. It was from Rosa, saying she needed to speak to me immediately. What did she want? I wondered. I hope not to tell me how happy she was being pregnant, or maybe she had dropped her load and thought I needed to know if she had a boy or girl. I didn't need to hear that shit. The last message was from Raymond, asking me to call him because he had great news. Since it was three hours earlier in Seattle, I picked up the phone. But before I could punch one button, I heard Raymond's voice on the other end.

"Basil. Did you get my message?" Raymond asked.

"Dude, this is strange. I just picked up my phone to call you and here you are on the other line," I said, laughing.

"Great minds think alike," he said.

"So what's the word?"

"Looks like you lucked out again," he said.

"Did Bitch Boy Bart take my offer?"

"Apparently not."

"Then how did I luck out?"

"His lawyer called me today and said she was dropping the suit," Raymond said.

"No shit," I said as I sat back on my bed. This definitely was good news.

"We're not out of the woods yet. It seems Bart and his lawyer have had a parting of the ways. I gathered from our conversations that she thought the suit was groundless and when he didn't take our offer, she dropped the case. He could get another lawyer, but I can't imagine any lawyers taking the case."

"Raymond, dude, I owe you big time," I said.

"Yeah, you do. I wish I could believe you've learned your lesson, but I won't even try to convince myself of that. Why don't you just find someone and settle down? Find a woman or a man, and save yourself and the people who love you some aggravation," Raymond said.

"It's gonna have to be a woman," I said.

"Basil, why are you so afraid of men?"

"I'm not afraid of men, I just don't trust them."

"Why?"

"Bart is a prime example. Besides, you know me, I like the thrill of the hunt. And I know the male animal all too well, 'cause I'm one of them. Whoever has the most blood in his balls wins," I said.

"I think one day you're going to have a life-changing moment, and then you'll surprise yourself and you'll be ready to settle down," Raymond said, his voice confident as usual.

"If that happens, you'll be among the first to know," I said.

"Okay. If you hear from Bart or somebody representing him, give me a call quickly and I'll try and work my magic again. Thanks for calling me to help out."

"Why are you thanking me?" I asked.

"For reminding me for a couple of days why I chose the

law," Raymond said. "This was fun. I mean, when I told Bart's lawyer that I didn't believe her client's claim for one minute, but that my client—that would be you—was too busy to defend himself against a frivolous lawsuit, man, I was feelin' it."

"So you're going back to practicing law full time?"

"I doubt it. I like the slow pace of academia. It was just nice working on your case. Sort of like visiting an old friend."

This was the opening I was looking for with Raymond, so I said, "Now that you mention old friends, when are we going to get together for a visit?"

"Who knows? Life is full of surprises," Raymond said before saying good night.

• • •

Tuesday was more like fall than winter, with the bright sun streaming in through the car's slightly open windows. Daschle and I were in the backseat of a limo on our way to Jersey to pick up his new BMW X-5. I was happy about the news I'd gotten last night, and I was glad to have Bart off my back. Daschle and I were two dudes rolling toward the future.

"Are you sure the car's going to be ready?" Daschle asked.

"I had Kendra double-check. They've got the tags on it. The sound system has been installed. In about thirty minutes, you'll be rolling big-time, D," I said as we slapped each other with open palms.

"What about the phone?"

"They told me it was installed, but you've got to fill out an application to get the service turned on," I said.

"Didn't Kendra fill out all the applications?" Daschle asked.

"Yeah, but she couldn't do this one. It won't take but a few minutes to fill it out," I said.

"Maybe I'll just get the phone turned on when I get back home," Daschle said.

I began wondering what the big deal was about filling out a simple application. Daschle pulled out one of the magazines in the back pocket of the car and began flipping the pages. I pulled out a copy of *Ebony* with Janet Jackson on the cover. I thumbed through the magazine and came to the article on Janet. I read a few sentences and then started laughing to myself. I playfully punched Daschle on the shoulder and said, "Hey, D, read this and tell me what you think."

"Read what?"

"Read this," I said as I pointed to the article.

"Is it about Janet Jackson? Dude, she's dope. One of the most beautiful women in the world," Daschle said.

"Yeah, you right. But read this," I insisted.

"Is it sumthin' 'bout her being single? You think I'd stand a chance when I'm flossing in the NFL, dawg?"

"Just read it and see," I said.

"I'll read it later," Daschle said as he pushed the magazine away. He leaned forward uncomfortably and placed his magazine back into the pocket.

"D, I need to ask you something," I said nervously.

"What's up, B?" Daschle asked as he looked out the left side of the car.

"D, uh, can you read?" I asked. Daschle turned to me and looked genuinely shocked by my question.

"What are you talking 'bout? Shit, yeah, I can read," Daschle said.

"Then read this," I said as I opened the *Ebony* magazine again and placed it in Daschle's lap. He quickly knocked the magazine to the floor of the car.

"Niggah, whatsup with you? Why you trippin'?" Daschle asked.

"Daschle, I'm concerned about you. If you can't read, then I can get you some help. I'm not the kind of agent who's only interested in getting a huge commission from my players. If that's what you want, then the big boys can do that. I'm concerned about you after your playing days are over. You can't be a baller your entire life," I said.

"You don't need to worry 'bout me. All you need to do is get me more paper than I know what to do with."

"But if you can't read, all the money in the world will be gone like this," I said as I snapped my fingers in the air. Daschle didn't answer, and his eyes looked cold and expressionless. The silence between us was as thick and hard as bulletproof glass. About five minutes passed, and when I looked up and saw we were coming to the exit for the car dealership, I thought I'd give it one more shot.

"D, listen to me. Man, I can get you a private tutor. It'll be just between you and me. It ain't nobody's business. Be honest, D. Can you read?"

"A little," he said softly.

"Do you know what level?"

"The last time I checked, a mutherfuckin' counselor said on a third-grade level. When they told me that shit, I just quit trying," he said. There was deep pain in his voice. I didn't ask him how he had gotten into college and managed to last two years. There was no need to. I knew that when someone was a gifted athlete, there were ways around anything, including entrance exams and required classes.

I touched Daschle on his knee, and he flinched like he had been pricked with a needle.

"Say, man, trust me. This is a problem we can solve," I assured Daschle.

"It might be too late, B," he said sadly.

"Naw, D, it's never too late."

• • •

Dealing with Dashcle and his problems had almost caused me to miss an event I was looking forward to: the Sportsman of the Year Awards, being held at Radio City Music Hall.

It was a cool winter evening as I walked down the red carpet frantic with sports stars like Derek Jeter, Alan Henderson, Jason Seahorn and movie stars like Samuel Jackson, Halle Berry, Angie Harmon and groups of fans smiling and waving as they walked into the auditorium.

I was looking mighty fly if I do say so myself in a midnight-black suit tailored to perfection by Everett Hall out of Washington, D.C., and a snow-white French-cuffed shirt, no tie. I was enjoying being out with my peers and I smiled proudly for the pool of photographers. The only thing missing was a beautiful lady on my arm.

I was halfway down the red carpet when I spotted one of the most startling bodies I'd seen in a long time. The young lady was wearing a body-fitting floral silk dress and was posing like a fashion model for the photographers. I stopped to just look at her. Her ass was calling my attention in one direction, and her robust breasts were calling me in another. When she turned around and smiled, I realized this golden brown woman with long black hair and the face of an angel was television hostess Ananda Lewis of BET and MTV fame.

Just as I was getting ready to make my move, I heard someone call my name. "Basil Henderson, can I get a few words with you?" a female voice shouted. I turned around with a huge smile for the press and saw a large black woman with a small recorder in her hand. I walked over to her and asked, "What can I do for you?"

She pushed the small recorder up to my mouth and asked, "What do you think of the song 'Any Way the Wind Blows'?"

"What?"

"You heard me. Your ex-girlfriend's hit song. Do you love it? Is it about you?"

"Who are you?"

"You know me. When are you going to tell the truth about yourself?" she shouted. I noticed people staring at me, including Ananda, and I was feeling uneasy.

"Tell me who you are," I said firmly as I used my body

to block this woman from view. At times like this it paid to have a big body.

"I'm LaVonya Young. Your neighborhood diva undercover and I'm not going to stop asking my questions," she said boldly.

I looked at her like I was Satan's newest soldier and whispered, "Bitch, if you don't get that recorder out of my face, you're going to have even more weight in that fat ass of yours. Leave me the fuck alone!"

Movin' On Up

I did something a diva should never do. I invited Desmond on a date and paid for everything. But I didn't really call it a date, because I didn't want him to think I was hard up for male company. Plus lots of men freak out when a woman takes charge, and I didn't know Desmond well enough to know how he'd react. I just gave him the lame excuse that I felt obligated to take him out and celebrate the news that "Any Way the Wind Blows" had reached number five on the *Billboard* pop charts. Desmond seemed only mildly impressed with my news.

I knew he'd appreciate my talents even more after seeing a Broadway musical. I told him I'd been given the tickets to *Aïda*, when in fact I had paid a broker top dollar to make sure we would get fabulous seats. At a time like this, I wished I'd done a better job of being nice to my Broadway associates so I could have gotten house seats or comp tickets.

Desmond and I both loved *Aïda,* even though I think he loved it more. He raved about the star, Heather Headley, and couldn't believe I thought she was just okay. "Trust me," I said, "I would have worn that role out."

When he kept talking about her elegance, I wanted to set him straight about one thing. I didn't want him to think for one minute I was cutting my hair "boy short" to compete with that lanky beauty. Why should I, as a black woman, have to cut my hair when black men seem to be holding on to their hair for dear life with their cornrows, dreads and retro Afros?

For the most part, the evening was pleasant. Desmond looked handsome with his dreads pulled back in a ponytail exposing his face in full view. He was wearing jeans, but they were tight and he was wearing them well. I must admit that I was a little disappointed when Desmond ended the night with the gentle kiss of a new friend, and not someone hoping to become my new lover or a casual fling. I knew I would have to enjoy my rose petal bath alone.

$$\bullet \quad \bullet \quad \bullet$$

After I finished my bath, I was having some herbal tea when the phone rang. Who is calling me this late? Maybe it was Desmond or Windsor, so I picked up the phone without looking at the caller I.D.

"Hello."

"Yancey, this is LaVonya. I need to confirm a little item I heard."

"Please contact Motown and schedule an interview," I suggested.

"Oh, this will only take a minute. When are you going to talk about your child?"

"Good night, LaVonya," I said as I hung up the phone. So it was LaVonya who was trying to rattle me. Could she be getting her information from Ava? And if so, how could I stop her?

I picked the phone back up and dialed the Plaza Hotel. An operator came on the line and I asked for Ava Middlebrooks. After a few rings, she picked up the phone.

"Hello."

"Ava, this is Yancey," I said.

"I know your voice," she said calmly.

"You got to stop this mess," I said.

"Stop what?"

"Stop sending me the pictures of the little girls," I demanded.

"What are you talking about? I've been busy trying to get my management business off the ground, and I don't plan to represent little girls. Are you going crazy? Maybe you need me to do more than manage you," Ava said.

"Someone has been sending me photos of little girls saying that one of the pictures is Madison, and tonight this columnist called and asked about her," I said.

"Who is Madison?" Ava asked.

"Your granddaughter," I said.

"I don't have a granddaughter."

"Cut the act, Ava. I know you're behind this," I said. I was so mad, I wanted to pull the phone out of the wall and hurl it through the window.

"Yancey, listen to me. First of all, I don't want anyone to think I'm a grandmother. I still have some bookings in Europe this summer. And if I've told you this once, I've told you a million times: Forget about that little girl and go on with your life. What would I have to gain by bringing her back into your life?" Ava asked.

"Then who could be doing this? How could the media know about this?"

"What about your manager, Basil the bisexual?"

"Basil wouldn't do that. He loves kids and he knows how hurtful this would be for her," I said.

"You have left plenty of crumbs behind for a lot of enemies to follow your trail," Ava said.

"That's not true."

"You can fool yourself if you want, but you're not the only diva out there who will do anything to get ahead. Of course, the others didn't have all the advantage of having me as a partner. Now, what about me taking over? I'll find out who's trying to spook you."

Maybe Ava wasn't behind the Madison photos and calls. She was right about not wanting Madison in her life any more than she wanted Basil in mine. Still, I didn't think I could trust her, and it made me sad because she was still my mother.

"I need to go. How long are you here?"

"Until I take care of my business," Ava said.

"Goodbye, Ava," I said as I hung up the phone.

•   •   •

I was at home, a couple days after my evening with Desmond, watching *The View*, when Michel called with more good news. He told me my CD had jumped five spots on the R & B chart and six on the pop chart. I still didn't understand why African American artists had to worry about two charts instead of who was selling the most records. The video was in heavy rotation on all the music channels, and he thought it was time to shoot the new video for the second single so that it would help the CD go platinum in less than a month. Everybody was telling me that if the video had been released with the single, my song would be number one by now, or at the very least in the top five.

"This is so exciting," I said.

"Yeah, it is. One more month before the second single drops, so we need to be one step ahead," Michel said.

"Tell me what I need to do."

"Just do what you do. Oh yeah, I think we might be able to get Billy Woodruff to direct number two. I'm not certain, but I've got a call in to his agent," Michel said.

"What about using Desmond again?"

"You want to do that?"

"He did a great job, and he's easy to work with. I say let's stick with a winner," I said. I was also thinking it would be nice to see Desmond and maybe find out why he hadn't called the morning after our *Aïda* date.

"I'll check with his agent. Also, I think we're going to do this on location. Right now, I'm checking out some spots in South Beach. So it might take a couple of days. Where would you like to stay?"

"The Delano. And make sure you put Desmond there as well."

"First I need to see if he can do it," Michel warned.

"I think he'd do it for me. Why don't you let me call him," I suggested. Desmond would be happy to hear my voice, especially when I was bringing him work.

"You want to do that? I mean, I can get my assistant to take care of those details."

"Let me do it. You handle the hotel and travel plans," I said.

"What about casting? Do you want to sit in on it? We could save a lot of time if we cast in New York. I know Miami has several agencies, but most of the guys down there are biracial," Michel said.

"You do it, even though it would be nice if we could find someone like Bart," I said, recalling the nightmare the first casting had been but how Bart and Desmond had made the video fun to shoot.

"Okay. I'll take care of that. I'll talk with you later on this afternoon."

"Fine. I love your calls with all this good news," I said.

"And I love giving it to you," Michel said.

Plaza Hotel. Where may I direct your call?"

"Ava Middlebrooks, please," I said.

"Is she an employee or a guest?"

"A guest."

After a few rings, Ava picked up the phone. "Ava speaking."

"Ava, this is Bart. We've run into a little snag. I need to get another lawyer. Do you know anybody in New York who would take my case?" I asked.

"What happened?" Ava asked.

I told Ava that Gail had decided to drop me as a client when I wouldn't take Basil's offer. I also told her how she was upset with LaVonya's blind items.

"What kinda lawyer wouldn't appreciate a little free publicity for their client?" Ava demanded. "And you better believe that won't be the last line in LaVonya's column."

"So what do you think I should do? Maybe I should take the money," I said.

"Listen to me. You don't want to let him off that easy. From what I know, fifty thousand dollars ain't shit to him.

That's like giving you ten dollars. If you settle, don't you have to sign some kind of agreement which says you can't speak about the case?"

"Yep, that's part of the deal. Take the check and keep my damn mouth shut," I said.

"And when your little lady lawyer gets her share, you won't have nada. Are you going to let Basil do that to you?"

"My lawyer thinks she can get him to pay legal fees," I said. For the first time, I was beginning to wonder if getting back at Basil was worth the trouble.

"What's all that noise in the background?" Ava asked.

"I'm heading toward the subway. I just left a go-see."

"Honey, you still riding the subway? That's why you can't give this thing up. You can make more money by writing a book."

"You think I could sell a book?"

"Maybe I'll even back your book. You know, I've been thinking about writing a book about my own career and life. I could call it something like *Diary of a Diva,*" Ava said, and laughed. She was going on and on about her life, and here I was not having a clue about what my next move should be.

"What about my lawyer?"

"Maybe we don't need a lawyer. Maybe we can really do some damage to Basil, and I'll take care of that little money he was offering you, plus some," Ava said.

"What are you talking about?"

"It's time to get personal. It's time to let his family, friends and some of his clients know what kinda freak Basil is," Ava said.

"I'll call you when I get home."

"I'll be waiting," Ava said.

I clicked off my cell phone and headed down the stairs of the subway thinking about one of my favorite childhood films, *The Wizard of Oz*. I just might be dealing with the real Wicked Witch of the West.

• • •

I stopped by Wylie's after I had a late go-see for a fashion show at Gucci. I didn't know why my agent had sent me on the call, since he knew I wasn't white-boy Gucci thin, but I went on those calls sometimes just to see what I could see. This was a wasted call on both counts: I didn't get the job and I didn't get leads on any other work.

I walked into Wylie's prewar midtown building. The doorman knew me and said he'd tell Wylie I was on my way up. On the elevator ride I was deciding if I should tell Wylie what Ava wanted me to do. I knew he would be judgmental, but I didn't give a shit because he didn't have my bills to pay. I pulled some lotion out of my bag and worked some into my hands just as the elevator stopped and opened into a large foyer. Just as I stepped out, I heard Wylie's voice: "What a wonderful surprise. I'm just having my evening *cock*tail."

"Now, that's a surprise," I said as I gave Wylie a kiss on the cheek and walked into his spacious living room. It was a casually decorated apartment with the appearance of money. It had thick Oriental rugs from Wylie's trips to Asia, and built-in bookshelves packed with books. The room had two soft couches in pastel colors and a beautiful mahogany bench that doubled as a coffee table until he replaced the glass-topped one some of his trade had broken. The end tables had lamps with Tiffany shades, and silver picture frames with photos of Wylie's family.

I took my jacket off and threw it over a leather high-back chair that didn't really fit the room's decor, but Wylie said it was his throne. I sat on the sofa, and Wylie came out of the kitchen with a glass of wine and swirling ice in a cocktail glass.

"So how was your day?" he asked as he sat down next to me.

"Another day without making a dime," I said as I took a sip of the wine. This was not the brand of wine I served or drank at my own place. It had a smooth buttery taste with a touch of fruit. I couldn't remember the name of it, but I knew it was over eighty dollars in the restaurant where I used to work.

"Don't worry, things will pick up," Wylie said.

"How much is this wine per bottle?" I asked.

"Oh child, I don't know. I usually buy it by the case," Wylie said casually.

"One day very soon," I said softly.

"Guess what?" Wylie asked with excitement in his voice. I knew this could only mean one of two things: a man or an exciting trip somewhere soon.

"I've got a date with that man I told you about," Wylie said.

"What man?"

"David Carroll. Remember I told you about him? He's from the Bahamas, and he wrote a workout book with the best pictures in the world. He's the one who was on the Bahamian gymnastics team."

"I thought you didn't date your clients," I teased as I sat my wine down on the bench.

"I don't date my *American-born* clients," he said, and smiled.

"Oh, I see. It's like that," I said.

"I can't wait. Where should I take him?"

"He's the author, let him decide. But you're a braver girl than me, 'cause I would never date a man who can do a split," I said, laughing.

"Oh, I ain't worried about him doing no splits. I just want to make sure those beautiful legs of his stay firmly on my bed and don't go swinging in the air before I can get mine up there," Wylie laughed. "What about yourself? Are you back in the dating game?"

"Naw, not just yet. I still got some unfinished business with Mr. Basil, and then I'll see," I said as I took a sip of the wine.

"Bart, come on, now. This is getting crazy. Move on and leave that child alone. I know he'll think twice before he tries to mess over someone again, but I'm beginning to worry about you," Wylie said.

I told Wylie I didn't know what Ava had planned but I was going through with whatever it was as long as it didn't include serious bodily harm.

"Bart, you can't be serious? This woman sounds cruel. You could both end up under the jail," Wylie said.

"I don't give a fuck, I'm getting back at Basil. Besides, where am I going to get the ten thousand dollars to pay Miss Ava back if I don't do it? Shit, I need that and everything else she promised me."

"Bart, you can go back to personal training. I mean, I hear some trainers are getting eighty and ninety dollars an hour now."

"Then they're doing something more than training, especially if they're black," I said.

"So when are you going to do this?"

"I'm going off to the Plaza tomorrow and follow Ms. Ava's plans," I said.

"Think about what you're doing. You are ruining another man's life," Wylie said, his voice tight, and there was a coldness in his face, like he was either sad or disappointed.

"It's easy for you to sit here and pass judgment on me 'cause it didn't happen to you. None of this happens to you. You collect your fat paycheck and come home to your fabulous home, sit on your fat ass and drink all week, and then go to church on Sunday. You're a trust-fund baby. When your parents die, you'll be set for life. I don't think you're in any position to judge me," I said firmly.

"Finish your drink."

"What?"

"You heard me. Finish your drink and leave," Wylie said. I could see tiny pools of tears forming in his eyes, and I wanted to take back what I had said. But I didn't. I just grabbed my coat and bag, then left like a gush of wind, without telling my friend, my only friend, goodbye.

Who Can I Turn To?

I was watching Shirley MacLaine in *Sweet Charity* on The Movie Channel when the phone rang. I looked at the caller I.D. and saw it was Michel, so I picked up the phone. Michel said he was calling with more good news. Both *People* magazine and *Vibe* wanted to interview me for a possible cover story.

"That's great!" I said.

"Yeah, it will help with the second single and the CD," Michel said.

"When do they want to do it? Before I go to South Beach or after?"

"Most likely when you get back. The writer who proposed the story is a reporter here in New York. You've probably heard of her. She writes a column called 'Lines from LaVonya' for the *Daily Press*." There was a long silence as my brief moment of joy turned into plummeting disappointment.

"Yancey, are you still there?"

"Yes, I'm here." I felt a shiver of fear race through my body at the thought of LaVonya dipping into my life, both past and present.

"What's the matter? This is great news."

"But why does LaVonya have to do it? She's a gossip columnist."

"She is the one who got them interested. What's the problem?"

"No problem. But I need to think about this."

"Think about what? This is free publicity. There is nothing to think about. You have to do it."

"Michel, let me call you back," I said as I hung up the phone. I needed someone to talk to, so I decided to call Windsor.

When Windsor answered the phone, I said, "It's Yancey. You feel like talking?"

"Sure. What's going on? You sound sad," Windsor said.

"Being a pop diva is starting to wear me down," I said as I sat on the edge of my bed.

"But Yancey, this is what you dreamed of. I was talking to Marlana the other day, and she was so excited because her record is out and it's doing well. You know, she really looks up to you," Windsor said.

"She does? She doesn't really know me," I said.

"But she's read about you and she's seen you perform. Plus I talk about you all the time," Windsor said.

"Be careful, Windsor. Marlana is competition now," I said, and laughed. I certainly didn't view Marlana as a threat. I hadn't heard her song or anybody talking about her.

"I don't think Marlana feels that way. She was saying how wonderful it was for two former Howard students to be taking on the music world."

"I guess that's nice. You know, Puffy Combs went to Howard also," I said.

"Yeah, I knew him. Don't forget I was Miss Howard," Windsor said proudly. There were many times when I wished I had a personality like Windsor's. Everybody that met her fell in love with her, and I was happy I had her for my first real friend.

I told Windsor about LaVonya wanting to do a story on me, but I didn't tell her what she had asked me. I tried not to think about Madison, so I never talked about her.

"Yancey, you can handle this woman. Whenever she asks you something you don't want to answer, just say, 'That's not something I'm willing to discuss.'"

"You think so?"

"Yes, I do."

"Oh, I forgot to tell you. I've got to leave town for a few days. I'm shooting another video," I said.

"That's wonderful."

"Windsor, are you getting nervous?"

"About what?"

"About having the baby?"

"I'll be fine," Windsor said.

"Well, childbearing is no joke," I said.

Windsor was silent for a moment, and then she asked, "Do you ever think about Madison?"

"Why would you ask that?" I asked as I moved quickly from my bed. My body suddenly felt warm.

"Yancey, I'm sorry. I was just thinking, with you becoming so famous, it's bound to make you think about her. I mean, how old is she now? She might be a fan of yours," Windsor said.

"I need to go and call Michel and talk about travel plans. Thanks for listening, Windsor," I said as I hung up, suddenly feeling like I didn't know whom I could trust.

The Big Payback

I rang the doorbell of Ava's suite the next day. I had decided not to call Basil's family, and I thought it was only fair I told Ava in person. I don't know if it was the fear of losing Wylie's friendship or holding out a small hope that Basil might give me another chance at being with him that made me back out of Ava's grand plan for revenge.

After a few moments, one of the double doors swung open and Ava greeted me with a wide smile and tousled, almost messy hair. She looked like the lost black Gabor sister in her strawberry-red nightgown covered with a matching robe with dyed fur trim. The air in the room was filled with a strange scent; it was hard to tell if it was expensive or cheap perfume mixed with a man's cologne.

"Bart, darling, come on in," Ava said as she waved her long cranberry-colored fingernails in the air.

"How are you doing?" I asked as I followed Ava into the living area of her large one-bedroom suite.

"I'm doing fine, darling. Are you ready for our big day?" Ava asked as she sat on one of the two matching sofas. I sat on the sofa opposite her and stared at the roaring fireplace I hadn't noticed on my previous visits.

"Bart, are you ready?" Ava asked again.

"Oh, I'm sorry. I was just thinking how nice it would be to have a fireplace in my apartment," I said as I smiled weakly.

"Baby, after we finish doing what we have to do this afternoon, you can have anything you want, including a fireplace in Harlem," Ava said.

There was no use holding back, so I said quickly, "I'm not going to make the phone calls. But since you've been so nice to me, I wanted to tell you in person." Ava raised her eyebrows as if she was totally shocked by my decision.

"Do you mind telling me why? I mean, we've made plans, and I know you need the money," Ava said.

"Yeah, I could use the money, but I do have to live with myself. Why don't you give that money to some charity up in Harlem?" I suggested, trying to soften my refusal.

"Give my money to somebody up in Harlem? Are you kidding? From what I've heard, with Disney and Magic Johnson putting money up there, Harlem don't need my money. Besides, my husband gives enough to the downtrodden. I'm only concerned with the uptrodden," Ava said with an artificial laugh.

"Don't worry, Ava, Basil will get his one day. He can't just go around hurting people forever," I said.

"I hope you're right," Ava said as she got up and walked over to the bar. She walked like she owned not only the suite, but the entire Plaza Hotel. She pulled out a bottle of champagne and popped the cork, then poured herself a glass.

She quickly emptied her champagne in one gulp and then turned toward me and asked if I wanted a drink.

"You got any brandy?"

"Of course, and if I don't, I'll call room service and we'll get some up here right away," Ava said.

While Ava was looking for the brandy, I walked over toward the windows overlooking Central Park. I gazed quietly at a winter blue sky without a cloud, as faint sunlight bounced through a large bay window. When I turned to walk back over to the seating area, I glanced toward the open door to the bedroom and the large canopy bed, layered with pillows and silk linens. My eyes moved toward the pale green carpet and I noticed a pair of men's boxers on the floor. I figured either Ava's husband was in town or she had gotten lucky.

"So is your husband coming to New York soon?" I asked.

"What?"

"Your husband. Does he ever come to New York to see you?"

"Naw, he doesn't like New York. What made you ask about him?"

"Nothing, really. I just figured he probably missed you or you missed him," I said as I sat back down on the sofa.

"Of course he misses me. There is only one problem, and that's the fact that I don't miss him. I mean, New York's got a lot of fine young men willing to spend the evening with a beautiful and rich woman," Ava said as she placed the brandy in front of me and took a small sip of her champagne.

"I'm so glad you're not really upset with me, and I'll start paying you back the ten thousand dollars in installments as soon as I get another full-time job," I said, not looking at Ava directly but at the arrangement of white orchids sitting on a beautiful rosewood desk.

"And when might that be?" Ava asked.

"Hopefully very soon. I just finished a video for a young diva that's going to be big, but they don't pay much no matter how popular the singer. I'm going to start checking with some friends of mine about catering, and lately my agent has been sending me out on a lot of calls for film work," I said. "It's only extra work, but one day I might get lucky."

"In starring roles, I hope," Ava said, her voice rich with sarcasm.

"Yeah, right," I said as I took a long sip of the wonderful-tasting brandy. The doorbell rang, and Ava hopped up from the sofa. As she rushed toward the door, she said, "Oh, I'd forgotten I had ordered more champagne and some caviar to celebrate."

While Ava dealt with the good-looking Italian room-service waiter wearing tight-tight black pants, I was thinking how long it was going to take me to pay Ava back. How many nights would I have to work on my feet serving ungrateful assholes who *might* leave me a decent tip? I thought about how many times I was going to have to raise my sweater and have greasy-looking clients admire my chest and how many times I would have to drop my pants and show my ass like I was a jail inmate. Was I being realistic thinking Basil might one day call me, or was it just one of my crazy, convoluted dreams?

After the waiter left, Ava swooped back over to the sitting area and poured me some more brandy. I took a sip and felt it tingling my nostrils and going straight to my head. I couldn't believe I was sitting in an expensive hotel suite sipping brandy and getting ready to eat caviar, something I didn't even really like. Ava prepared the caviar on toast points like she had been doing it her entire life. When she looked at me and blinked, I noticed the first signs of crow's-feet at the corner of her eyes and wondered if she worried about aging gracefully.

"So Bart, are you sure you don't want to get back at that bastard? I would hate to spend time finding somebody else Basil has fucked over, and I've already invested a great deal of time and money in you," Ava said in a soft voice that sounded both seductive and menacing.

"I'm sure," I said as I took another sip of the brandy.

"Is there anything else I could offer you?"

"What else could you give me besides money?" I asked. I hoped this dragon diva didn't think I wanted sex from her.

Ava took another sip of her drink and pursed her lips, then took a deep breath. "What if I helped you find your parents?" she asked flatly, without emotion and with a slight tightness in her voice. How did Ava know about my parents? As far as I was concerned, they were dead. There was a long silence, and my heart was beating with a bulletlike quickness.

"You look like you're surprised that I know you were given up for adoption," Ava said.

"I wasn't given up for adoption. I was abandoned," I said. "Who told you about that?" I demanded. I knew Ava was dangerous if she had been snooping around my family tree. But how much did she know, and did she really know where my parents, and I use the term lightly, were?

"Now, Bart, baby, honey, sweetheart. You're talking to Ava. I know everything there is to know about you, baby. Well, almost everything. My sources told me you were adopted."

"I was almost adopted," I said mournfully.

"What happened?"

"I don't want to talk about it," I said firmly.

"I understand, baby. But haven't you ever wondered about your biological parents? I mean, they were young. Maybe now they've come to their senses and would welcome you back into their life with open arms. I could find out for you," Ava said.

"You could do that?" I asked. What was I thinking? I didn't want to meet two people I didn't remember. Maybe Ava didn't know as much as she thought. She obviously didn't know my parents. Two people who had dropped me off at day care, never to return. Two people who had left me to grow up in a foster care system most of my adolescent life. When I was eight, a couple teased me with adoption plans, only to return me when I was eleven because they caught me with their thirteen-year-old son in a questionable position and thought I was a bad influence. Why in the fuck would I want to meet my parents now? I didn't give a shit how young they were. Nobody asked them to bring me into the world.

"You've talked about your sister, but do you have any children of your own?"

"Honey, look at me. Does this body look like one that belongs to a mother?" Ava asked as she stood up and posed with her hands on her hips.

"I guess not. So you really think you could find my parents? I mean, if they're still alive?"

"Darling Bart, Ava can do almost anything," she said confidently.

"Then why don't you get even with Basil without me?" I asked.

"Because he would come after me, and then my sister. Lord knows she's been through enough. I'll be honest with you, he's holding some information he has on me. I know this might surprise you, but Ava hasn't always been a good diva. Have you thought about what you're going to say to the people on our list?"

"I was just going to say whatever you thought I should say."

"What if I make a call, maybe to one of his clients? You listen to me and see how easy it is, and then you give it a try," she said softly. She made it sound so easy, but when I still hesitated, she added toughly, "Basil doesn't give a shit about you, and if you think he's going to brand that beautiful ass of yours, then it's just wishful thinking. He's probably fucking some great-looking man right now."

"Yeah, you're probably right, or some stank-ass female," I said. My anger toward Basil and his partner was returning, aided by Ava and the alcohol.

"This is what I would do," Ava said. "I would just call—say, for example, this new client of his, Daschle Thompson. I would say, 'Do you know that your agent is a faggot?' Don't say 'bisexual,' because those dumb-ass jocks might not know what you're saying. You need to use terms like 'dick-suckers' and 'butt-fuckers.' Don't mention women, 'cause that might turn their sick asses on. Same thing with his father. He's from the old school and won't know what words like 'bisexual' and 'gay' mean. You have to talk on their level and use terms like 'sissy' or 'punk,'" Ava continued. She was drinking, and I continued drinking, and all of a sudden Ava's plan sounded like a lot of fun. I took another gulp of my brandy, and with glassy eyes and slurred speech I looked at Ava and said, "Give me the numbers and pass the phone."

• • •

I woke up with a throbbing hangover, but I couldn't let that stop me. Bart, old boy, you got some serious shopping to do. I took a quick shower and put on my leather pants and off-white turtleneck sweater. I called Wylie and left him a message asking if he could meet me at my apartment later that evening. I had some apologizing to do.

I walked down to Sylvia's soul food restaurant even though the winter wind was blowing without mercy and I had left my skullcap at home. I reached Sylvia's and was warmed by the packed restaurant and the rich scents coming from the open kitchen. I ordered chicken livers, scrambled eggs, grits and toast. I drank two cups of black coffee and then reached for my wallet and pulled out my little gift from Ava. A check for one hundred thousand dollars made out to Bartholomew Dunbar. I felt a little bad about what I had done to Basil, but I also felt I had earned every penny Ava had given.

I whipped out a little notebook and wrote down a "to do" list. I wrote down: *Go to bank and deposit check; shop; pay rent for two months in advance; shop; go to gym and get haircut;*

shop some more. Just as I finished my list, the waitress placed a piping-hot plate of food in front of me and I began to chow down.

When I finished eating, I pulled out a crisp fifty-dollar bill and gave it to my waitress and told her to keep the change. My kindness caused an unexpected reaction. She started crying and said, "I've just got to hug you. I need some extra money so I can get my son some Jordans for his birthday. Thank you . . . thank you," she said as she hugged me tight.

"Glad to do it. I'm a waiter too, and I know how hard you work," I said.

"You wait tables somewhere up here in Harlem?" she asked.

"Naw, I worked downtown. But I don't have to wait tables anymore," I said cheerfully.

"What happened? Did you hit the lottery?"

"I guess you could say that." I grinned as I put my jacket on and walked out of the bustling restaurant.

I stopped at the bank and deposited my check. When Mr. Bell, the banking officer, confirmed the funds' availability, he approved a personal check for ten thousand dollars. I left the bank with one hundred crisp hundred-dollar bills bulging in my wallet, and stuffed it in my backpack. I then hopped on the number 6 train down to Fifty-third, transferred to the E and got off on Fifth Avenue.

I walked to Fiftieth and stopped in at Saks Fifth Avenue, where I quickly spent over three hundred dollars on new scents and various facial products I had only dreamed of being able to use. I left Saks and stopped at Versace, where I didn't buy anything because even the doorman acted snobby. I moved over to Banana Republic, where I dropped seven hundred dollars in fifteen minutes on sweaters and slacks.

I had the most fun at my last two stops. First, I picked up a beautiful pen and silver cardholder for Wylie from Tiffany's. My last purchase was three pairs of nylon mesh underwear from Gucci. Never before had my ass been caressed by underwear that cost one hundred and ten dollars, but my ass had earned them.

Before catching a cab uptown, I stopped in an American Express travel office and bought a first-class ticket to Santo Domingo for the following week. I had a feeling I might need to be on the DL when Basil figured out who was responsible for his outing. I saw no reason why I shouldn't surround myself with gorgeous men while figuring out my next move.

Judgment Day

Kendra buzzed me on the intercom and told me my sister, Campbell, was on the phone.

"Put her through," I said. I moved the forms I had been studying to the right of the desk and leaned back in my chair, then pressed the speaker button.

"What's the good word, baby sister?"

"How you doing?"

"Great. What about yourself? How is Austin and my little man Cade?" I asked.

"Everybody is doing good. We miss you, and I must say, we even miss Brooklyn. But I'm getting used to Pittsburgh. I mean, the real estate market out here is really good, and there aren't a lot of women of color selling high-end real estate," Campbell said.

"You know you can come back to New York anytime you want to," I said.

"I plan to visit sometime this summer. Are you sure everything is okay?" Campbell asked with some concern in her voice.

"Yeah, everything is cool. Business is great. Social life is okay. I have no complaints. Why do you ask?" I wondered if Campbell had heard Yancey's song.

"I was just asking because I got a strange call last night," Campbell said.

"What kind of call?"

"Some woman, or it could have been a man pretending to be a woman, called and asked if I was your sister. When I asked who was calling, this person just repeated the question. So I hung up the phone. A few minutes later, the same person called back and said, 'I have some information about Basil Henderson you need to know, especially since you have a young son.' When I asked again who I was speaking to, they got smart and told me to shut up and just listen. So I hung up again," Campbell said.

"Did they call back?"

"No, but it was really eerie. When was the last time you spoke with Yancey?"

"Not that long ago. Did it sound like Yancey?"

"Not really. I was just wondering who had a reason to be mad at you, and Yancey was the first person that came to mind," Campbell said.

"Yancey is too busy with her career to worry about me. I wouldn't call us friends, but I think we've both moved on," I said.

"That's good. I just wanted to make sure everything was okay. Last night made me wish I had caller I.D. or something so I could find out who's playing games with me and my family," Campbell said.

"Yeah, you need to step into the new century, sis," I said.

Before Campbell could respond, Kendra used the intercom to tell me Daschle was on the phone with an urgent call. I was hoping he had finally agreed to meet with the tutor I'd found.

"I know you're right. Give Cade a call when you get a chance. He asked about you this morning," Campbell said.

"I'll do that this evening. Hey, gotta go, sis. I need to take this call," I said.

"Okay. I've got to get out and make some money. I love you," Campbell said. Every time I heard her and Cade say those words it made my heart a little softer, and I had to keep myself from becoming some emotional punk.

"You know, it's all love. I'll talk to you later," I said as I punched line two on my phone.

"D. Whatsup? You got some good news for me?" I asked.

"What are you talking about?"

"Have you thought about the tutor?" I asked.

"Not really," Daschle said.

"Then what's going on?"

"I'm signing with PMK," he said coldly.

"What?"

"I don't want you to represent me anymore."

"Why not?" I asked. I couldn't believe my trying to help this mofo better himself was going to cost me a client.

"Let's just say I got some information that don't sit right with me."

"What kind of information?"

"I don't want to go into that right now. I'm with my girl," Daschle said.

"Is she the reason?" I asked, remembering how I had suggested Daschle wait until he got his signing bonus before he started buying fleets of cars for his girl and family. He had agreed, and he didn't seem to me like a man who was whipped when it came to the females in his life.

"Naw, I make my own decisions. And if this information I heard gits out, I think some of your other people gonna jump ship too," Daschle said with an ominous tone. What information was the dude talking about? I wondered.

"D, dude, I thought we were tight. Tell me what happened. If I've done something to offend you or your crew, just tell me. I'm trying to make sure you get the best not only with the league, but with your life as well," I said.

"Looks like to me you need to get your own life straight. Later," Daschle said, without even saying goodbye.

• • •

I was approaching Brison's office to tell him about Daschle's defection when I heard Nico talking loud. This was not usual for Nico, but as I got closer, I heard him say my name, so I stood right outside the door to hear what he was saying.

"Brison, I'm telling you, if this shit is true, then we need to cut our losses and buy Basil out. Not only will he hurt the client base we got right now, but it will hurt any chances we have to sell the firm down the line," Nico said.

"Don't bring up that 'let's sell' shit. Tell me what Jamal said."

"He said that somebody called him and told him B was a fucking faggot. Has been for a long time. Now that I think about it, he was never really against that faggot you tried to bring in the firm last year. What was his name?"

"You talking about Zurich Robinson?"

"Yeah, whatever."

"How does Jamal know this? I mean, it could just be gossip. Basil is our partner. We can't try to buy him out based on a rumor. Every famous person around has been accused of being gay at some point. And what if he is gay? He still brings in clients. He's a good partner," Brison said.

I was proud that he was defending me, but what in the fuck was Nico talking about? And what was Jamal Haywood, one of our top baseball clients, doing spreading rumors about me? I felt like some little bitch eavesdropping, and for a moment I started to just bust in the office and confront Nico. Instead I cleared my throat and knocked on Brison's door. There was a sudden hush, and then I heard Brison ask, "Who is it?"

"It's me, Brison," I said as I walked into his office. Nico nodded and then looked away.

"What's going on?"

"Looks like we got a little problem," I said. Nico turned around and just looked at me like I was the lowest of the low. I wanted to punch his punk ass out, but I resisted.

"Problem?" Brison quizzed.

"Daschle is leaving the company," I said.

"What? When did that happen? And why?" Brison asked.

"Yeah, tell us why, Basil," Nico said. His voice sounded so businesslike and official and not like the man I regularly called buddy.

"I don't know, but I think it has something to do with me confronting him about not being able to read," I said.

"Daschle can't read?" Brison asked.

"No, he can't, and I called him on it and tried to get him some help," I said.

"What's so surprising 'bout that? A lot of our mutherfucking clients can't read or add two plus two," Nico said. "None of them have left the firm 'cause they're dumb as dirt."

"Are you sure he can't read? How'd you find out?" Brison asked.

"Several small things happened. He never read any contracts I gave him, and he was always getting Kendra to fill out applications for him. Whenever we went out to eat, no matter where, he would just say, 'Order me a hamburger or chicken,' without reading the menu. Eventually I just figured it out. I did trick him into confessing, and I think he's embarrassed."

"He's going to be more than embarrassed when he signs with one of the big boys and they take him for everything he's worth," Nico said.

"That's sad, and I hate to lose him, but we got to move on," Brison said as he moved from behind his desk.

"Daschle is going to be a number-one draft choice. We can't just let him walk out. Didn't he sign a contract?" Nico asked, raising his voice even more.

"Yeah, he did. But our policy has always been to not force clients to stay if they didn't want to be here," I said as I looked over at Nico, who was looking at me with narrowed, distrustful eyes. I felt awkward, like I was on trial.

"I think there's more to this than his just not being able to read. We need to make him honor his fucking contract, and we need to just confront him face-to-face, and see why he *really* wants to leave," Nico said as he looked at Brison and then cut his eyes at me.

"Let's take the night and think about this and decide what to do in the morning," Brison said in a guarded voice.

"Cool," I said as I turned and headed toward my office as I felt the walls of my life of lies and denials closing in on me.

Bart's Escape
from New York

I was wiped out after a grueling session at the gym. In preparation for my trip to Santo Domingo, I had hired a trainer for a few sessions just to make sure my body was in peak form for the boys and the beach.

I dropped my gym bag on the new leather sofa I had purchased and checked my answering machine. There was a message from Wylie thanking me again for the gift and saying a proper thank-you note was on the way. There was also a message from Yancey B, asking me to call her immediately. I couldn't believe I had the voice of one of the hottest singers on my answering machine. She even left her number. I needed to tell her that a true diva left only her assistant's number. A girl had to be prepared for anti-diva terrorists lurking around, and there were a lot of diva-haters in New York.

I wrote the number down on a pad and then saved the message. I knew it was a message I would never erase, along with the two messages I had gotten from Basil when we first met. There was still something about that sexy voice of his.

I dialed Yancey's number, and after a few rings, a female voice picked up.

"Hello."

"Is Yancey B in?" I asked.

"Who's calling?"

"This is Bart Dunbar returning her call."

"Oh, Bart. This is Yancey. Thanks for calling me back so soon," Yancey said.

"No problem. How's it going?"

"Everything is fine. You know, my record is in the top three, number one on the dance charts, and we're getting ready to drop the second single," Yancey said.

"I've been keeping up with you on the radio and *Billboard* magazine," I said.

"I'm so excited. I think the album might go platinum soon, thanks to the songs and video. Have you seen it?"

"Yep, I have, and it does look great."

"It sure does. That's why I'm calling. The guy we had scheduled to do the next video got sick, and we need to find a replacement fast," Yancey said.

"So how are things going with you two?" I asked.

"Slow but steady. Anywho, I called your agency, and they said you're not working for the next couple of weeks," Yancey said.

"Yeah, I'm going on a little vacation."

"When are you leaving?"

"In a couple of days."

"I need to ask you a big favor. Will you come and do the shoot with me? We need somebody with a stunning body, and that's you," Yancey said with the charm of a morning talk show hostess.

"You want to use me again?" I asked. I was always

shocked when an unsolicited and unexpected job just fell into my lap, but I guess Evanston being an asshole had worked to my advantage. During the first break when we were shooting Yancey B's first video, he acted like he was the star. I was through with him when I asked him what part of town he lived in, and he looked at me and said, "You don't need to know that. I'm in a stable relationship, and I don't date black men. Too much confusion, if you get where I'm coming from." I wanted to tell that dumb snow queen he was the one who was confused.

"Yeah, there was a little concern since you were in my first video. Don't want the public to think you're my boy toy." Yancey laughed. "But it's a location shot, and I hope you won't be offended, but we won't see your face. Just your backside."

"Where are you shooting it?"

"In South Beach, and we leave tomorrow afternoon. We would need you for two days."

"South Beach. I haven't been there in a while, and I could just leave from there and go to Santo Domingo."

"So will you do it? We're traveling first class," Yancey chimed.

"Of course. For you I will do anything," I said.

"You're a sweetheart, Bart. Start packing! Someone will give you a call later with your travel plans."

"Cool, I'll look forward to seeing you. Thanks for thinking of me."

"No, Bart, thank *you* for saving the shoot."

When the Worm Turns

It felt good to be in a city like South Beach, with warm weather and even warmer bodies. I was enjoying a faded blue sky, the sun gushing through dancing clouds, while eating lunch with Bart. We had been up since 6 A.M. so Desmond could get the exact lighting for my video. I had hoped to share lunch or something better with Desmond, but he was busy editing, so Bart volunteered to join me when he heard me say I was going to order room service and I didn't want to eat alone.

We found a cute sidewalk café in the carnival-like Lincoln Road area, a few blocks from our hotel. Bart quickly turned the conversation to my skyrocketing career. Of course, I didn't have a problem with that.

"How does it feel to be you, Yancey?" he asked after we had ordered and the waiter and Bart had exchanged flirtatious smiles.

"Wonderful. Now that my music career is off and running, I'm getting ready to do my Janet Jackson move and turn my attention to my movie career," I said as I took a sip of water.

"You got anything lined up? I hear it's tough out in Hollywood."

"I got my eyes on a couple of things. There's going to be a remake of *Sparkle,* and even though I swore I wouldn't do television, HBO is doing a film version of *Jelly's Last Jam.* I heard Vanessa Williams turned them down for the female lead, so it's time for me to swoop in, even though I hate taking someone's leftovers," I said.

"I saw *Jelly's,* and you'd be the one-one in that! You'd play the hell out of the role of Sister as well," Bart said with a sweet and sincere smile.

"Think I'd make them forget Lonette McKee?"

"Lonette and Miss Irene 'I'm gonna live forever' Cara." Bart laughed.

"I can't thank you enough for filling in at the last minute," I said.

"Are you kidding? I get to be with the number-one pop diva and spend a couple of nights in a fabu hotel. I should be on my knees thanking you. Plus, I can learn a thing or two being around someone like you. I hope just a little bit of your success rubs off on me," Bart said.

The waiter brought out our drinks, and I began to notice the good-looking men walking up and down the open-air mall area holding hands with each other. It was like being in the Village in New York on a Saturday night. I decided this was a fine time to ask some questions about gay men, since it looked like I would never be able to keep them out of my life completely.

"Have you hung out since we've been here?"

"I went out last night, and the men are just okay," Bart said as he sipped his iced tea through a straw.

"Just okay? These men are gorgeous. Look at him," I said as I pointed to an attractive golden-brown man wearing white shorts and nothing else. He looked like he was Puerto Rican or maybe Brazilian.

"You see men like that all the time in New York. I've dated white men, and Hispanic men too, but for me there is nothing like a black man. I love the way they look and smell," Bart said with a broad smile.

"Are you dating anyone now?"

"No, I broke up with someone a couple of weeks ago, and it left a pretty bad taste in my mouth. Please pardon the pun," Bart said, and giggled.

"Why do you think so many men are gay? Or, more importantly, bisexual?" I asked.

"I'll tell you what I think if you answer a question for me," Bart said.

"What?"

"Have you ever dated someone who was gay or bisexual, and if the answer is yes, is that where your song came from?"

"You promise not to tell anyone?"

"I promise on the gay boy pledge of silence," Bart said as he playfully raised his hand in the air like he was taking an oath.

"Yes," I replied quickly.

The waiter interrupted Bart's next question when he placed two fried-oyster salads in front of us. I had not received the kind of service Bart and I were receiving in a long time. Every minute the waiter was standing over us and checking to see if everything was fine. I told Bart he should just go ahead and give the guy his number so that we could eat in peace. When it seemed the waiter was finally giving some service to his other tables, Bart had a question.

"Was he someone famous?"

"Who?"

"The man you dated?"

"Sorta."

"This is getting good," Bart said as he took his fork, picked up an oyster and dipped it in the tartar sauce.

"But that's all I'm saying about my past," I warned Bart.

"That's fine. Baby, your song is making the kids cry out. I mean, everybody is talking about the song and the video and wondering who you're singing about. And the club version of 'Any Way the Wind Blows' is just *over* the rainbow and back again," Bart said as he snapped his hand quickly in the air.

"Do you think someone could really be bi? I mean, if a guy loves women, then what can a man do for him?" I asked.

"Bisexual men are just selfish jerks. They want everything. I think you women are partly responsible," Bart said.

"What do you mean?"

"I think sometimes men try it because the first time they see a woman roll her eyes back and shrink with pleasure while she's being drilled, he thinks, I want some of that," Bart explained confidently. Now, that was something I had never thought of, but the thought of two men making love still caused a certain degree of disgust within me. Maybe it was because every time I imagined two men together, one of them was always Basil.

I was a bit surprised when Bart called me out, so to speak, by telling me that I was the kind of woman who thought gay sex was nasty.

"Why do you say that? I believe in letting people live their lives. And I couldn't be homophobic and be in show business," I said.

"I'm not saying you're homophobic, but you strike me as the kind of woman who thinks dicks don't belong anywhere but between the legs of females. And I feel just the opposite. Ain't nothing wrong with that. I just get sick and tired of people talking about what is wrong and what's right about sex. What God had planned, and so on and so on. I want to tell them if God thought gay sex was so nasty, then why did he create a body part that brings me so much pleasure?" Bart said. His voice was quiet and steady.

"I hadn't thought of that," I said softly. I was getting ready to ask another question when Bart's cell phone rang.

"Excuse me for a second," Bart said as he popped open his silver cell phone. I was thinking about how I was going to get Desmond to spend some downtime with me. I was so happy to get away for a couple of days from cold-ass New York.

I turned around to ask the waiter for more iced tea when I heard Bart's voice change suddenly. He started yelling, and several people turned around to stare at our table.

"What do you mean I'm overdrawn? I just deposited a check for two hundred thousand dollars about five days ago. Yes, I think you better check your records," Bart said as his eyes blinked in a very nervous fashion. I pulled out my cell phone and called Windsor, but I kept one ear on Bart's conversation. Windsor's line rang a few times, and I was expecting Windsor to answer, but instead it was her aunt.

"Toukie, here. Can I help you?"

"Ms. Toukie? This is Yancey. How is Windsor?" I asked.

"Call me Aunt Toukie, baby. We just like family seeing how I done slept in your house. You want to talk with Windsor?"

"Yes, can I?"

"Naw . . . she's asleep. Not feeling well today. But she's trying to keep that baby in her stomach for a few more weeks at least, and then her doctor says we might be okay. I'm kinda worried how it's gonna look. But all we can do is pray. She and Wardell found a good doctor down here. How is New York? You made any more of those minimovies?"

"I'm in Florida, finishing up a video, and it's going fine," I said as I looked over at Bart, whose face was so contorted he looked like he was in pain. He had lowered his voice, but I could tell he was in a conversation that was not making him happy. Just as I was getting ready to tell Ms. Toukie goodbye, I heard Bart shouting and his voice trembling with anger: "What do you mean the bitch stopped payment on my check?"

. . .

Ten minutes later, Bart and I were walking back to the hotel, and he seemed to be in a stunned silence. Every few minutes he would pop open his cell phone and dial a number and then mutter, "Damn."

"Is everything all right, Bart?" I knew it was a dumb

question, but I wanted to know what had happened to change his personality in a matter of minutes.

"Somebody's trying to run a game on me, and I ain't having it. This bitch don't know who she's fucking with," Bart said as he looked straight ahead, like he was traveling in his own private bubble.

"Do you want to tell me what happened? Is there anything I can do to help?"

"I'm thinking. First, I got to contact this bitch, but she's not answering her phone," Bart said.

"Who is she?"

"Some wanna-be diva who I did some work for," Bart said. I was wondering what kind of work could net $100,000. I needed to meet her. I wondered if it had anything to do with drugs or sex, but I decided to let Bart spill the details when he was ready.

When we reached the hotel, I suggested we go and sit by the pool so he could calm down.

"I'll meet you in ten minutes. I got to make sure my credit cards are still working. I'm leaving the country when we're done here. At least I think I am," Bart said. Now he looked sad instead of angry.

• • •

About thirty minutes later, Bart came down to the pool area, and I could tell from the look on his face that he was still in some type of trouble.

"Any luck?" I asked.

"No, she's still not answering the phone. I thought if I

came back to the hotel and called from here, she might not know it was me and pick up. The only numbers I had were a hotel number and a cell phone and she already checked out of the hotel," Bart said as he sat down next to me in front of a hypnotic pool with pure turquoise water. The pool was surrounded by overly tan white people, mostly women, and mostly topless. I figured they were European and didn't hesitate to remove their tops on the beach or near a pool.

"You want to use my cell phone? She wouldn't know my number," I said.

"I might do that later. Right now, I just got to figure out how I'm gonna deal with my bank. This check I deposited and got some funds against was returned with a 'stop payment.' Now the bank's threatening to bring in some investigators," Bart said.

"Bart, do you mind me asking what you did for this lady?" I asked.

He was silent for a moment, and the only thing I heard was foreign chatter and faint sounds of water splashing until Bart began talking. "I don't want you to think badly of me. I like you, Yancey, and I'm not proud of some of the things I've done lately."

"Trust me, I understand. I like you too, and I'm trying to figure out how I might help."

Bart told me how he had helped some rich lady get back at some man they had both dated. The man sounded horrible, sleeping with them both at the same time. The man was a powerful businessman, and Bart said the lady had cracked the guy's computer system and then contacted several of his clients and told them about his double life. For a brief instant

I became lost in my own thoughts with some of the schemes I'd done with Ava. Thankfully, I didn't miss those days.

"Have you heard from this guy?"

Bart rolled his eyes and took a deep breath and said, "No."

"Then why would the lady want to double-cross you?"

"I don't know. I did what she asked me to do, including something I didn't want to do," Bart said softly.

"What was that?"

"I called the man's father and told him his son was a homo and a child molester."

"Was he?"

"I don't know. The guy certainly liked what I was serving up. I don't know if he's a child molester, probably not. Ava thought it would really do him in, even if it was a lie."

"Ava? Did you say Ava?" I felt a sudden chill in the air and pulled my towel over my shoulders.

"Yeah, Ava," Bart said. I started to ask for a last name, but I thought I'd see if I could get more information first.

"Is Ava from New York? I knew an Ava once," I said as I turned toward Bart to see if he was trying to play me.

"No! I think she's from California. Which part I don't know."

"Is she a middle-aged lady?"

"I would say so, but she wouldn't. No, that goddamned Ava doesn't know her days of being a girl are over," Bart said.

I stopped my questions, because I had the answer I needed. I knew there were a lot of women in both New York and California with the name Ava. But I also knew there was only one "goddamned Ava."

I walked into my office building on another dreary, gray day, as winter headed into its final slide. When I walked into the suite, Kendra greeted me with several messages and said Brison and Nico were waiting for me in the conference room.

"Do we have a meeting scheduled?" I asked. I didn't recall a meeting, and I had taken my time getting to the office. I had been trying to get in touch with Daschle, who wasn't returning my calls. I wanted to find out who he had spoken to and wanted to make sure he'd gotten in touch with the person who could help him with his reading. He didn't have to be my client for me to try and help him out, I told myself.

I walked into my office and took off my overcoat and sports jacket, grabbed a legal pad and a cup of coffee, then headed to the conference room. When I opened the door, Brison and Nico were huddled at the end of the maple conference table.

"When did we schedule this meeting?" I asked.

"Basil, we got some major problems," Brison said.

"Yeah, dude. Two more clients have left, and the basketball player I was about to sign called me last night and said he couldn't sign with a firm that was run by faggots," Nico said with an air of superiority.

"What are you talking about, Nico?" I said, looking directly into his eyes and ignoring Brison.

"I'm talking 'bout you, man. You got to come clean with us before we lose everything. I told you guys we should have sold the firm when we had a chance. Who is going to want to buy a company whose clients are leaving by the hour?" Nico said.

"You're overstating the facts," Brison said.

"I don't know who's spreading these lies, but I'm not letting somebody else's bullshit run my life. Who left the agency and why did they leave?"

"Martin Gill and Terrence Allen. Both said they were called and told we had a child molester running the firm," Brison said.

"So now I'm not only supposed to be a faggot but a child molester as well?"

"Aren't they one and the same?" Nico asked with a smirk. He was now sitting on the edge of the table with his arms folded across his chest.

"Nico, be cool," Brison said.

"Brison, you don't have to protect me from Nico. I can handle myself," I said as I slapped the pad on the table. A fire-hot burst of anger came over me, and I wanted to punch Nico in his fucking mouth. I thought about it for a few seconds and knew punching Nico was about as stupid as this conversation. I also thought about Yancey and Bart. I still hadn't determined which one was responsible. I was wondering how a person could tap into our company's database, contact our clients and spread lies about my life.

"What are you saying, dude? You want some of me?" Nico said as he unfolded his arms and moved toward me until Brison moved in front of him and pushed him back.

"We're not going to handle this like little kids," Brison said.

"Say what you want. But I don't think somebody's lying on him. I mean, I listened to the song by that woman he was going to marry, and the story is pretty clear if you listen to the words," Nico said. "What else could lyrics like 'you want him and not me' mean? It ain't the kind of love song I'm used to."

"What song?" Brison asked as his expression grew uncertain.

"He's talking about Yancey's song that doesn't have jack to do with me—it's about making money. That's what they do in the music business," I said.

"And that's what we should be doing, but we can't, as long as your ass is a part of this firm," Nico said.

"Then buy me the fuck out. I never stay anywhere I'm not wanted. Write me a mutherfuckin' check and I'm out of here," I said.

"So you are a fucking faggot," Nico said as he pointed his finger in my face like he wanted to poke my eyes out in disgust.

"Nico, point your finger in my face again and you're

going to pull back a nub. I mean that." I glanced over at Brison for support, and he reacted quickly.

"I think we need to just chill. Basil, why don't you take the day off and think about what you want to do. Then we can sit down as a firm, as partners, and come up with a plan that'll be acceptable to everyone," Brison said.

"Cool. This room is beginning to feel stank anyway," I said as I picked up my pad and walked out of the conference room.

• • •

A couple of hours later, I was standing in front of Yancey's town house taking a deep breath before I rang the bell. After I had left the office, I went to the Upper West Side to watch *Remember the Titans* for the third time. I left midway through the movie, when the Titans were close to their emotional state championship game. It took everything I had to keep the tears in my eyes, and I realized what an emotional disaster this day was turning into. I don't know if I had come close to tears because of the confrontation with Nico and Brison, or because the movie triggered memories of a happier time in my life, when I was a star on the University of Miami national championship team. Maybe it was the realization that as wonderful as the experience was of playing with the same players for over four years, I was at risk of losing the one friendship I had managed to maintain with another player. I deeply treasured my relationship with Brison, and now some mofo was trying to ruin it and my life. I realized that with the exception of Raymond there was no one in my life I could trust with my true feelings, my true self. I was on the verge of some kind of mental melt-down that I had avoided since the first time my uncle Mac crawled into my bed and "touched" me.

• • •

I got home a little after eight o'clock. I was going to make myself a drink and then order some dinner, when I felt the vibration of my beeper on my belt. I thought with the bad day I'd had, the evening was only going to get worse. I didn't want to see who was calling, because I figured it might be another client telling me they were jumping the XJI ship as well. Then I decided that if my clients wanted to leave because of what they'd heard and not how I repre-sented them, then let 'em jump.

I looked at the beeper and could tell from the 816 area code that it was my Pops calling. He never paged me unless it was an emergency. I thought I should check my answering machine first to get an indication of what was going on.

Sure enough, there were two messages from my father, one from Brison saying he was just checking on me and that everything was going to be fine and another call from Rosa. What did this woman want? She hadn't called me this much when we were dating. My Pops's voice sounded paper-thin, and all he said was, "Call me, son. It's important."

I picked up my phone and hit speed dial. After a few rings my Pops answered the phone.

"Pops. What's going on? You called twice and beeped me? Are you all right?"

"How are you, son?"

"I'm fine. Is everything all right?"

After a few moments of silence, my father asked, "Basil, are you a homosexual?" I was stunned into silence for a few seconds and then I said, "Pops, what are you asking me? Hell, no. You know me. It's me and the ladies, and why would you ask me something like that?" I could feel thin beads of perspiration begin to form around my neck, and if Nico had started the burn in my body, my Pops's question was about to ignite a certain explosion. Yancey and/or Bart had taken this little game of revenge too far. It was okay to mess with me, but this was my Pops. He was my heart.

"I didn't think so, son. But a couple of nights ago, some young man called me and told me you were a homosexual. That you'd been one all your life."

"What young man? Did he say who he was?"

"No."

"Pops, I think it's somebody from one of our rivals who's upset that we won't sell them our firm. They've called several of our clients, telling them the same thing. Trying to run us out of business. But it's all bullshit," I said as I started to unbutton my shirt. So Bart was behind these calls, but how did he get my Pops's number? As far as I knew, he didn't even know where my Pops lived.

"I asked him how he could say something like that about my son, but he just yelled for me to shut up and listen."

"Why didn't you just hang up?"

"I did. Then he called back and said something that just broke my heart. Basil, you got to be honest with me. Did my brother . . ." My Pops paused, and his voice sounded strained, like it was pleading for answers.

"What, Pops?"

"Did my brother, your uncle Mac, do unnatural things to you when you were a little boy? Did he make you homosexual? Tell me the truth, son."

"No, Pops. It never happened," I said quickly as I lowered my body to the floor in my dark and silent apartment. I couldn't believe how my life was unraveling right before my eyes, hour by hour. As I sank to the floor, I felt shame and embarrassment wash over me like some stank body wash. I wanted to step into a steaming shower and never leave.

"You promise me? 'Cause if it did happen, I will go and dig the sick sonofabitch out of his grave and kick his ass," Pops said. My heart began to pound at each word, and I could feel the pain in his voice.

"Pops, don't do this to yourself. I promise it didn't happen," I said as I began to rock my body back and forth in anger.

"I spent all day just thinking back. I used to leave you with Mac so many times when I was on the road driving all the time. But it was the only thing I could do. I couldn't take you with me and keep you out of school. It wouldn't have been right. I also 'member how once your mother asked me if Mac was funny. I know he had his ways. But he was married. He was a man."

"Yeah, he was. Don't believe this stuff, Pops. Remember Uncle Mac the way you used to. It's just playa-hating at the highest degree. It's a lie," I said in a reassuring voice.

"I believe you, son. I'm sorry," he said, and then he added as an afterthought, "I'm supposed to go out and do a little bowling. Drink a few beers with my lady friend."

"You do that, Pops. I'm going to come and see you soon. We still got to take our trip to Las Vegas," I said.

"I look forward to it, son. We need to spend more time together. You ain't gettin any younger." He laughed nervously.

"I know that, Pops. I got to go. Roll a strike for me."

• • •

One hour later, I was on my way to Harlem with an aluminum baseball bat in hand. As I walked the two blocks to the garage where I kept my car, I felt the coldness of the wind rushing from the dark sky, but my body was still warm with anger.

After I hung up with my Pops, I located the piece of paper with Bart's number and his address from our first encounter. I called him a couple of times, and when I tried for a third time, an automated voice informed me the answering machine was full.

When the attendant drove my silver Porsche in front of me, I hopped in without even tipping. As I drove toward the West Side Highway, I became more convinced that Bart was behind the phone calls. And that Yancey was helping him. She was the only person besides Raymond who knew what my uncle had done to me. If it was in fact Yancey, then how did they know each other? I thought about all the press Yancey'd gotten recently, the store promotions, and wondered how their paths had crossed. I also remembered Bart talking about doing some videos and how Yancey had some men in her video but you couldn't really see their faces. Was Bart one of them? I made up my mind that somebody was going to answer my questions or else there was going to be a massive beat-down. I didn't give a damn if I had to spend the rest of my life behind bars. Somebody was going to pay for messing with the Henderson men.

I exited on 125th Street and turned south. I came to a stoplight near the train station and turned west again when I got to 122nd Street. I drove cautiously, looking at the numbers on the buildings. When I came to the end of the street, I saw a brownstone tucked neatly in a curve at the end of the block with the numbers Bart had printed neatly.

I looked out my window and then the passenger's side. I reached in the tiny backseat and pulled out the bat, which had been a gift from one of my major league clients, Purvis Turner. I looked at the metallic blue lettering, which said "1999 All-Star Game," and Purvis's signature scribbled in black Magic Marker.

I zipped my jacket to the top and got out of my car. I beamed the key toward the lock, and I heard the sound of my car doors locking automatically. As I walked up to the brownstone, I looked at the buzzers. I realized there were three floors. I pulled out the paper with Bart's address and noticed the *B* next to his name and figured he lived in the basement apartment.

I stepped quietly down toward the basement apartment with the baseball bat in my hand. I was determined to do damage to Bart and anything he owned. When I got to the door, I noticed a black mailbox with the name "Bart Dunbar," and I suddenly felt my heart begin to beat at a rapid pace.

I knocked on the door forcefully and waited for Bart to answer. A few minutes went by, and then I knocked again.

When Bart didn't come to the door, I looked in a window covered with black bars. I didn't see any lights or hear any movement in the apartment. Bart must not be home. But he had to come home sooner or later, and I had nothing but time. I gripped my bat tighter and headed back to my car.

Two hours later and still no sign of Bart. He must be shaking his ass at some gay bar in the village, I thought. I was listening to *The Quiet Storm* on WBLS, when I decided to check my messages at home. Another call from Rosa, and one from Raymond saying he was just thinking about me. I looked at the clock and saw that it was only 10:20 in Seattle, so I dialed Raymond's number. I knew from the events of the last thirty-plus hours that with my luck, Raymond's partner would probably answer the phone. So I was a bit surprised when Raymond picked up himself.

"Hello?"

"You lookin' for me?" I said.

"Just checking in. How are you doing?"

"Chillin'."

"Where are you? Sounds like you're on a portable."

"I'm in my car."

"Is it cold there?"

"It's winter, so you know it's cold. But I'm hot as hell," I said.

"Why?" Raymond asked. It sounded like he was whispering. Maybe old dude was close by.

"Would you take a criminal case if it was somebody you loved?"

"Who are you talking about?"

I spent the next ten minutes telling Raymond about my

day and evening. I told him how difficult it was hearing the pain in my Pops's voice and how I had never been so mad in my entire life. I wanted to punish Bart and Yancey for making me look weak and soft in front of my Pops and business partners.

"Why didn't you just tell your father the truth? You know he loves you. Basil, what your uncle did to you wasn't your fault," Raymond said.

"And it wasn't my Pops's fault either."

"Basil, do me a favor. Turn on your car and go home. Don't make matters worse. How is your father going to feel with you in jail? He'll know you were lying to him. What about your business? Please don't do this."

"I got to, dude. People can't fuck me over and expect me to just walk away. You know that's not how I roll," I said.

"Would you do it for somebody who cares a great deal for you?" Raymond said.

"Who?"

"Me."

I thought about what Raymond had asked. The sincerity and concern in his voice were powerful, but I couldn't stop thinking about Bart. I pictured him and Yancey celebrating as they completed each call. Finally I said, "Naw, Raymond. I know you're right, but I can't do it. Not even for you."

I'm a Survivor

So, Bart, are you really going to move down here?" Yancey asked.

"I'm pretty sure that's what I need to do. I really don't have much of a choice," I said. Yancey didn't respond as she took a bite of the salmon omelet we both had ordered. We were having breakfast on a deck near the hotel pool. With the state of my finances, I realized the three-egg omelet with skillet potatoes and onions might be the last decent meal I was going to enjoy.

I had spent the previous evening trying to reach Ava, without success. I tried her cell phone number when I woke up, but a recording told me the number had been disconnected. Ava had pulled a fast one. I was very depressed, and I was overdrawn by $33,000. I figured I could buy a little time by not returning to New York right away. With all the criminals in New York, I didn't think my bank was going to send the police to South Beach to get me. Besides, they couldn't prove that I was trying to defraud the bank. I deposited the check from Ava in totally good faith. I decided to move into one of the cheap hotels on South Beach and try to find work as a waiter and model.

The only saving grace was that I had paid my Visa down to a zero balance, and the $7,500 check had cleared. After a few bites of my omelet, I looked over at Yancey and thought how wonderful her life must be. Adored by fans both male and female, she was most likely blessed with a big bank account as well.

Yancey was wearing all white, a sleeveless sweater and capri pants. Her face was beat to perfection, like she was getting ready for a photo shoot. She had her hair styled in a long sophisticated ponytail fastened with a tortoiseshell clip. Her eyes were a warm brown, with little flecks of gold and long lashes. Yancey stopped eating and looked over at me. Her smile was soft, like she was watching a newborn baby sleep. She touched the top of my hand and offered, "Cheer up, Bart. Things will work out."

"I wish I had your confidence," I said. "I guess I'm getting what I deserve. I did a horrible thing."

"Are you sorry for going after this guy?" Yancey asked.

"Should I be? I mean, is he sorry for what he did to me? I doubt it. He's probably lying up in his fabulous apartment, in his big king-size bed, with someone else," I said. I was so mad at Ava that I had forgotten about Basil in the last twenty-four hours. I wondered why Yancey was so concerned about the feelings of his bisexual ass. Maybe she was thinking about the man who had dumped her. Maybe it was a good thing I had added a little twist to my story by telling Yancey the guy was sleeping with both Ava and me at the same time. Women hated that. Besides, now I wasn't so certain Ava was telling me the truth about why she hated Basil so much.

"You must have really loved him," Yancey said.

"As much as I'm capable of loving. I do think I learned something from this."

"What's that?"

"I think I fell for this guy, like most of the men I fall for, because I know deep in my heart they're unattainable. These men are never going to be involved in a faithful relationship with another man no matter what. Maybe that's why I love and *hate* bisexual men with such a passion. They don't think they deserve love, and I know I don't," I said, suddenly wondering if my pineapple juice had some type of truth serum in it.

"Do you think Ba—I mean the guy—loved you?" Yancey asked as she coughed like she had something caught in her throat.

"Are you all right?" I asked.

"I'm fine," Yancey said as she looked down into her lap and then took a sip of water.

"He loved what I did in bed," I said.

"You don't have anyone you can borrow the money from?"

"No, I don't," I said. I had decided against asking Wylie for the money because he would ask too many questions. If I told him the truth, not only would he not give me the money, but this would probably be the last straw of our already fragile friendship.

"How much do you need?" Yancey asked.

"About forty-five thousand dollars," I said. My heart started beating rapidly at the thought of Yancey offering me a loan. I figured I'd better inflate the figure in case she was in a generous mood.

"What about your parents?"

"What parents?" Yancey wanted to talk about parents, and I wanted to discuss a payment plan. Then I realized that unless she was independently wealthy, she probably didn't have that kind of money. I knew it took most recording stars years to make any money, with all the expenses of promoting an album. Yancey had already spent a lot of money on the two videos. Not on me, of course, but I know she dropped a small bundle on her outfits alone.

"Your parents are dead?"

"As far as I'm concerned," I said coldly.

"Why don't you tell me about it?" Yancey asked.

I was silent for a few moments, and then I figured since I had told her so much, I might as well tell her the story of my miserable life.

"You know, I don't know why I'm telling you all this stuff. But somehow I feel like I can trust you. Can you explain that to me?" I asked.

"Maybe we have some things in common," Yancey said quietly.

"Children never forget," I said, and then I paused for dramatic effect. I leaned back in the wrought-iron patio chair and enjoyed the warmth of sunshine on my face for a few moments. Then I began talking to Yancey like she was my therapist and she could make everything in my life right.

"The last time I saw my parents was when they dropped me off at day care. I think I was four or five. Well, that's not exactly true. I saw them once again when I was seven. They

were on television. In handcuffs, being led out of a court-
room. My birth parents had robbed a bank. Who in the fuck
did they think they were? Bonnie and Clyde?" I stopped for a
moment. That was usually my punch line, but Yancey wasn't
laughing. Her eyes were full of sympathy, so I continued,
spilling out details.

"Anyway, my father ended up killing one of the guards.
When I became older, I went back and read some of the
newspaper accounts. He was sentenced to life without
parole, but my mother was given fifteen years. She's probably out now, I don't know. I haven't tried to find her, and
I'm sure she hasn't been looking for me. I try not to think
about them," I said as tears began to form in the corner of
my eyes. I began blinking repeatedly, like someone was
flashing a bright unwanted light in my eyes. I couldn't
believe I had finally told someone the true story of my criminal parents. When Wylie had pressed me for details, I had
told him an equally sad story, but in the version I told Wylie,
my parents were drug addicts and had both died from AIDS.

Yancey had tears in her eyes. When she looked away, she
picked up the linen napkin from her breakfast plate and
dabbed the corners of her eyes. She then looked at me and
said, "Bart, we can't choose our families."

"I know. But I couldn't even catch a break when I was
placed in foster care. Every time I came close to getting
adopted, something went wrong. Where in the hell was
Rosie O'Donnell when you needed her?" I joked, trying to
lighten things up.

Yancey smiled and then said, "I hope this doesn't sound
cruel, but you're not the only one who had a rough child-

hood. I say that only because I really know where you're coming from."

"I know, but that still doesn't stop me from being angry. I mean, there is another part of the story," I said.

"I'm listening,"

"I had a baby sister. She was about eight months old. Amanda was her name," I said softly.

"What happened to her?"

"She was adopted right away. The family didn't want me. Neither did my grandmother on my father's side. My mother's parents disappeared too. So don't believe that shit about black folks never turning their backs on family."

"Oh, baby, you're talking to the choir here. I know that."

"And the foster homes were just like prison camps. I had to fight all the time to keep the boys off of me. I mean, the ones I didn't like," I said.

"Do you think that's why you're gay?"

"Oh, hell no. I'm gay through and true. I would have been gay even if Cliff and Clair Huxtable from *The Cosby Show* had been my parents. I spent so many years praying to God for parents, and when he didn't answer that prayer, I began pleading that if I'm going to be an orphan and gay . . ." I paused, because tears the size of grapes were rolling down my face.

"It's okay, Bart," Yancey said as she patted my hand.

". . . then let someone like me, love me," I said as I tried to stop crying. I wanted to cut out this pity party, but all I could manage was a weak smile as Yancey held my hand. It was time, once again, to figure out yet another plan for survival.

You Make Me Feel Brand-New

I wonder what people see when they look at me. I studied my face in the mirror after removing the ton of makeup I'd worn for the shoot. It had been a very long day, but if the dailies Desmond and I had just watched were any indication, the second video was going to be a bigger hit than the first!

My eyes looked tired. I wondered what Desmond saw when he looked at me. Tired eyes? Or the face of a cover girl? I guessed it was best that most people saw only what they wanted to see and no more. I was damn glad I didn't have the kind of face that tells your whole life story. My career would be over!

I peered in closer and ran my finger across the faint scar over my left eyebrow. No one ever noticed it, but I always knew it was there. My grandmother had said it was an accident and that she hadn't meant to break the skin or draw blood. What she had meant to do was beat the living devil out of me with an extension cord when I was eight years old. Whipping me was a common occurrence when my grandmother thought I'd looked at her the wrong way or, even worse, "been fast" with a neighborhood boy.

On that particular day many years ago when I tried to pull away from her grasp, she let me go and I fell, hitting my head on the sharp corner of the kitchen counter. She'd never hesitated to raise big red welts on my legs and back, but when she saw the blood running down my face, it scared her so badly she put the extension cord away for at least a week.

Sometimes I can't look at my own face. I'm afraid of what I'll see there. I can brush my teeth, put on my makeup and fix my hair without ever looking into my own eyes. Most of the time people don't look any deeper than my pretty face. But I've learned that beautiful people don't always lead beautiful lives.

I thought Desmond had broken the family code earlier today, when he was looking at me so intensely that I wanted to tell him my life story. The true version—not the one I'd carefully crafted for the outside world. It made me nervous. I thought maybe Desmond could see Ava, my grandmother, or even Basil in my eyes; that he could see the lies I've told, the deceptions. Could he see the hurt little girl who lives inside of me? He kept looking at me and searching my face, but I realized suddenly that he was just trying to get the lighting right. I was so relieved that I let out a deep sigh. "You okay?" he asked. "Fine," I lied, avoiding his stare and giving him one of my best diva smiles.

I surprised myself by being so concerned with what Desmond thought of me. Besides his looks, he's talented, smart, down-to-earth and totally unimpressed with me as a woman. At least, that's the way it seems. He's had plenty of opportunities to make a move. I know he knows how, but so far, nothing. I guess I should be glad that he hasn't jumped all over me, like most of the men I've met. Desmond has a homeboy quality mixed with the air of a southern gentleman that makes him almost irresistible.

• • •

I'd spent so much time working and thinking about Desmond that my stomach had to remind me it needed food to survive the long days. I was tired of the room service thing again, and Bart had already switched hotels. I walked out on the balcony and soaked up the amazing view in Miami: the pool, the beach and the open-air café and bar below. I decided that I needed to get away from Yancey B tonight, so I put on my peach-colored tube top to show off my tan, and a blue- and peach-flowered sarong that showed plenty of leg and thigh when I sat down. Then I slipped on some barely-there sandals.

I dropped my cell phone in my bag and glanced over the balcony to see if the café and bar were too crowded or if I should walk down to the Lincoln Road area again. Suddenly my eyes landed on Desmond. The man even looked good from nine stories up. He was sitting casually at a table and talking with one of the production guys. Just as I began to savor the view, he rose to leave. I watched him for a second to see which direction he was going. When it looked like he was headed for the beach, I quickly raced from my suite and rushed to the bank of elevators. I pushed both the down button and the up button. Moments later I heard a *ding!,* but the up arrow was lit. I thought about taking the stairs, but I knew I'd be sweating like a pig once I reached the lobby. Seconds that seemed like minutes passed, and finally, the next *ding* signaled a down elevator. When the door opened, an elderly white man gave me a smile as he moved to the back of the elevator. He stood directly behind me, even though there was no one else in the elevator. I could feel his eyes on my butt, so I moved over so we were standing side by side.

I was getting really agitated when the elevator stopped again and a young black man with blond hair, talking on a cell phone, stuck his foot against the door to hold it open for his slow-moving girlfriend, who was wearing a Wal-Mart special pale pink short set. She was smacking gum, and I looked away so she wouldn't see me roll my eyes at her and her boyfriend. But then she looked up at me like she knew me, and I began to pray that the elevator would reach the lobby quickly.

"Ain't you Yancey B?" she asked me in a loud voice. I nodded and smiled.

"Bitch, you're the bomb with a mushroom cap. I heard yo song. Me and all my girls listen to your CD all the time. Can I get your autograph?" she asked as she started pressing her elbow into her boyfriend's side. Of course, this wasn't the first time someone asked me for an autograph, but Broadway fans and hoochie mamas were very different in their approach.

"Sure. Do you have a pen and paper?"

"Tuwan, give me a piece of paper and a pen," she demanded.

"LaTonya, I ain't got no pen and paper. Who do I look like, yo assistant or sumthin'?"

LaTonya looked at the white man and said, "You got a pen and paper, ole man?"

He smiled and whispered, "No."

The elevator finally reached the lobby, and LaTonya grabbed my hand and said, "Come on, let's go to the front desk. They better have some pens and papers up there."

I wanted to tell LaTonya that we would have to do this later because I had a man to catch, but I also realized that keeping my fans happy was part of being an entertainer. Three autographs later (for LaTonya and her two best friends, Trina and Bedonna), I headed for the hotel café, passed the pool and began to frantically search the long stretch of white sandy beach for Desmond.

The moon was hanging full and glorious over the water, and the sun had dipped below the clouds and bathed the distant cruise ships and small boats in gold. I kept looking all around, in front, behind and then up the beach. I started to run south, when I suddenly spotted Desmond's tall, lean self as he walked along the water's edge. He was walking slowly, but his stride was so long, I had to run to catch up to him, quite by accident, of course.

When I got within a few feet, I stopped and caught my breath, brushed some of the sand off my feet, and smiled as I mumbled to myself, "You got him, girl!" I felt a little bit like a stalker, but I enjoyed the excitement of following him. Desmond was wearing cream-colored linen slacks and a matching linen shirt that must have been unbuttoned in front, because it flared out as he walked. During the shoot, his dreads had been tied back away from his face, but now they swayed freely to the left and right as he glided along, beckoning me to follow.

The warm night air was humid, kissed by the softest of breezes. The farther we walked from the hotel, the more quiet and peaceful it became. I could hear my own heart beating rapidly. I wondered if Desmond could hear it too. Perspiration was dripping down my back, collecting just above the waistband of my sarong. I told myself I better make my move before I was completely drenched. But it was Desmond who made the first move.

He turned in toward the water and stopped. He let his shirt fall from his shoulders to the sand, kicked off his sandals, then stepped out of his slacks. His almost naked body cast a fierce silhouette against the moon, which seemed to hang in the sky just inches above the water. For an instant, I thought he was going to throw back and beat his chest like he was Tarzan. And damn if he didn't look like Tarzan dipped in chocolate and caramel.

I had assumed that Desmond was on the thin side of lean, but now, seeing him with next to nothing on, I realized how his usual oversized clothing masked a fabulous physique. Desmond looked like a sculpted Hershey hunk of muscle, not bulky, mind you, but well defined. Arms, back, thighs, calves, ass—especially ass—smooth flawless skin pulled taut over rock-hard muscle. It was not a Basil look-at-me body; it was more natural, less forced and much, much sexier. I was slightly aroused, but was more overwhelmed by the pure, almost spiritual nature of his looks.

"Desmond," I wanted to say, but the words got caught in

my throat and no sound came from my mouth. I coughed to clear my dry throat, and he heard me. He turned around and tilted his head slightly to the side with a quizzical look on his face. When he recognized me, a broad smile spread across his face. I knew I was caught, but the brilliant contrast of the stark white swimsuit he was wearing against the brown hues of his skin had my full attention. His crotch bulged almost obscenely, or maybe my eyes had suddenly become as big as cookies. "Desmond," I said again with mock surprise in my voice, "fancy meeting you here."

"That's pretty weak, Yancey," he said, laughing at me with his eyes. "How long have you been standing there? Are you following me?"

"Following you? Of course not. I mean, it *is* a free beach. You're not the only one who decided to take an early-evening stroll on the beach. Look around," I said as I whirled around with my arms spread toward the other people walking along the beach.

"True. True," he said. "Let's not get defensive."

"Defensive. There's nothing to defend. I was on my way to dinner, but that beautiful moon and sea air called out to me. I wasn't looking for you," I said unconvincingly.

He walked over and took my hands in his. He looked deep into my eyes, and I could see my face reflected in his pupils. "You are a very beautiful woman, Yancey Braxton. And a very lucky one as well."

"Lucky? How so?" I asked as I looked at him with affection and just a little fake contempt. I still didn't want him to think I had chased him down the beach like a brazen schoolgirl.

"Because you are here with me under the alluring spell of the full moon," he said, pulling me to him.

He wrapped his arms around my waist and I held him around his neck, nestling my head into the space between his head and shoulder. His body was protecting me from the slight night breeze like a shield. We spoke no words, yet we communicated a great deal to one another. I found strength in his raw masculinity, and security in his sensitivity. Within moments, the tiredness and tension that I'd held in my body all day were replaced by calm and peacefulness.

A few moments later, Desmond asked me if I was a swimmer.

"It's my second-favorite exercise," I said with a seductive smile.

"Oh, you're bad, Yancey Braxton." Desmond laughed as he waved his index finger a few inches from my nose.

"No, I'm very good."

After a few moments of awkward silence, Desmond looked at me and said, "Let's go for a swim."

"I'd love to," I said. "But I'm not wearing a swimsuit."

"Your point would be?" He laughed again.

I hesitated a second, then unwrapped my sarong and tossed it in the direction of his clothes piled on the sand. Desmond stood there perfectly still, then slowly looked me up and down like he was checking for places to kiss. After he'd taken me all in, he nodded his approval. I stood there in my tube top and robin's-egg-blue thong underwear, but felt no awkwardness with this man who seemed to see right through me.

"Very beautiful, indeed," he said. "And here, too," he

added as he placed his hand over my heart. He took my face in his hands and brushed his lips softly across mine. He pulled back for an instant and studied my face, running his thumbs over my eyelids, along the scar on my eyebrow, over my mouth, and then leaned in and gently parted my lips with his tongue.

It was a kiss I didn't ever want to end, even though I knew it could lead to something better. Desmond's pillow-soft lips suddenly left mine, and he took my hand gently and walked me into the ocean. Goose bumps rose all over my body as we entered the deep, cool weightlessness of the water. Before we began to swim, I pulled Desmond toward me and looked into his eyes and said, "I haven't done anything in my life to deserve someone like you."

Desmond smiled at me and touched my bottom lip and said, "Just be Yancey. The Yancey no one has ever seen."

You've Got a Friend

Bart was hiding from me, and my anger was still very much alive. I came home the next morning around nine when it was clear he wasn't going to show. I got undressed, crawled into bed and drifted into a heavy child-like sleep.

I woke up renewed, determined that I was not going to allow life to wrestle me to the ground. I ate a bowl of cereal and then took a shower. I stood for a long time and let the warm jets of water beat on my body in full force.

When I came out of the shower, I wrapped a beach towel around my waist and readied myself for some important calls. I needed to speak with Brison. He had called several times to express his concerns and assured me I was still wanted and considered a partner. When I reached him, I asked, "What about Nico?" He took a moment before replying, "Nico is an idiot. We got the votes to overrule him. Don't walk away from what we've accomplished." I asked him to give me a couple of days to think and I would get back to him.

I called my Pops to make sure he was all right, and he didn't even mention our last conversation. When I mentioned I was thinking about moving back to Florida, he sounded excited, and talked about the two of us going fishing. That was a good sign, I thought, unless he was simmering like me.

I went into the kitchen for some orange juice, but there were only a few drops. I was getting ready to get dressed and run to the store when the doorman rang the intercom phone. I started not to answer it. The day before, Rosa had shown up. Why I don't know, but I'd told the doorman to tell her I wasn't feeling well. Even when she told him it was important, my response was a firm no.

I figured it was probably Rosa again, so I decided I might as well deal with her. Her constant phone calls during the last couple of days and then showing up unannounced probably meant only one thing. She had gotten a call from Bart too.

"Yeah."

"Mr. Henderson. I have a Mr. Tyler here to see you," the doorman said.

"A mister who?" I heard the doorman ask someone to repeat his name, then a voice in the background say, "Raymond Tyler."

"Mr. Raymond Tyler," he repeated.

"Are you sure?"

"That's what the man said."

"Send him up," I said.

I raced to my bedroom and then decided it was too late to get dressed. Damn, Raymond had seen me half-naked before, anyway. But what was he doing here? I wondered as I moved to my bathroom to brush my teeth quickly. Just as I was getting ready to wash the excess toothpaste from my mouth, the doorbell rang, so I quickly wiped my mouth with the back of my hand.

I went to the door, and I felt my heart pounding. I took a deep breath and pulled open the door. There he stood, Raymond Tyler, looking handsome with cool grape-green eyes and unblemished skin. He looked at me with a nervous, sexy smile. I looked at him in disbelief.

"Raymond, what are you doing here?" I asked.

"I came to collect my pay. You didn't get my messages?"

"I haven't checked my machine in a while. You called?"

"Several times."

"Why are you here, seriously?"

"If you let me in, I'll tell you," Raymond said.

"Dang, I'm sorry, come on in," I said as I grabbed hold of my towel to make sure it was tucked tight.

Raymond followed me to the living area, and we both took a seat on the sofa as I maneuvered my towel to make sure I didn't get Raymond excited. Although the boy looked good, I knew he hadn't come all the way from Seattle just to get a little piece.

"Be real, why are you here?" I asked.

"I was worried about you," Raymond said seriously.

"Why? You know me. I can handle my business."

"I'm glad to see you're not in jail or something."

"That's 'cause I haven't caught up with that mofo Bart. But trust me. His days are numbered."

"What's that going to solve?"

"It's going to show a mofo he can't fuck with my family and then just walk away. How would that make me look?"

"Don't know. You tell me," Raymond said.

I didn't answer, and my loft began to vibrate with the still air of our unspoken words. A few moments later, the stillness was beginning to feel overpowering, so I finally said, "Can I get you something to drink?"

"You got any OJ?"

"Naw, I was on my way to get some," I said.

"Why don't you get dressed and let me take you to breakfast," Raymond suggested. Maybe my towel and I were getting to him.

"So you came all the way from Seattle to take me to breakfast. I'm impressed," I joked. But Raymond wasn't going to let me take things lightly.

"Basil, when are you going to really deal with life? Are you going to joke, fight or fuck yourself out of every situation?"

"What are you talking about?"

"Basil, I got on a plane and left my home and job to come here to check on you, because the last time I talked to you, you were talking about beating some dude's ass because he did something you didn't like. Dude, this is a new century. We're getting older. We've got to stop playing and acting like little boys."

"I'll stop acting like a little boy when I finish with Bart," I said.

"I bet you will, because from what I hear prison changes boys into men or into something I know you don't even want to hear. And jail is where you're headed if you don't deal with this fool in a civilized way."

"So you think it was civilized of him to call my clients, my friends and most importantly my family? What if someone did that to you?"

"They can't! I tell the truth to the people I love. Life is full of surprises, and they sure don't need any new ones from me," Raymond said calmly.

I thought about what Raymond was saying about living a life of truth, when suddenly I was distracted by a rush of memories of a night I had spent with Raymond at the pool of my rented Atlanta town house. It had been more than seven years ago, but I remember the night like it was yesterday.

It had been a humid night, with Anita Baker's voice filling the air, under a full moon, and stars sprinkling the sky like tiny pins in a black velvet cushion. I was wearing neon-green shorts and a jock to keep my jimmie tight. Raymond, who had not come prepared for a swim or seduction, was wearing his black boxer briefs. I remembered feeling the solidness of his body pressed against mine and the sensual warmth of the water. I thought of the ripples of pleasure my body felt when Raymond practically forced me to kiss him. A kiss I will never forget, because it was the first time I had kissed a man. I hadn't kissed a man like that since.

"Basil? What are you thinking about? Did you hear what I said?" Raymond asked with concern.

"Yeah, I hear you, but that works for you," I said.

"And it can work for you."

"All I know is it makes me realize that there are two kinds of men I don't know whether to envy or hate," I said, trying to keep my voice even and not let my anger creep in. I knew Raymond was only trying to help.

"Two kinds?"

"Yeah, men like yourself, who have accepted their fate in life and still found a way to love themselves and find love. And mofos, like most of the men I know, who have never ever spent a second thinking about hittin' it with another hardhead."

"I have my days of doubt," Raymond said; his voice was deep and soothing as a massage.

"And there is one type of mofo I most certainly hate— mofos like that fucked-up Bart. Those type of niggahs needed to be destroyed."

"Why? Because he's not ashamed of being gay?" Raymond asked.

"No, because he's a mutherfuckin' evil asshole," I said.

"So you're determined to get revenge. Sounds like you and that girl you were going to marry were a perfect match."

"You don't understand people like Yancey and myself. We had tough childhoods, and it made us tough. We didn't have a *Father Knows Best* life like you and your brother. Your father would never turn his back on you. He's too proud of you," I said.

"And your Pops wouldn't turn his back on you. He's just as proud of you. What's the worst thing he could say or do?"

Silence chased Raymond's question and a heavy emotional weight covered the room for a few minutes. Finally I said, "He would probably ask me how can I bring this kind of shit into our family. He would tell me I'm not the son he raised. Alone."

"And he could say what my mother said: 'You're my son and I love you no matter what.' Have you thought about him saying that? Besides, if he knew what your uncle did, and I believe deep in his heart he knows, he would have to accept you. I mean, why else would he take Bart's words so seriously?"

"I will never tell him what Mac did to me," I said firmly.

"Why?"

"Because it would hurt him. I have never brought pain to my father, and I never will. I can still remember his face the first time I scored a touchdown in Pop Warner football. I saw that same face in junior high, high school, college and in the pros. It's the only look I ever want to see on his face."

"That's joy for him, but what about some joy for you? Think of all the pain you've gone through. Think how your uncle made you feel nasty about your sexuality. It's like you're still trying to purge him from you. I think that's why you have to sleep with all those women and even the men. Why you're never able to say 'I'm gay' or 'I'm bisexual.' And Basil, as sure as I'm sitting here, it won't get any easier. There will be more Barts and Yanceys," Raymond said.

"Why can't there be more Raymonds and Yolandas?" I asked Raymond, reminding him of the woman I loved before Yancey.

"You have to be ready when they show up. And as much as I love you as a friend, I can tell that right now, you'd chase them away if they landed on your doorstep."

"Why do you say that? Are you saying I'm not good enough to have love in my life?"

"Not when you're consumed with lust and willing to do any- and everything to protect your secrets."

"Were you ever in love with me?"

"I take the Fifth." Raymond smiled.

"I'll take that as a yes."

"Basil, I know you. If we got together, I know that one day I could come home and find you in our bed with either a hot-looking lady or a guy. Being in a relationship with you would mean that I would have to accept your shit, even though it goes against everything I believe about love. Some nights I look at Trent and I ask myself, Who is this man I am in love with? Does he love me? Or does he love who he thinks I am? And when I don't really know the answer, it makes me sad."

"What do you do?"

"I keep breathing. I keep believing in love, no matter what the world tells me. I have my own standards for love. I don't depend on anyone else to love me just because I say I love them. I have to feel it here," Raymond said as he tapped his chest.

"So what do you think I should do?"

"Move on. Forget about Bart and concentrate on the people who love you. Like your Pops. Reconnect with friends who would love you no matter what. People who will love the whole you. People like me," Raymond said.

"What if my Pops rejects me?"

"He won't."

I thought about the pain in my Pops' voice when he had asked me if I was a homosexual. I thought how saying yes would have been like driving a stake through his heart. I know that. Raymond could believe in that "love will save the day" shit all he wanted to, but my life wasn't his. I was getting ready to tell him that when he started to speak again.

"You know, a couple of years ago my Pops had a stroke and we almost lost him. And the only thing I could think about was the last thing I had said to him. Was it something loving or was it something out of anger? Was it the truth or was it a lie? Now, your Pops could outlive the both of us, but that's not promised. Do you want that lie about your life hanging out there, unprotected from people like Bart? A lie that can be used to make you act in hate and not love? Let it go, Basil. Let it go!"

I suddenly felt the full weight of my sadness, all the years of never feeling anyone could love me if they knew everything about me. They could never love the whole me. How could I ever release those feelings? I looked at Raymond and the loving concern in his eyes. I felt tears come, and it startled me. I had not cried since I was a little boy. I didn't cry at happy times in my life, like winning big football games, and I would never cry if we lost. Tears were a sign of weakness, I had always thought. I tried to blink back the tears with every fiber within me. I couldn't let Raymond see me cry, and so I looked down for a few moments at the towel I was wearing. Then I heard Raymond repeat himself: "Let it go. True love can only begin with truth."

And the tears I had tried to stop turned into uncontrollable sobs and Raymond moved quickly to embrace my naked shoulders. I couldn't look at him, but I let him hold me as sobs racked my body like an earthquake. These tears felt cleansing, and I felt so intimate with Raymond, so secure in his strong, solid arms, and I wondered if this was what it felt like to make love with someone you knew loved you.

There's No Place Like Home

After almost two weeks in South Beach I had learned one thing. Today, yesterday and tomorrow had a couple of things in common: torrential rain and brilliant sunshine. And both were driving me nuts.

I did like a couple of things about South Beach. Like New York City, it was a city that never slept. I loved the calmness of the beach early in the morning and late at night. I had spent a great deal of time thinking over the last several days. Opening up to Yancey had brought back so many memories I thought I'd tucked safely away. I wondered about my parents and what kind of people they were. Were they sorry for what they'd done? Leaving me and my sister in the arms of a system that didn't have time to care? Or was I just a wild plant from a family that only produced bad seeds? Why hadn't my parents gone on welfare instead of robbing a bank and committing murder? Was I, their son, capable of killing another human being? There were so many times when I felt pure hatred for the men I fell for, as well as the women who welcomed them back into their beds.

I wondered if my sister, Amanda, had grown up in a family of people who loved her, and if she now had love in her life. Maybe she was some big superstar who had changed her name to Nia, Aaliyah or Brandy. Had her new mother educated her about the ways of the world so she didn't fall in love with men like Brandon and Basil?

I thought about the woman who had been like a mother to me and wondered if she was still alive and if she could ever forgive me. Her name was Hattie Kaufman, and I had spent five years with her, from age thirteen until I left for Morris Brown. Hattie was a wonderful lady with a big heart. She had over nine foster children, and even though I didn't like any of them, Hattie made me feel like I was an only child. Back then I rejected her love because she was white and Jewish and I felt there was no way Hattie could love me like a real mother. Now I thought I had been wrong. It was Hattie who had encouraged me to attend a black college because she wanted me to know my community. Our neighborhood and most of her foster children were white or Mexican, which to me, at that time, were one and the same. Maybe Hattie treated me special because in a house where I was the darkest thing there, I was special.

So when I got to Atlanta and Morris Brown, I fell in love with black people. I soaked up every drop of being black, and in my new world, there was no room for white women with hearts of gold.

Seeing all these old Jewish ladies take their daily walks along Lincoln Road and around South Beach made me think of Hattie, and I hoped that wherever she was, she realized I hadn't known how to love her.

I still hadn't landed a job, although I had a second inter-view scheduled at the David Barton gym in the Delano Hotel. Being a trainer would allow me the flexibility to wait tables and do a little modeling on the side. If I was lucky I could support myself and start saving to replace the money I owed my bank.

Most of my days had been lonely. A lot of gay men down here don't speak English, or they don't speak to black men, or else they suffer from the "too cute to speak" syndrome. I had spent the night before at a gay nightclub filled with syn-thesized R & B music, flashing lights and a lot of men look-ing for one night only. Love here in South Beach seemed the same as in New York: a guilty pleasure based on physical attraction.

But this was the bed I had made for myself, so I was determined to make it work. I still had to get some of my possessions from my Harlem apartment without the risk of being caught in case the police were looking for me, and so once again I needed Wylie's help. I hadn't called him and told him I was moving, but I had to now so he could ship me my clothes.

I booked a room at a hotel called the Betsy Ross. It's a boutique hotel that looks like the big house on a southern plantation. It was an okay hotel—definitely not the Delano, where I had been staying with Yancey B and her crew—but for now it would have to do.

I picked up the phone and punched in the numbers from my phone card. It was early evening, and I was hoping I would get Wylie and not his answering machine.

After a few rings, I got my first break in a couple of days.

Wylie answered the phone, and I suddenly missed New York terribly.

"Wylie, this is Bart. How ya doing?"

"Where have you been? Do you know your answering machine is full and your cell phone is off? Where are you?"

"I'm in South Beach."

"Are you still shooting that video?"

"We finished a couple of days ago."

"Don't tell me you met another confused man?"

"No, not yet. But I'm not going to let that stop me from moving down here," I said, laughing. It was the first time I had cracked a smile in days.

"What? You can't move down there. What am I going to do? I need you," Wylie said.

"Oh, you'll be fine. I need a change. It's all for the best," I said. I wrestled with the thought of telling him what I had done to Basil and what Ava had done to me, but I didn't want to hear his "do right and good things happen" speech.

"Bart, you can't do that. I've been calling you every hour on the hour. I have a problem," Wylie said. I noticed his voice was unusually loud and trembling.

"Wylie, what's the matter?"

"I don't want to talk about this on the phone. When can you get back to New York?"

"I can't do that," I said firmly.

"I need you, Bart. For once in your life, stop thinking about yourself. How many times have I been there for you?"

"Then tell me what's going on. You expect me to just change my plans for you because you say so?"

"You know me, I wouldn't ask you if it wasn't important. I need to talk to someone, and you're the only one I can turn to."

"Tell me what's going on."

There was a long moment of silence, and then Wylie said, "I think something's wrong with . . ." with hesitation in his voice, and then he was just silent.

"Wylie, are you still there?"

"Yes. Bart, please come home. I think I have HIV," Wylie said.

I didn't know how to respond, and my stomach began bouncing like a trampoline. I could hear Wylie crying softly on the other end of the line. He sounded like a little boy crying because he'd suddenly been separated from his parents in a huge mall or park. I didn't know what to do or say, so I whispered, "I'll have to call you back."

Happy Birthday, Yancey

Since it seemed like I wasn't going to get Desmond into my bed, I would go to his. After a very tense meeting with Michel over my not doing the interview with LaVonya, I'd become upset when he said this might hurt my career. I called Desmond and invited myself to his apartment, and he didn't object.

We were sitting on his sofa, getting ready to watch a movie, when my cell phone rang. I looked at the number and said, "I better get this. It might be Michel."

"Or one of your boyfriends," Desmond joked.

"Hello."

"Yancey, this is Michel."

"Are you still upset with me?"

"We need to schedule your interview with LaVonya," Michel said.

"I still haven't decided if I'm going to do it," I said.

"This is free publicity. Yancey, you have to do it. The higher-ups are furious about your not wanting to do the interview. Mr. Hudson is talking about coming in from Los Angeles to talk some sense into you."

"Like I told you earlier, I think LaVonya has an ulterior motive."

"What?"

"I can't talk about it right now," I said as I looked over at Desmond to see if he was looking at or listening to me. He had moved over to his DVD and CD collection and was searching for something.

"Yancey, I need to give you some advice. Take it or leave it, but not doing this interview would be a very big mistake, and it might alter your relationship with Motown. People will start to consider you difficult to work with, and trust me, there's a long list of difficult divas that are no longer in the business. You need to call me in the morning and set a time for this interview," Michel said firmly.

"I'll call you," I said as I clicked off my phone. The nervousness I was feeling in my stomach must have moved to my face, because Desmond turned to me and asked, "Is everything all right?"

"It will be fine."

"Is there anything I can do?" Desmond asked as he sat down next to me on the sofa.

When I looked into his eyes I decided that I was going to try something different. I was going to try the truth. The whole truth.

I began by telling Desmond about my dilemma with Motown and *People* magazine. I told him I had some secrets about my past I was sure LaVonya was going to ask me about, and how those secrets could end my career.

He took my hands and said, "We all have secrets. But you can't let your past haunt your future."

"Some of the things I have to say might change the way you feel about me," I said softly.

"How could they? Is there something in your past that you've done to me? My family?"

"No."

"Then how could it change the way I feel about you?"

"Let me ask you something. Why didn't you make love to me when we were in South Beach?"

Desmond responded quickly, "Because it wasn't time. I want to make love to the entire you. Your body. Your soul. I'm still learning that. Any man could look at you and love what he sees on the outside. I want something more."

"What if I can't give you that?"

"Then we both would lose a great deal," Desmond said as he sweetly touched my face with the back of his hand.

I spent the next hour telling Desmond about my sordid past. I started out on the sofa with Desmond holding my hands, and then I got up and walked around the small living room as I recounted stories of how my grandmother used to beat me. I told him how my mother wasn't interested in being a mother. I told him what I had done to Basil, and even Nicole.

I started talking and I couldn't stop, and I felt cleansed. Like I was finally able to remove old photos from a scrapbook I was too afraid to open; tearing up the pictures, which brought me pain. Desmond listened both silently and intently. Several times during my monologue I wanted to rush over and fall into his arms, but I wanted to get everything out into the open. Once and for all. When I finally stopped talking I was exhausted. Desmond moved toward me, rested his arms on my shoulders, delicately pushed my hair back and asked, "So I don't understand why you don't want to talk with this reporter. None of us had perfect childhoods. But we survive. We change."

I took a deep breath and moved away from Desmond's embrace. For a moment I had my back to him, and then I suddenly turned and said, "I had a child. I gave her up." And then I began to cry body-shaking tears.

Desmond rushed to me and held me in his arms. One was covering my head and the other was wrapped tightly around my waist as he whispered, "Let it out, girl. Everything will be just fine. Let it out, baby." I clung to Desmond like he could save me.

Then he kissed me. Deep and hard, like he was making love to me. I had never been kissed so passionately, so lovingly. When he paused, he wiped the tears from my face with his open hand and said, "You said you felt like you were changing. You can. You mentioned feeling like you were shedding the layers of your past. Your grandmother's beatings. Your mother's deceit and lies. But Yancey, as long as you keep those lies inside you," he said as he gently tapped my heart, "you won't shed anything. If it's causing you this much pain, let everything go."

"But I can't," I said.

"Yes you can. I know you can. Stop trying to be perfect. Let Yancey out!"

Desmond spent the next hour convincing me that telling my story would help others and would allow me to enjoy the rest of my life without fear. It was not the first time I'd been told this. But I heard Desmond's words in a new and different way. His sweet-smelling breath caressed my face like a fall wind and everything made sense to me. He told me that I wasn't the first woman who had given up a child and I surely wouldn't be the last.

Desmond assured me that keeping Madison would have been the wrong thing to do, since I was worried about passing on the legacy of bad parenting. That it would be better for her to be in a healthy and happy environment and not in a home haunted by secrets and fear.

He also suggested that if I didn't want to have LaVonya tell my story in *People* I should consider offering my story to *Ebony* or *Essence*. "Think of all the young girls you can help. Our community is still overwhelmed by teen pregnancies, and now we have AIDS to worry about. If you, Yancey B, came forth and talked about the importance of healing by facing our past, just think how much good you could do."

I spent the night, my first in Desmond's bed, with his arms holding me tight. I felt safe, protected and new. No, I felt reborn. I promised myself I'd make the most of my rebirth.

We Fall Down

I arrived back in New York and caught a cab straight to Wylie's apartment. When I got out of the cab, fear clutched my insides as the warm spring air brushed over my face. I was worried about Wylie, because he hadn't returned my calls.

All I could think about was one evening when Wylie and I were discussing one of his friends who had the virus. Though a little tipsy, Wylie had said he would kill himself before he took his family and friends through AIDS. I still couldn't believe Wylie had slipped and had unsafe sex while always reminding me to be careful.

My heartbeat slowed a bit when the doorman called Wylie's apartment and then nodded for me to go up. That was a good sign, I thought, unless someone else had answered his phone, like a member of his family.

When I reached his apartment, I knocked on the door quickly, and a few moments later, Wylie opened the door and I breathed a sigh of relief.

"Wylie, why haven't you returned my calls? I've been

worried about you," I said as I walked into his apartment and dropped my luggage beside the front door. I gave Wylie a hug, but his body felt lifeless and his usual smile was absent. His puppy-dog brown eyes looked empty. He must have bad news, I thought.

"Come on in, Bart. I was hoping you'd have the guts to show up," Wylie said as he pulled himself from my embrace and headed toward his sofa, where I noticed a half-empty glass of wine. The first thing I thought was that I needed to talk to Wylie about his drinking, but I wasn't going to pile on with what he was going through.

"Why didn't you call me?" I repeated.

"Because I don't like lying and I need to say what I need to say to you face-to-face," Wylie said. There was a sharpness in his voice I had never heard before. It was like our fight a few weeks ago.

"What are you talking about? Have you been to the doctor?"

"No."

"Why not, and why do you think you have AIDS?"

"I get a physical every six months. I don't have AIDS."

For a moment I didn't believe I had heard Wylie correctly, and I looked at him with a disbelieving look. I suddenly felt a lightning-flash moment of anger and then I asked Wylie to repeat himself.

"I don't have AIDS."

"Then why did you tell me you did?"

"Because you've got something you need to take care of here in New York. I had to figure out a way to get you back."

"What the fuck are you talking about!" I screamed as I leaped for the sofa. "What kind of sick game are you playing? AIDS ain't no joke."

"And neither is going to jail," Wylie said calmly.

"Going to jail? What are you talking about? Have you smoked all the weed in New York City, or do I need to talk to you again about your drinking?" I said.

"You can't talk to me about shit until you get your own house clean," Wylie said

I was in a state of semishock. In all the years I had known Wylie, I had never seen him mad or this feisty. Something was up, and I needed to find out.

"Wylie, just tell me why you lied to me."

"Did you take some money from a lady named Ava Parker Middlebrooks?"

"That's none of your business," I snapped quickly.

"Is that why you hightailed it out of the city? Did you know she was going to stop payment on the check?"

"That's my business," I said.

"No, it's *our* business, and we're going to take care of it," Wylie said.

Wylie spent the next ten minutes telling me how the bank had called him about the check Ava had given me and the money I had received from the bank. When I asked him why they would call him, Wylie reminded me that because of my bad credit he had helped me get an account and now they were looking to him to either replace the funds or get in contact with me.

"But you didn't do anything," I protested.

"What you did was bank fraud. And they are going to arrest your ass if you don't come up with the money."

"But I don't have it," I said. "That bitch Ava double-crossed me."

"That's just too bad. I told you to leave Basil and that lady alone. But you couldn't do that. You had to go out and try and hurt somebody, and now look what's happened. I warned you your ass could land up in jail. What did you do to make her give you a check? And I want the truth!"

I told Wylie how I had called several of Basil's clients, his sister and his father. Wylie looked at me in disgust and kept shaking his head and muttering, "Bart, how could you do this to someone you barely knew?"

I didn't answer Wylie, but I suddenly felt tears spring from my eyes. I didn't know if they were tears of guilt about how I had hurt Wylie or for being so stupid to think that I could get something for nothing.

I remained silent as the tears continued to flow and Wylie didn't say a word. He went over to his CD player and pushed a button, then came back to the sofa with the remote control and said, "I want you to listen to this song and then I want you to think how you're going to change your life. Your actions and anger have caused me a great deal of pain. And that's what happens, Bart, when someone like family lets you down."

For the next half hour, Wylie remained silent as a gospel song played over and over. Every time the song ended, Wylie would lift the remote in the air, press Repeat, and play the song again. It was a great song and the singer had a wonderful voice. The chorus was powerful and painful as the voice sang, "We fall down, but we get up."

"Who is that?" I finally asked after about the tenth time Wylie played the song.

"It's Donnie McClurkin and it's my theme song, and now it's got to become yours. You've got to change, Bart. That's the only thing that's going to save you from possible jail time and, at the very least, expensive legal bills."

"The song is nice and all, but how is that going to get me the money I need to give back to the bank? And they still might press charges," I said. My body felt warm and sweat was pouring out of me and my knit shirt felt uncomfortable against my skin. I wanted to run from Wylie's apartment and back to South Beach on foot. But it was clear Wylie wasn't playing and I was going to have to face up to what I had done.

"If you tell the bank what happened, maybe you can turn things around."

"They won't listen."

"I've talked with Mr. Bell at the bank, and we can work something out, but you've got to play by my rules. And I mean the first time I get an inkling that you're not playing the game like decent folk, then you're on your own, and our friendship is over," Wylie said, sounding sympathetic but firm.

"What do I have to do?"

Wylie told me that he was willing to pay back the money to the bank, but I had to come and work for him until the money was paid back.

"What am I going to do for you?" I asked.

"Whatever I tell you, and you're going to do it with a smile on your face. The first time I hear someone at my company say something about Bart being shady, then it's over. You're going to treat people the way you *say* you want them to treat you. Am I making myself clear?"

"I hear you," I mumbled. I felt like a child being disciplined by the school's headmaster.

"None of that 'I hear you' bullshit. It's either probation with me or a chance of probation with the state of New York after some time in the joint."

"I'll do what you want, and somehow I'll make you proud."

"I'm already proud of my life. Take that pride and save it for yourself," Wylie said.

I didn't answer, because I was too busy crying, wondering if I could really get up, or had I fallen down too far?

Promises, Promises

After Raymond's visit, things in my life changed. My heart had softened, but I wasn't soft. There was still a part of me that wanted revenge against Bart. Even though I'd promised Raymond I wouldn't do anything stupid, I still had pangs of great anger.

Raymond and I had spent a couple of days working out and walking around Manhattan, just talking about life and what the second half might hold for the both of us. There was no sex, no kissing, just a lot of intimate moments without physical intimacy. Raymond told me he missed the East Coast and talked about some major changes in his life. When I asked him to elaborate, he turned lawyer on me and said he couldn't talk about it until he'd worked something out with Trent, his longtime partner. He told me when everything was settled he would give me a call. While I wasn't holding my breath, I had to admit to myself that I was looking forward to the day when I would pick up my phone and hear Raymond say he had moved back to New York. Solo.

I also found out who was sending me those nasty e-mails.

Some mofo named Sean, a sportswriter from Chicago who I assumed had some dealings with Zurich Robinson, an ex-pro quarterback I tried to get with. Sean gave himself away when he sent me an email telling me to keep my clothes on when I was around somebody else's man. Since Zurich was the only one I had given the full monty, I gave him a call. When I told him the e-mail address, he knew immediately. SWALZ-Sean will always love Zurich. Before I hung up, Zurich assured me I wouldn't be getting any more e-mails.

I guess the most amazing thing to happen was that I actually had a very civilized and cordial meeting with Yancey. She had called and said she had something very important to tell me. At first I told her I didn't have time, and then she pleaded, saying it would be the last time she would bother me. I was ready to move on, and so I agreed to meet her.

We met at the entrance of Central Park at Columbus Circle and spent an hour walking through the park. It was a warm, beautiful day; spring was pretending to be summer with its eighty-plus temperature. We stopped and got some lemonade and then sat down on a bench to talk more. When I finished my drink, Yancey nervously shifted the conversation about what she had done wrong with me and her life.

"I'm trying to make a clean break, and I've decided to go public about Madison," she said. Her voice was both intimate and sad, she had a wounded tone, and not the sexy, sometimes bitchy, tone I was used to.

"Does that mean you're going to become a part of her life?" I asked.

"I don't know. It might be a little hard," Yancey said softly.

"Why?"

Yancey told me that she had called her former boyfriend Derrick to give him the news about her going public. She told him the record company wanted her to do a cover story with LaVonya, and she had agreed to talk about the daughter she gave up. When she spoke with Derrick, he didn't object but told Yancey not to reveal Madison's name or where she lived. Derrick had met a woman and was ready to get married and his new bride wanted to adopt Madison.

"How do you feel about that?" I asked.

"It's probably the best thing. Derrick said his fiancée, Beverly, is a wonderful woman and she loves Madison. All I ever wanted for her was to grow up differently from the way I did. To have someone who really loves her. Sounds like she will finally get that," Yancey said.

"So you still don't want children?"

"I still don't think I'm capable, emotionally or physically," Yancey said. Then she touched my knee delicately and with a slight hesitation asked, "What about you? Do you still want children?"

"More than I can explain," I said.

"Then I hope you get a whole football team," Yancey said.

I looked at my watch and noticed it was almost five. "I guess I better be heading home. I'm going to Jacksonville to spend some time with my Pops."

"How's he doing?" Yancey asked.

"Everything is cool, but the older I get the more I realize I have no idea how much time we have left," I said.

"I'm sorry about what happened," Yancey said softly.

For a moment I looked at her with a puzzled expression, wondering what she was talking about, but then she said, "I know what Bart did. But he wasn't alone. Ava talked him into calling your father. I wasn't involved, but I think something I did caused Ava to put the plan in place," Yancey said.

"What are you talking about?" I asked suddenly, feeling leery again about Yancey. Maybe she was still acting with me, every word rehearsed.

"Ava wanted to manage my career, and I wanted no part of that. When she came to New York and wouldn't take no for an answer, I told her I was letting you manage my career. I guess that tipped her over the edge and she wanted to get you out of my life once and for all."

"But how does she know Bart?"

"I don't really know. But I think LaVonya had something to do with it."

"How do you know Bart?"

"He was in my video. He still doesn't know that Ava is my mother."

"How are you going to stop her?"

"I think going public with my secrets will do it. That way she can't hold anything over me. She's used my secrets against me to keep me under her control. I won't let her do that ever again."

"Yancey, I can help you."

"What?"

"I've still got the tapes. Maybe if Ava knew you had them, it would keep her in her place," I said.

"You would do that for me?" Yancey asked.

"Sure. My days of trying to get back at people are over. But Ava and Bart still need to be taught a lesson," I said.

"So you really are trying to change. That's wonderful. So am I," Yancey said as she touched my knee again, but without hesitation.

"I'll send you all the tapes by messenger when I get back," I said as I leaned over and gave Yancey a simple kiss of forgiveness on the cheek. She looked into my eyes with a grateful smile, and we walked hand in hand slowly out of the park. I realized that the love I had for Yancey would never end as long as I kept the good memories, like today, close to my heart.

• • •

When I got home I realized my day of surprises was far from over. Standing in my lobby, looking like she was carrying an exercise ball in her stomach, was Rosa.

"Why haven't you returned my calls?" Rosa asked.

"I've been busy," I said as I headed toward the elevator.

"Basil, I'm not leaving until we talk. It's important," she said, her voice getting louder.

I turned around and looked at Rosa; she was staring at me so intensely, like she was demanding that I notice and listen to her. I didn't want a scene in the lobby, so I said, "Why do you need to talk to me? Did you get a phone call too?"

"A phone call? What are you talking about?"

"Never mind. Come on up. You've got five minutes," I said.

Rosa and I rode up the elevator in silence. When we got

to my apartment, I stood in the foyer and looked at Rosa and said, "Now tell me what's so important."

"Can I sit down?"

I started to say no, but it looked like she could drop her load any minute and I didn't want to deliver some other man's baby in the foyer of my home.

"Come on, and make this quick. I've got some packing to do," I said as I walked to my sofa and sat down.

Rosa stood silently for a few moments and then she moved toward the living area and took a seat on the sofa next to me. I didn't want to look at her, so I just looked around my living room like I was seeing it for the first time. I noticed the new Paul Goodnight painting my art dealer had sent for approval, a tall metal and glass lamp in the corner of the room, next to the maple armoire that held my television and DVD player. I wanted to look anywhere but Rosa's face.

After a few moments of silence, I heard Rosa's voice. "I know what I did was wrong, and I hope you'll forgive me. But, Basil, I lied to you. The baby I'm carrying is yours," Rosa said, her voice breaking over the words.

I turned around, stunned, and looked into Rosa's eyes. They were shiny with tears, and my heart was beating faster with a strange mixture of rage and excitement. I didn't know if Rosa was playing some kind of sick game with me or if she was telling me the truth.

"What did you say?"

"This baby is yours," Rosa said as she gently patted her stomach.

"Rosa, what kind of game are you running on me?" I yelled.

"Basil, I lied to you because I thought if you found out I was carrying your baby, you would want to get married. I don't want to get married."

"What about this other guy you told me about?"

"There was no other guy. I was lying. This is your baby. I'm a hundred percent positive."

I jumped up from the sofa and started shaking my head from side to side. The anger had passed, but I suddenly didn't know how I should feel or what I should do. A part of me wanted to rush over and hold Rosa in an unbreakable embrace, and yet I didn't trust my emotions.

"Rosa, are you sure?"

"I'm sure. I'm sorry, Basil. I realized I had made a mistake the moment the lie left my mouth. I was being selfish. I know how much you want children, and so do I. I suddenly didn't want to share my baby with anyone."

"What made you change your mind?" I asked, determined to detect any falseness in her voice, before I surrendered to my dream of being a father.

"My father. He told me a child needed both parents. I realized that even if we weren't married we could still make this work."

I moved over to the sofa and sat down and looked at Rosa. Tears were pouring from her eyes, and I pulled her to my chest. Stroking her hair softly and gently, I whispered, "We're gonna make this work for the baby."

The Diva Is Dismissed!

"How did you find out about Madison?" I asked as I took a sip of my herbal tea. I was sitting on a brown leather love seat in a suite at the Four Seasons, directly across from LaVonya.

"Let's just say a little birdie told me," LaVonya laughed as she placed a slice of Muenster cheese on a cracker.

I stood up and said sternly, "I don't have time for games. I don't care if it's *People* magazine or a reprint of the Bible. I'm not talking until you tell me where you got your information."

"Cool your heels, honey. Sit down. If it's that important, I will tell you. But I better not hear of you telling anybody that I revealed my sources," LaVonya said.

"This is the only story of yours I am concerned about."

"It's one of your rivals," LaVonya said.

"I don't have any rivals," I said. "My record is number one for the third straight week, it just knocked Destiny's Child from the top spot."

"Yeah, you're the flavor of the moment, but keep your

eyes in the back of your head. There's a young lady named Marlana who's on your tail. And just between me and you, I don't think she likes you too much," LaVonya said as she took a sip of sparkling water and then dabbed her lips with a cloth napkin.

"How does she know about Madison? I barely know that girl," I said.

"But your former roommate, or house-sitter, what's her name, whatever, told her," LaVonya said.

"Windsor told her?" I asked as I suddenly felt my face become warm.

"Yeah, that's where she got her information. But I wouldn't be upset with Windsor. She loves you and didn't do it to hurt you. She was trying to encourage Marlana not to give up her child for adoption. She used you as an example of someone who might have regretted giving up her child. Marlana tells me Windsor really loves you and thought sharing information about you would help Marlana. This Windsor sounds like she should start some type of diva rehabilitation service. Helping divas who have lost their way. It's such a shame that Marlana used the information against you, but it will all wash out in the end. I just sorta took over when she got busy with her career and couldn't harass you anymore," LaVonya said with a satisfied smile on her face.

"How kind of you," I said sarcastically.

"So are you ready? Can I turn my recorder on? *People* and *Diva* can't wait to get this story."

I stood up again and said, "Sorry, but I think they'll have to wait."

"What are you talking about?" LaVonya asked as she clicked her tiny recorder off.

"I'm on my way to another floor, where I have an interview with Monique Greenwood of *Essence*. I'm giving them an exclusive. And I thank you so much for the information," I said as I grabbed my purse and headed for the door.

"Wait a minute. You can't walk out on me like that. I'm getting paid big money for this story."

As I reached for the doorknob, I turned around, looked at LaVonya and said, "You *were* going to get big money. I don't think it's a good idea to work with a writer who reveals her sources so easily."

• • •

Club Mix (The Finale)

I Learned from the Best

A lot of good came from seeing Basil. For the first time I feel as if I have a clean slate and a real chance for love with Desmond. It feels wonderful to not have secrets. The response to the *Essence* article has been overwhelmingly positive and I looked fabulous on the cover.

In a couple of weeks, I leave to do my first feature film in North Carolina and Desmond will direct me. I'll play the trophy wife of an older man in a film the studios are calling a black *Big Chill*. Denzel Washington is playing my husband. So I must be livin' right.

Before I start filming, I'm going to visit Windsor and Wardell. Recently, she delivered a healthy eight-pound baby boy, Kelson Adams-Pope. When I spoke with her, she sounded happier than I've ever heard her, and for someone like Windsor, I guess that's what's called being delirious with joy. I decided not to tell her about what Marlana did, because in the end Marlana helped me shed some more layers of my past. Besides, I know Windsor would never do anything to hurt me. Every time I talk to Windsor or see her, she teaches me the power and beauty of friendship.

My CD is currently multiplatinum and my second single, "I'm Not in Love," hit number one on all the charts—pop, contemporary and R & B. The first triple number one for Motown in a long time, so life is good.

Basil sent me the tapes, and I called Ava to let her know I had them. The conversation was an Ava special, and she yelled, hollered and called me all kinds of names. She told me I didn't have the sense God gave a goose, and reminded me she knew where all the bodies were buried. I knew she was talking about Madison, so I sent her a copy of the *Essence* article and copies of the tapes, and enclosed a little warning that the masters were now in *my* hands. Still, nothing gave me more satisfaction than finally getting in the last word with Ava. I said, "I bet you're having second thoughts now about trying to be my friend rather than my mother."

"You're such a bitch," Ava screamed.

"Thank you. I learned from the best," I said as I hung up the phone, with the knowledge I'd also learned some lessons from people like Basil, Desmond and Windsor that Ava could never teach me.

Every Time I Feel
the Spirit

After Warden Wylie releases me, I've got big plans. I'm going to buy me a used car and travel across the United States and see what I can learn about this country and myself. I plan to visit Cleveland and maybe look up Hattie, and then West to California. I think Hollywood might be interested in the stories I can tell.

Spending so much time with Wylie has not been the ocean of time I imagined. I've actually learned some things about the public relations business. Wylie suggested I read a book called *The Personal Touch* by this sister named Terrie Williams, and I picked up a few things about life and business. I'm also seriously thinking about finishing up my education, 'cause this body ain't going to last forever.

Nothing much about my day-to-day friendship with Wylie has changed. Well that's not totally true. He makes me work and I make him go to the gym. He's lost about twenty pounds and if he keeps it up, we might wind up competing for male attention. We still laugh a lot and he hasn't turned me into a saint. And quite frankly, I think Wylie likes it that way.

I still have a lot of questions about my life, and whenever I'm searching for answers, Wylie quickly shares some wise saying his mother told him or something from the Bible.

One day when I was musing over why I'd met people like Basil and Ava, Wylie quoted me some scripture and told me to read John 3:8. I looked it up and found: "The wind blows wherever it pleases. You hear its sound, but you cannot tell where it comes from or where it is going. So it is with everyone born of the Spirit." Wylie told me he thought it meant that people come into our lives for different reasons, good and bad, and if you're in the Spirit, you can survive anyone and anything. I don't know if I believe that or not, but it's probably one of the reasons Wylie has remained my friend.

A few weeks ago, Wylie took me to see August Wilson's *King Hedley II,* on Broadway. I was enjoying the play and leaned over and whispered, "Thanks for being my friend, Wylie. Thanks for showing me tough love and not giving up on me." The old lady sitting in front of us turned around and shushed me. It was a normal reaction for me to shout, "Bitch, don't shush me." She was so startled, she huffed her way out of the theatre. I looked at Wylie, ready for him to tell me how wrong I was, but instead he just burst out laughing and said, "I guess you told her." We were laughing so hard I was surprised they didn't kick us out of the theatre.

At that moment I realized I had spent my life looking for love that could never be true and missed things that were right in front of my eyes: a good laugh, words that make you think (even lines from the B-I-B-L-E) and friendship. That's all love, all the time.

That's the Way Love Goes

Any man who doesn't respect a woman after watching her give birth isn't a man. The new love of my life was born today: a beautiful baby girl, Talley Alexandria Henderson, weighing in at 6 pounds, 3 ounces. With just one look at Talley, I knew she was mine. I can tell already she's going to be a heartbreaker, and the first heart she'll break will be mine, her daddy's.

There's no way to describe the way I felt watching her come into the world. I felt humble. I felt scared. It was an amazing event that covered my body with a chill as cold as winter, and then when I heard her scream, I felt a warmth that felt like the sun was shining just on me and my daughter. When Rosa, with tears streaming down her face, passed Talley to me and I looked into the baby's face, I cried, but this time the tears that streamed down my face were tears of pride and joy. This crying thing ain't that bad after all. I know I might be alone again in my life, but I will never be lonely. The girl I've been waiting for has finally arrived.

Raymond was right: One person can alter your life

forever when you least expect it. It was finally time to embrace life and never question where or to whom it might lead.

I've learned that you have to be able to flow. Any way the wind blows is cool with me.

ALSO BY E. LYNN HARRIS

The Invisible Life Trilogy

INVISIBLE LIFE

In his last year at law school, Raymond Tyler seems to have it all, but there are secret, terrifying issues for him to confront. Being black is tough enough, but Raymond becomes increasingly conscious of conflicting sexual feelings: He is completely committed to Sela, his longtime girlfriend, but his attraction to his friend Kelvin has become more than mere friendship. Fleeing to New York to escape both Sela and Kelvin, Raymond finds new relationships—both male and female—that give him enormous pleasure but keep him from finding inner peace and lasting love. The horrible illness of a friend forces him, at last, to face the truth.

Fiction/0-385-46968-3

JUST AS I AM

Just As I Am picks up where *Invisible Life* ends. Raymond struggles to come to terms with his sexuality and with the grim reality of AIDS. Nicole, an aspiring singer/actress, experiences frustration in both her career and in her attempts to find a genuine love relationship. Both Raymond and Nicole share an eclectic group of friends who challenge them to look at the world through different eyes. In this vivid portrait of contemporary black life, with all its pressures and the complications of bisexuality, AIDS, and racism, E. Lynn Harris confirms the power of love to thrill and to heal.

Fiction/0-385-46970-5

ABIDE WITH ME

In this masterful conclusion to the Invisible Life trilogy, E. Lynn Harris traces the evolving destinies of Nicole and Raymond and reintroduces readers to their respective lovers, best friends, and potential enemies. *Abide with Me* moves between the worlds of New York City, where Nicole has recently settled in order to pursue her dream of returning to the Broadway stage, and Seattle, where a late-night phone call from a U.S. Senator is about to change Raymond's life dramatically.

Fiction/0-385-48658-8

NOT A DAY GOES BY

John Basil Henderson has always played the field—both as a professional football player and as an equal opportunity lover. After retiring his jersey for a career as a sports agent, the dashing playboy is finally settling down and getting married to his new love, Yancey Harrington Braxton. Yancey is a fiercely driven, emerging Broadway star who would seem his ideal counterpart, but she is also an insatiable opportunist with a vicious streak, and when Yancey joins forces with her mother and unearths Basil's most carefully guarded secrets, she finds more than she bargained for.

Fiction/0-385-49825-X

AND THIS TOO SHALL PASS

In *And This Too Shall Pass*, E. Lynn Harris takes us into the locker rooms and newsrooms of Chicago, where four lives are about to intersect in romance and scandal. At the heart of the novel is the celibate Zurich, a rookie quarterback for the Chicago Cougars whose trajectory for superstardom is interrupted by a sexual assault charge made by Mia, a sportscaster with her own sights on fame. With his career in jeopardy, Zurich hires the high-powered attorney Tamela to defend him, while Sean, a gay sportswriter, covers the story and uncovers his heart.

Fiction/0-385-48031-8

IF THIS WORLD WERE MINE

Four friends keep a collective journal they call "If This World Were Mine," and meet for monthly gatherings filled with humor, gossip, and affirmation. Yolanda, a media consultant, has a no-nonsense attitude that is balanced by the theatrics of Riley, a former marketing executive whose marriage has reduced her to a "kept woman with kids." Computer engineer Dwight's anger at the world is offset by the compassion of Leland, a gay psychiatrist. But after five years, the once-strong bonds of friendship are weakening, and the group must face the challenges of work, love, and a stranger in their midst.

Fiction/0-385-48656-1

⚓

ANCHOR BOOKS
Available from your local bookstore, or call toll-free to order:
1-800-793-2665 (credit cards only).